Also by Loren D. Estleman

BLOODY SEASON

PEEPER

WHISKEY RIVER

Gift

of

The Arizona

Daily Star

MOTOWN

Loren D. Estleman

BANTAM BOOKS

New York · Toronto · London · Sydney · Auckland

MOTOWN

A BANTAM BOOK/SEPTEMBER 1991

Library of Congress Cataloging-in-Publication Data

Estleman, Loren D.
Motown / Loren D. Estleman.
p.   cm.
ISBN 0-553-07421-0
I. Title.
PS3555.S84M68   1991
813'.54—dc20   91-6924
CIP

Published simultaneously in the United States and Canada

Bantam Books are published by Bantam Books, a division of Bantam Doubleday Dell Publishing Group, Inc. Its trademark, consisting of the words "Bantam Books" and the portrayal of a rooster, is Registered in U.S. Patent and Trademark Office and in other countries. Marca Registrada. Bantam Books, 666 Fifth Avenue, New York, New York 10103.

PRINTED IN THE UNITED STATES OF AMERICA

RRH   0 9 8 7 6 5 4 3 2 1

For Barbara Beman Puechner,
who has never acquired the knack
of separating being an agent
from being a friend.

We may be able to pacify every village in Vietnam over a period of years, but what good does it do if we can't pacify the American cities?

—MAYOR JEROME P. CAVANAGH,
July 30, 1967

Chapter 1

Candy-apple red GTO.

Steel front, divided grille, stacked headlights, 389 V-8 engine under a Tempest hood. Bench seats, for chrissake, and a chicken-leg family-car steering wheel, in partnership with a mill and four-speed trans that cried out for bucket seats and padded leather.

A crime.

Unlawful incarceration.

Every time Rick took it out he wanted to pull into a garage somewhere, gut the interior, and do it over in black leathergrain Naugahyde, punch a hole in the hood and drop in real twin scoops in place of the factory dummy. Let the big 389 breathe.

Instead he drove it down to the corner and washed and rinsed it for fifty cents and parked it behind the bays and Turtle-Waxed it and brought it home.

He was pulling down the garage door when Mrs. Hertler came out of the house and stood in front of him, kneading her hands in her apron. She always did that when she had something unpleasant to pass along, a nasty job that needed doing or a visit from one of Rick's old associates.

Except when she went out, in her cloth coat and gray felt teardrop hat with a blue feather in the band, he had never seen her without an apron. She was a gravity-bound woman of Eastern European background with hair like copper wire pulled back and twisted into a knot behind her head. Her eyes were a startling blue in the faded face.

"Bob is coming home," she said.

He turned the door handle, locking it, and straightened. "When?"

"Next week, Tuesday or Wednesday. They're discharging him a month early. He thinks he can get a ride on a mail plane." She kneaded. "I'm sorry, Rick."

"You shouldn't be. It's always good news when a son comes home from the army."

"Do you think you can find a place?"

"Sure. The only reason I haven't looked before this is I got spoiled by the rent. I'd have been glad to pay more."

"No, I liked having someone in Bob's room. And I know he'll be grateful you took such good care of his car. He's so proud of it."

Then why didn't he pop for a four-barrel carburetor instead of air conditioning? Aloud Rick said, "I've enjoyed it. I like cars." He paused. "I'll miss your cooking."

"You don't have to. You'll always be welcome at our table." As she said it—"*our* table"—he knew the invitation would never come to anything. The presence at home of Specialist Robert C. Hertler would cut whatever cord bound Mrs. Hertler and Rick Amery. She let her apron fall. "Are you home for dinner tonight?"

"I thought I'd go to the movies. If it's all right. I know I just had the car out."

"Take it, you don't have to ask permission. Are you going with someone? Julie?"

"No, I thought I'd go alone."

"I liked Julie," she said. "I thought—well. I guess I have to be someone's mother, don't I? What are you going to see?"

"*Grand Prix.* It's playing at the Galaxy."

"Isn't that a long way to go to see a movie? I'm sure it's playing somewhere closer."

"Not at a drive-in. It's going to be too nice a night to stay indoors." He didn't tell her he preferred to watch racing pictures from behind the wheel. Putting it into words would have made it sound as stupid as it probably was. Anyway, he had just plucked the title and theater out of his memory when asked which picture he was going to; he'd seen it advertised in the *Free Press* but hadn't thought about going until that moment. He had planned on staying in before hearing the news about Bob.

"Well, if you change your mind." She shrugged in the continental fashion, without sarcasm, and went inside. The screen door wheezed against the pressure of the spring and clapped shut. He suspected she wasn't fooled.

He took the outside staircase to the room he'd been using on the second floor of the frame saltbox. Mrs. Hertler had explained that her late husband had built the steps and cut the outside door into Bob's room when their son, attending the University of Detroit then, complained about lack of privacy. That was the point where Rick had decided he wouldn't like Bob. Grown men who lived with their parents held no place on his private scale. Grown men who lived with someone else's mother rated scarcely higher.

The room was large and comfortable, with a west window and its own bath and a double bed under the slant of the roof. The dresser, massive in black walnut with a mirror framed in Baroque gilt cherubs, had come across the Atlantic with Mrs. Hertler and now belonged to Bob, whose other possessions had been moved to the basement when Rick took the room. Most of his own possessions were in storage at his sister's house and had been since he was forced to give up his apartment in Redford Township. Everything in the room that belonged to him he had carried there in two suitcases, one of them borrowed from his sister. She had offered to make room for him as well as his furniture, but the offer had not been as sincere as his hatred for his brother-in-law and so was easy to decline.

Answering Mrs. Hertler's *Free Press* classified last summer, Rick had seen the GTO parked in the garage with the door open, its tires soft and a skin of gritty dust on the finish, and had convinced her of the wisdom of getting someone to drive and maintain her son's car while he was away. She had offered to knock twenty dollars off the rent if he agreed to do this. The deal was set before he had even seen the room. But he would have agreed to it without the discount and stuck to the bargain even if his quarters had turned out to be a hovel. As he had said, he liked cars.

Which was the source of all his troubles.

He stretched out on top of the bedspread in his clothes and read Hunter S. Thompson's *Hell's Angels* until the light through the window faded, when he didn't bother to switch on the bedside lamp to read further. The book was a disappointment: not enough bike stuff. He lay there for a while with the book open facedown on his chest and his eyes closed, not sleeping nor trying to, then put on the lamp and showered and pulled on black chinos and a red sport shirt and his P. F. Flyers and picked up the keys to the Pontiac on his way out.

At thirty-seven, Rick Amery looked twenty and was routinely carded when he ordered a drink in a bar. He was less than six feet tall but seemed taller because of his spare, hipless build. He cut his sandy hair aggressively short to stand out from the proliferation of long-haired teenagers and wore aviator's glasses with graphite rims when he drove; these had a maturing effect on his features. In the car he slid them from their visor clip, checked them for dust, and put them on. The amber lenses gave the gathering shadows a coffee tint.

He didn't go to the movies. Instead he took a succession of side streets to Woodward, emptying now of rush-hour traffic, and started down toward Jefferson, teasing and bullying the big engine by turns to avoid stoplights. At that hour, as the light shed by the gooseneck streetlamps whetted its edges on the granite dusk, the pavement turned rich black, like the clean surface of a long-playing record. He felt as if his tires were rolling across virgin asphalt, leaving a clear intaglio behind.

At Warren he missed the yellow by two seconds and stopped with a squelch of rubber. While he was waiting, listening clinically to the dub-dub-dub of the GTO at idle, a black '66 Mustang cruised up next to him in the outside lane. He could see the streaks of glue on the little backseat window where the price sticker had been peeled off. The car's long hood and spoiler rear made its profile a shallow wedge, like a shark's.

A sudden gunning of the Mustang's engine drew his attention to the driver, for him the least important component of any car. He saw a man in his early twenties wearing mirrored glasses and a lot of black hair pushed back behind his ears, grinning at him. The engine roared again.

It wasn't the first time Rick had been invited to drag on Woodward. The avenue's broad expanse was like a strip, as straight and flat as an airplane runway and divided into blocks of equal size. The V-8 Pontiac—even the early model Rick drove, wider and boxier than later GTOs and loaded down with chrome—just naturally attracted challengers. Maybe it was the scarlet paint job. He returned his gaze to the windshield. He never raced.

The window on the driver's side of the Mustang squeaked down. The kid with the hair was shouting something. Rick looked at him again.

"Ford's town, asshole! Crap or get off the can!"

Rick turned his head just as the light changed.

Well, hell.

He popped the clutch and squashed the footpedal to the firewall.

The swell of the 389 boxed his ears. The tires shrieked, bit, and hurled the car forward; Rick felt the sickening lift and jar as the front wheels left the earth and slammed down. The steering wheel yanked his arms straight, his neck whipped, and the gray Detroit scenery became a white wipe.

He didn't look to see if the Mustang was keeping pace. This kind of driving required two hands on the wheel and both eyes on the road. He shifted without being aware that he was shifting. The changes in pitch were like gulps of oxygen.

They tore across Hancock, nicked a red light at Forest, and closed in on Garfield seconds too late for the yellow. Rick clutched and braked, baring his teeth at the cry of tires. To his right the Mustang, a beat behind, barely slowed and took the corner on two wheels and a fingernail. The phrase *sore loser* came to Rick just before he saw the red throbbing in his mirror. The wail of the siren reached him then like a crucial piece of information remembered too late.

He had the registration out of the glove compartment and his driver's license in his hand when the officer approached, a big man in the loose blue uniform with brown leather patches whose design hadn't changed in Rick's memory. The officer hovered just behind the window post with his fingers on the black rubber butt of the Smith & Wesson in his holster. His head was somewhere above the Pontiac's roof.

"Who's your friend, punk?"

"We weren't introduced."

The silence was long enough to tell him that that was the wrong answer.

Finally the officer accepted the items Rick had been holding through the open window. A flashlight snapped on.

"Your name's Richard Amery?"

"That's right."

"Who's this Robert Hertler on the registration?"

"My landlady's son. I'm taking care of the car while he's away."

"He know *how* you're taking care of it?"

Rick said nothing to that.

"Hold on. Are you *Rick* Amery?"

He caught the officer's change in tone.

"Most of the time," he said.

"Hell, I didn't know you. I guess you don't remember me either." Abandoning the safety zone behind the window post, the officer stepped forward and bent down, framing his face in the window. Rick turned on the domelight. A broad face, not young but not yet middle-aged, with a thick brown moustache rounded off at the ends. Rick didn't know him.

"Roger Kornacki," the officer said. "I was the officer on the scene on that nun killing at St. Benedict's."

Three years ago. "Oh, hello."

They shook hands. Kornacki's was twice the size of Rick's, a big red palm built for wrapping around the handle of a welding torch at Dodge Main.

"That was some kill, that was. I lit a candle every Sunday for a month, but we never got the son of a bitch." The big face flickered. "I'm sure sorry about that punk crack. I thought you were one of these dumb kids."

"No, just dumb."

Kornacki handed back the license and registration. "Saves me a lecture. So what are you doing these days?"

"Piecework. Mechanics mostly."

After a short pause a throat cleared. "Well. Lay off the foot-feed, okay? We got to set an example, Christ knows why."

"I didn't even hear you coming. When's the department going to install those new yelpers?"

"Commissioner says we're getting all-new Pontiacs next spring."

"Just as soon as Rock Hudson gets into Doris Day's pants."

Kornacki brayed. "You nailed that one. Well, remember what I said. It was good seeing you, Sarge."

"Rick."

The light had changed several times while they were talking. When it turned green again Rick went ahead without looking back at the blue-and-white.

It had been ten months and two days since he had been forced to throw in his shield.

Chapter 2

Barry McGuire singing.

Singing very low in that broken-gravel Dylan voice, saying someone was telling him he didn't believe we're on the eve of destruction. But the lyrics weren't audible at that volume, only the buzz of the bass and the thump of the drums, making the tiny illuminated legend FM STEREO on the dial flicker with each note that fell below the staff.

The department band radio was also turned very low. The bored, one-sided conversations that lisped intermittently from the speaker weren't intelligible to civilian ears. Lew Canada, who had not been a civilian since Corregidor, monitored the calls while watching the fire door in the alley across from the weedy lot where his Plymouth Fury was parked. The car was unmarked, black, with minimal chrome, only the concave grille gleaming softly in the reflected light, like the meshed teeth of one of those undersea predators that swim aimlessly with their mouths gaping, scooping up plankton and small creatures as they go.

The two radio frequencies belched and crackled like the digestive tract of that same animal. It made Canada, who knew nothing of the sea, think of evenings on his Uncle Herman's beet farm in Mecosta

County, lying with his head on the chest of Dolf, Herman's bull mastiff, and listening to the double crash of the dog's great heart pumping blood through arteries as thick as packing cord. Dead thirty years now, Dolf, the farm whose boundaries he marked with one leg in the air gone to the developers. But Uncle Herman lived, a hostage to his decomposing body, in a nursing home in Stockbridge, listening to the sounds of his own heart and waiting. When had Canada visited him last? Long enough ago to have forgotten its occasion. Canada had shot Dolf himself when the dog grew too old to walk without whimpering. That was the major advantage animals had over humans.

"You buy that, Inspector?"

He looked quickly at the man sitting behind the wheel. He wondered for a moment if he'd spoken his thoughts aloud. In the shadows, Sergeant Esther was a dark pile of inertia in a coat too heavy for late spring and a hat with a brim too broad for 1966, who always smelled of Ben-Gay. "Buy what?"

The sergeant gestured toward the radio. "What the pukes say. The end of the world and like that. Think there's anything to it?"

"Kid stuff. They always think the fun's going to be over before they can get in on it."

"I don't know. That thing in Cuba had me scared shitless for days."

"It came out okay."

"Then some puke goes and shoots Kennedy."

"What do you care? You voted for Nixon."

"Doesn't mean I wanted some asshole to scatter his brains all over his wife's dress. Talk about your hard-to-get-out stains." Esther shifted his weight on the seat. The car leaned over on its springs. "The other day my daughter came home and called me a pig."

"Did you hit her?"

"Not hard enough. If I ever called my old man a name like that I'd still be walking funny. That cocksucking Spock book Beth brought home when she was pregnant screwed us for life. The scroat raises his own army of spoiled little sons of bitches, then marches them on Washington to protest the fucking war. It'd do the little bastards good to ship out and worry about getting their balls shot off."

"I wouldn't wish combat on Khrushchev."

Esther cleared his throat. "Sorry, Inspector. I was just talking."

"They're just kids. They like to listen to that monkey music and light up reefers and get their little carrots dipped. They'll grow out of it."

"You got kids, Inspector?"

"Not in my worst nightmare."

"I got three, and the only time they grow out of anything is when they grow into something worse."

Canada made no response and the pair settled into a mulch of silence. They had been watching the alley for an hour and a half. Two stray dogs had entered it an hour apart, sniffed around the base of the two painted trash cans standing by the fire door, then moved on. In between them an emaciated Negro in a streaked World War II army coat whom Esther vaguely recognized from some time or other in the squad room at 1300 had stumbled in, taken something from one of the cans the dogs had snubbed, and stumbled out after a minute wiping his hands on his coat. There had been no other activity. The alley ran behind an auto parts store on Gratiot.

The sergeant's Ben-Gay burned Canada's nostrils. The inspector had a sensitive nose, made more so by his personal cleanliness. His nails were always pinkish white and his black hair, barely splintered with silver at forty-nine, glistened, although he used nothing on it but hard water and Lifebuoy soap, a lot of Lifebuoy soap. His dark inexpensive suits and white shirts were never anything less than immaculate. "You could eat off the son of a bitch," he had overheard his wife complaining to her sister on the telephone shortly before she walked out on him. She'd told him then that if she wanted to live in a bandbox she'd have married a haberdasher, and advised him to see a psychiatrist. He didn't need to see a psychiatrist. He knew why he was the way he was.

"This snitch of yours reliable?" asked the sergeant.

"How reliable is a snitch?"

Esther didn't answer. "Nineteen years I been a cop, I never saw a tip come to anything but crap. Tips don't compare with good police work."

"You know the drill. We run 'em out."

"What I don't know is what an inspector's doing on a nickel stakeout like this. Day I make lieutenant I put my feet up on my desk and don't take them off till the department buys me dinner."

"That's the day LBJ makes Eartha Kitt ambassador to South Vietnam."

"I still think we're—"

Canada touched Esther's knee.

A late-model Pontiac had coasted to a stop in the alley just under the edge of the light from the lamp on the corner. The door on the passenger's side caught the light on its markings when it opened. DETROIT POLICE.

The sergeant said shit.

The door on the other side came open almost simultaneously and the officer who had been driving moved to the back of the car. That end was in darkness, but the flatulent creak of a trunk hinge in need of oil reached the men in the unmarked Fury. A moment later the officer came back into the light carrying a chrome-plated pinch bar.

The sergeant said shit again.

Both officers were at the fire door now. Canada thought he knew which was which. Their faces were out of focus at that distance and they were built similarly, but he knew there was a fifteen-year difference in their ages, and older officers always carried themselves the same way; a legacy of the automobile industry's inability to design a seat that didn't ruin a man's back after years of eight hours' daily contact. The man with the wrecking tool—it would be Wasylyk, a year or two behind Canada at the Academy—slid it between the lock hasp and the jamb and tore the screws out of the wooden frame after two tries. He tugged the door open by its handle. He handed the pinch bar to his partner, accepted a black rubber police flashlight in return, and went inside. The other officer leaned his shoulders against the door and crossed his ankles. He flipped the pinch bar end over end twice and slid it into the loop on his belt designed for his baton.

"Cool as a can of Schlitz," Esther said. "I wrote that little fucker Drachler up for a commendation two years ago."

Canada said, "He probably earned it."

"When do we go in?"

"Not yet."

After a few minutes the younger officer stirred from the door and Wasylyk pushed it open from inside, stooping to prop it in place with a box the size of a beer case. He went back inside and came out carrying another box, which Drachler took from him and carried back toward the rear of the patrol car. By the time he returned empty-handed, Wasylyk had another box for him.

Canada handed Sergeant Esther a pair of binoculars. "Can you make it out?"

"Disk brakes. I'd have picked radios."

"They don't stock them. I checked."

"Let's take 'em down."

"Hold your bladder. Let me know when they unprop the door." The inspector slumped down and tilted his narrow-brimmed hat onto the bridge of his nose.

"They got more horsepower than us. If they get out of that alley—"

"Don't let them."

Esther watched for a few more minutes. "There goes the door."

Canada sat up and pushed back his hat. He'd actually been asleep. "Well, don't wait for Christmas."

The sergeant dumped the binoculars and hit the ignition. The Fury's motor gunned, its rear tires kicked up divots of grass laced with condoms and broken beer bottles, and they shot across Gratiot behind a Sinclair oil tanker with a brontosaurus painted on its side.

Esther jerked on the lights just as they entered the alley. The high beams washed the blue-and-white and the brick wall on either side in blinding platinum. Quick-frozen in the glare, the two uniformed officers stood white-eyed, holding on to both ends of a box of disk brakes.

The crunch of the Fury's tires as Esther braked ended that. The box hit the pavement with a crash and Drachler and Wasylyk scrambled for the doors of the marked Pontiac. Canada piled out of his side an instant ahead of Esther and locked both arms across the top of the open door with his blunt-barreled Chief's Special clenched in both hands.

"Guess who, motherfuckers!" he shouted.

The sergeant had assumed the same stance with his own revolver trained across the top of the door on the driver's side. "Police! Hold it right there!"

No imagination.

Halfway across the front of the patrol car, Drachler faltered, then stopped and threw his hands straight up. "Jesus, don't shoot me!"

Canada lost interest in him then. He was watching Wasylyk's face behind the patrol car's windshield. A pouchy face, grayish in the light—probably in any light—looking years older than Canada's. It sagged before the inspector's eyes like a tent collapsing. Slowly an arm came out through the open door with the departmental Smith & Wesson dangling by its butt from between thumb and forefinger. The hand kept going up and laid the gun on the roof of the car. Wasylyk started to get out.

"Now the throwaway," Canada said.

In a moment a nickel-plated Browning .25 automatic with black sidegrips had joined the revolver on the roof. Wasylyk came out with his hands over his head and the two plainclothesmen left cover. Sergeant Esther flung Drachler facedown across the hood of the patrol car, handcuffed him, and relieved him of his sidearm and the pinch bar on his belt.

"I'll call it in," Esther said, panting a little.

"Not yet." Canada, who had not cuffed the older officer, put away the Chief's Special and told him to lower his hands. When he obeyed, Canada touched his arm and they moved away from the car.

"Piss-poor, Ed," Canada said. "Break in someplace and loot it, then call it in as a B-and-E. I'd have thought thirty years with the department would teach you something more original."

"Twenty-nine," corrected Wasylyk. "Feels like fifty." His voice, coarse and thick with phlegm, sounded like a flooded carburetor.

"I pulled your jacket. You've got commendations up the ass. I've got to ask why this."

"You know what the job pays."

"Screw that. A street cop can pull down a thousand a week just by knowing what doorways to stay out of. A couple of hundred in parts? Don't insult me."

"Let's just get to the booking. I got the same rights as any asshole junkie and one of them's to keep my mouth shut."

"If I wanted to book you, you'd be on your way downtown by now. Answer the question, shithead."

Wasylyk looked down the alley. There were white whiskers in the creases of his cheeks. "They passed me over for detective again. My wife and I were counting on that promotion for a decent pension when I retired next year. Then she went and died."

"Bullshit."

"You son of a bitch."

"I don't mean bullshit she died. I mean bullshit you don't care any more. You just got too lazy to do the job by the numbers."

No response.

"What would it take to light a fire under your lazy butt?" Canada asked.

Tobacco teeth showed in Wasylyk's sneer. "You recruiting me to spook for Internal Affairs?"

"I'm not with Internal Affairs."

"The hell you're not. Everyone knows you run it."

"Some college punk with a slide rule runs it. I work for the mayor."

"Ain't that a coincidence. So do I."

"I mean directly."

The officer looked at him for the first time. "Cavanagh?"

"When no one's around I get to call him Jerry."

"The hell you do."

"You're too good a cop to hand over to those pricks in I.A.D. They'd just bust your ass and send me out for more." Canada gave one of Wasylyk's blue collar-ends a flip. "It's a chance to get out of the bag."

"Detective's pension?"

"Don't be greedy."

Wasylyk glanced toward Drachler, still cuffed with Esther standing behind him. "What about the kid?"

"I'll get him put on Stationary Traffic. He can't steal anything there but fire hydrants. I don't need him."

"Okay by me. We just turn out together. We ain't exchanged vows."

"Is that a yes?"

The officer showed his teeth. "If I don't like it, can I come back here and take the fall for the brakes?"

Chapter 3

Jed Clampett smoked Winstons.

Granny was reluctant, but he talked her into poking the filter end into the bowl of her corncob pipe and she agreed with him that it tasted good, like a cigarette should.

That was the impression Quincy Springfield got anyway, with the sound turned off on the thirteen-inch set in the corner and the black-and-white images clomping around silently in burlap and gingham and those big scuffed-leather honky shoes that TV people associated with Southern wardrobe. Quincy had been to Alabama once and folks down there wore baseball caps and flannel shirts buttoned to the neck and stiff blue jeans and tenny-grippers, just like in some places in Detroit. Negroes too. But then the only Negro on TV wore a white coat and ironed Jack Benny's pants, so what did TV people know?

The commercial ended and the show came on, with the same two people conversing over a big smoking kettle that the old lady was stirring next to a swimming pool with statues of naked white people scattered around it. Nobody was lighting up now. Quincy lost interest and turned his attention to the man seated in front of him behind the glass-topped desk.

The man's name was Devlin, but Quincy was sure he was Jewish. He had the nose, a broad soft face with a hooking chin, and combed his dark hair across his scalp in a way that reminded Quincy of Mr. Rappaport, a pawnbroker he had liked twenty years ago because he always paid a fair price, or did anyway until somebody from outside the neighborhood let out his intestines with a Barlow knife when he didn't open the cash register fast enough. But Quincy had no affection for Devlin. The man wore highly inflammable suits with loud patterns and ties you could mop your face with and still have enough dry material left over to wipe your hands. People with money who didn't spend any of it on their appearance wore their contempt for their fellow human beings like a six-hundred-dollar suit. Quincy himself favored colored shirts—it was lavender today—jackets with natural shoulders, peg-top pants, and ostrich half-boots that zipped up inside the ankles. He never wore a hat. Hats were for pimps.

At six-three and 220 pounds, Quincy was a hard fit, which was why tailors received much of his income. The skin of his face was blue-black, almost plum-colored, and stretched tight over thick bones with chiseled edges. His prognathous jaw, which resembled the underslung bucket of a steam shovel, frightened the people he wanted to frighten, but when he smiled—not often—it receded, transforming his features. There was gray in his modest Afro. He was thirty-five.

Devlin removed the last packet from the satchel, stripped off the rubber band, and counted, his meaty thumb separating the bills with scalpel precision. He could have done it much faster, but he obviously enjoyed making Quincy wait. In so far as it was possible for a man like Devlin to enjoy anything. Any other courier would have been dismissed upon delivery, to be recalled later if there was a discrepancy in the count; and in fact the delivery itself would have been handled by a bag man, not by a boss like Quincy. But since the day three months ago that one of his couriers had pocketed fifteen hundred dollars, nothing would do but that Quincy carry the cash himself, one of many humiliations he had had to endure because he was Bass Springfield's son. It made no difference that Quincy had apprehended the greedy bag man and made him curl his fingers around a doorjamb while Quincy kicked the door shut. If the man had eight broken fingers, his boss had suffered as much in loss of esteem.

When he finished counting, Devlin grasped the arms of his chair, reddened from his hairline to his collar, and stood up. He went out through the door behind the desk without excusing himself.

On the television screen, a blonde in a slippery gown was hanging all over a man who was shaving the way no sane man would ever shave if there were a blade in his razor. Quincy ignored it and looked instead at the view from the forty-third floor of the Penobscot Building. The river glinted in scallops of reflected sunlight between the block buildings of the warehouse district and Windsor on the other side. Quincy had never been to Canada, three minutes away across the Ambassador Bridge or through the tunnel. Despite the similarity of the Windsor skyline to Detroit's, he pictured the country as a land of moose and snowy mountains and honkies in tight uniforms and Smokey the Bear hats who rode horses and sang to each other in deep fruity voices. He'd seen that in a movie his mother had taken him to see when he was five years old and the images were now more real than many of the other events of his childhood.

Devlin returned and lowered himself derrick-fashion into his chair. His body was bullet-shaped and like his face gave no indication that there were bones beneath. "Patsy wants to talk to you."

The door behind the desk led into a corner office twice as deep as the one Quincy had just left. The adjoining windows would have presented the same view of Canada and another of downtown Detroit if they weren't cloaked in blinds and drapes of some heavy green material with gold threads that glittered. There was a moss-green Brussels carpet wall-to-wall—Quincy had made a study of such fine things—and brushed aluminum panels on the walls that made the room look like something seen in a clouded mirror. Neither of its two occupants got up when the visitor entered.

"Your receipts are off six percent this week," Patsy said.

He was looking at Quincy with both hands resting flat on top of an absolutely bare desk with a deep gloss that reflected the perforated ceiling and its recessed circles of light; a small man with delicate bones who always seemed to be shrinking inside his beautifully tailored suits, his neck overcome by a high collar and the big knot of a silver tie. His black hair, waving back intricately from a straight line across his forehead, was his best feature, but it looked artificial. He had large, glistening, mahogany-colored eyes almost entirely without whites, a nothing nose, and the thickest pair of lips that Quincy had ever seen on a white man, very red against a complexion that ranged from saffron to orange depending upon the intensity of his emotions. Although Quincy knew that the man was several months younger than he, there was something about him that always made Quincy think of an old man in a room in a hospital, waiting.

"Did you hear me? I said your receipts are off six percent this week."

Quincy unbuttoned his jacket. Rooms that contained Patsy Orr were always uncomfortably warm. "That's because five-twenty-seven came up," he said. "Five plus two equals lucky seven. Every brother with a rabbit's foot in his pocket plays it. Lydell and me was up till two this morning paying out."

"They were off four percent last week and eight percent the week before that."

"Hard times. It's like the market, only opposite. Next time the Supreme Court hands down a desegregation decision, you watch them numbers climb, Patsy."

"Mr. Orr," someone corrected.

The someone, reading a paperback book in a tan stuffed leather armchair by the door, was called Sweets, and he was the only white man who unnerved Quincy as much as Patsy Orr. He was bullet-shaped like Devlin, but stretched out, a .44 long as opposed to a squat magnum round, with a head that came to a perfect point. It

was the point that bothered Quincy; he found it impossible not to
stare. The condition must have been congenital, as he could think of
no mishap that would plane a man's head on all four sides. Colorless
hair grew straight down from the point and curled on Sweets's
forehead, which sloped without a crease to glass-blue eyes and a
brief Irish nose and a long upper lip split in the middle like a cat's.
His suit was monk's-brown and sack-shaped—a dead giveaway that
he was carrying—and he wore one of those short diamond-shaped
ties Quincy hadn't seen since the forties, red and blue in vertical
halves with a musical clef embroidered on it, red on the blue background, blue on the red. Quincy craned his neck a little to see the
paperback's cover. *The Warren Commission Report.*

"Times must be especially hard in your neighborhood," Orr said.
"Nobody else's receipts are off by as much as yours."

"Hey, what else is new? Hastings Street ain't Grosse fucking
Pointe."

"Mr. Orr don't like that kind of language." Sweets turned a page.

"How long have you known Lafayette?" Orr asked.

"Lydell? We was in school together. They threw us out at the same
time. You're skinning the wrong frog there, Mr. Orr." He tried the
smile.

"Your judgment of human nature hasn't impressed me in the
past." The small man removed his hands from the desk. They left no
patches of moisture on the shiny top as Quincy's would have; as any
man's would have who had blood in his veins instead of engine
coolant. Quincy thought that if someone poked him full of holes
with an icepick, the holes would bleed for a second and then stop,
just like the radiator in the Zerex commercial. "I'm sending you a
man next week," Orr went on. "He's what we call a doctor. He'll look
at your organization and suggest changes."

"That ain't necessary, Mr. Orr."

"I wasn't asking your opinion."

"Well, is he black or white?"

"His name's Gallante. Will you make him welcome?"

Another fucking dago. "I got a choice?"

"Everyone has a choice, Springfield."

Four hundred fifty feet down, a horn squonked in the street.

"Anything else?" Quincy asked.

"Not just now." Orr went on looking at him.

Sweets said, "That means go."

Quincy went. Devlin's extravagant buttocks greeted him in the outer office, where the bookkeeper was bent double in his chair putting the bricks of currency into the floor safe under the kneehole of his desk. The view was entirely in keeping with Quincy's opinion of the man.

Alone in the office with the bodyguard, Orr made a gesture and Sweets laid aside his book, fished the twin aluminum canes from under his chair, and got up to bring them over. Orr finished securing his leg braces and allowed Sweets to help him to his feet and support him while he clamped the canes to his wrists. The operation was conducted swiftly, with a minimum of efficient-sounding snicks. The small man had not walked without artificial aid since he was four, the year polio struck down four thousand children in Detroit alone. His legs, and in fact his whole body, were little more than bone and withered gristle beneath the padding built expertly into his suits.

"Want the car?" Sweets asked.

"No, I'm just going across the street."

Sweets, whose brachycephaly didn't interfere with his intelligence, asked no more questions. Across the street was a public telephone booth where his employer took calls at prearranged times from an exchange in Puerto Rico; the booth contained the only untapped line convenient to the office. The man whose head came to a point left Orr to manage his canes and braces and went ahead to hold the door.

"How's things?" Lydell Lafayette asked.

Seated at the wheel of Quincy's candy-apple green Sting Ray with the top down, Lafayette had on a charcoal double-breasted that made him look like a colored banker, the brim of a pearl-gray hat snapped low over his eyes. His concession to color—a sizable one—was a lemon silk hatband and necktie to match. He had a hairline moustache like Little Richard's that accentuated the width of his mouth, which threw off the symmetry of his narrow face when he smiled. Which was all the time. His teeth were blue-white, each one the size of a pigeon's egg.

Quincy walked around the car and leaped into the passenger's seat without opening the door. "Fine as pine wine," he said, "if you like spies." He told Lafayette what Patsy Orr had told him.

"Little gimp. What you say?"

"I said, 'Feets, do your stuff,' and shuffled out of there along with what's left of my balls. What you expect?"

Lafayette turned the key and let the 327 bubble. "When's the guinea set to show?"

"Next week sometime."

"Shit, and we run out of olive oil just this morning."

Quincy slid his knees up above the dash and rested his head on the back of the Naugahyde seat. He grinned, softening his big-jaw profile. "You never guess in a million years what white folks watch on TV."

"I won't never 'cause I don't plans to try."

The Beverly Hillbillies."

"Shiiit," said Lafayette, and popped the clutch. The Corvette laid glistening black tracks to the stoplight on Fort Street.

Chapter 4

"Rick? Rick Amery?"

Rick had just tossed a tube of Ipana into his cart and was comparing prices between Brylcreem and Lucky Tiger when he heard his name called. Dan Sugar stood at the end of the aisle next to a stack of Post Toasties.

He had aged in two years, spreading below the equator and losing some of his coppery hair, which made his big, raw-hamburger face look bigger, rougher, and ruddier under the fluorescent lights of the A & P. He had on a stiff double-knit suit the color of surface rust, with wide lapels like the kids wore and a broad Jackson Pollock tie that reminded Rick of the Formica in a cheap diner. The material of the jacket hung poorly over the gun under his left arm.

A young man's voice on the PA system interrupted "The Ballad of the Green Berets" to remind shoppers that lamb chops were on sale that week only for seventy-nine cents a pound.

"How are you, Dan?" Rick did his best to sound as if he were in a hurry. Caught in the middle of the aisle, he couldn't back out without looking as if he were fleeing.

Sugar came down the aisle and shook Rick's hand across the shopping cart. His palm was warm and as soft as fresh dough.

"What's it been, a couple of years? Hell, no, it's been three since I left the C.I.D. Jesus, you don't get any older. I bet you still got your cherry in a jar somewhere."

"I heard you went into private security."

"If you call working for GM private. Best deal I ever made. I got sixteen people under me. I heard you left too."

"Yeah. Well, listen—"

But the other man had grasped his right upper arm. He was a grabber, was Dan Sugar; and that was one of the things Rick had liked best about him. "I never believed that shit they said. It was a bum deal."

"Not so bum." Rick drew back, but Sugar didn't take the hint. His grip tightened.

"Why you think I got out when I did? Commendations, medals, seniority, they don't mean shit when it comes down to you or the brass." He let go. "So what are you up to these days? How's Charlene?"

"Charlotte. We broke up. I'm working part-time at the Kwik-Pro Garage on Livernois."

"Jesus, I'm sorry."

Rick couldn't tell if Sugar was sorry for the breakup or for what Rick was doing to live. "Well, I'm due back." He started to push the cart.

"You don't report till two."

Sugar's waffled face was without expression. Rick stopped pushing.

"What do you want, Dan?"

"There's a spoon around the corner. We can walk."

Rick made his purchases in the express lane, locked the bag in the GTO parked two spaces down from the glass doors, and accompanied Sugar across the lot and down a block to a flat-roofed building with windows all around. They slid into a red plastic booth and Rick ordered coffee from a waitress in a blue uniform with red hair stacked and sprayed into a granite arch. Sugar chewed a cheek over the spotted menu for a moment, then asked for link sausages and hash browns. The waitress left with their menus.

"I'm slipping," Rick said. "How long have you been tailing me?"

"I put a couple of boys on you ten days ago. I had to be sure you were staying clean. I guess you know the Kwik-Pro's all mobbed up. They can boost a Camaro and change the paint job up on that second floor quicker than you can yell call the auto club."

"I work on the first."

"I know." Sugar looked embarrassed. "You drive a nice set of wheels for a grease monkey. I had to be sure."

"The wheels belong to my landlady's son. They go back next week."

"I know that too."

The waitress returned with Rick's coffee and two orange tumblers full of water, which she set in front of them. She told Sugar his meal would be ready in a minute and went away again.

Sugar sipped from his tumbler and set it down. "I never bought that story I.A.D. cooked up. I mean, everybody's got his price, but I don't think you'd sell that cheap."

"You're not that stupid, Dan. Of course the story was true."

"For a *car?*"

"No, not a *car.*" Rick mocked him. "A T-bird. A salesman at Schaeffer Ford was duping off Mustang keys and selling them at a thousand a crack. Every time they changed the padlock on the back gate he made a copy of that key too. I went undercover in the service department and popped him after a week. Burt Schaeffer was so grateful he offered me a year's free lease on a white sixty-four Thunderbird. I took it."

"Against department regs, but if you weren't doing any special favors—"

"Sixty-five was an election year. Internal Affairs let me keep it six months, then canned me. I guess you could say I helped re-elect Cavanagh."

"You should've gone to the union."

"My first civilian act. I get a letter from the D.P.O.A. every couple of months, telling me they're working on it."

Sugar watched him drink coffee from the thick white cup. "What is it with you and cars?"

"I like them. You like ugly suits, I like fast cars. The job lost a little of its shine when I came out from behind the wheel of a blue-and-white and put on plainclothes. If that T-bird deal hadn't come along, I might've quit in a few months."

"In that case you ought to be happy things turned out the way they did."

"Quitting and getting the boot aren't even related," Rick said.

The sausages and hash browns came. Sugar speared a link and chewed on it, face full of thought. "I can't get over how young you look. What are you, thirty-five?"

"Thirty-seven."

"You could pass for nineteen, twenty."

"I use Pond's. What's the skinny, Dan? Someone stealing cigar lighters from the Chevy plant? I don't smoke."

"Take it easy. I invited *you* to lunch, not your chip." He put down his fork. "You remember when Vice borrowed you for those marijuana busts at the U of D? You were moled in there three weeks."

"It seemed a hell of a lot longer. I was on Homicide then and I was glad to get back to good domestic murders. Sending a bunch of kids up to Jackson for smoking reefers wasn't my idea of police work."

"Forget them. They're out by now, probably smashing some poor dean's office. What I'm talking about is, none of them ever suspected you for a narc. I saw their faces when you testified. Just now I need a good undercover who can pass for a dumb kid." He grinned baggily. "You weren't hard to track down. I just sent the boys to every bar in town where the clientele have grease under their nails and talk cams and hemis."

"What's a nightwatchman need with an undercover?"

But no irritation crossed the pockmarked face. "That's another department. I'm a security vice president. I never see a plant except when I take the tour. Hey, you think I don't know your situation? This time next week you won't even have a place to live."

"I can always get a bunk at the Y."

"You can get the same thing at Mother Wattles', with soup and a sermon to boot. But she won't give you a car."

Rick laughed. It was the first time he had felt like laughing since Mrs. Hertler had told him her son was coming back from the army. "You're a joke, Dan. You got someone to pull my file downtown and now you think I'd walk bareass down Woodward for a spin in a VW."

"Camaro."

When Rick didn't respond, Sugar reached into his right pants pocket and held up a pair of brass keys attached to a leather holder. "Z-28," he said. "Experimental. This one won't even hit the pavement till next year. It's parked in front of the A & P. Canary yellow, with black racing stripes; you can't miss it. Go ahead, take it out. I'll have pie while I wait."

"Just because I look like a kid doesn't mean I think like one." But the keys fascinated him. They caught the light like brushed gold. "What's the job?"

The other man shrugged and put them back in his pocket. "Ever hear of Wendell Porter?"

"He wrote a book. *Hell on Wheels.* I read it."

"What'd you think?"

"He didn't say anything that anybody who knows about cars hasn't been talking about for years. They're rolling coffins if you don't treat them with respect. Which almost nobody does."

"He came down hardest on General Motors. As if Ford and Chrysler were making them any safer. The boys in the bean department figure that book cost us three million in sales last year."

"That comes to what, half an hour on the assembly line?"

"Fuck the three million," Sugar said. "The feds are starting to listen to him, especially since he got up that consumer group. All kids, of course; seems protesting the goddamn war isn't enough for some of them. They make a lot of noise. Washington's talking about getting up a Congressional committee to investigate safety in the auto industry. If they come out on Porter's side it means retooling for things like seat belts and padded dashes and airbags, and that means halting production, layoffs, a recession. We could wait and fight it on the floor of Congress, but that's a lot of juice. It's way cheaper to take Porter out now."

"Take him out how?"

Sugar picked up his fork. "Lower that chin, son. When GM starts killing off its enemies, a twerp like him won't make the top one hundred on the list. You don't ice the Porters of this world. You find out where they're dirty and smear it all over them."

"*You* meaning me."

"You got the cover experience. More than that, you got the looks. No one's going to suspect Beaver Cleaver of being a plant." He ate some of his potato.

"What would I do, just walk up to Porter and ask if he's hiring?"

"Basically, yeah. Most of his people are volunteers, they don't get squat. He doesn't have so many he'd bounce you for eating peas off a knife. It's too much like work for the hippies and the squares want cash. Impress him with your youthful fervor. Squirts like Porter are suckers for that earnest dodge."

"What am I looking for?"

"Whatever's there. Gambling, a little tapping from his own discretionary fund, late hours with his secretary—he's married to a lady lawyer—who knows, maybe he keeps himself some dark meat down on Twelfth. Use your imagination. I've got people researching his history looking for the same thing, but I need someone inside."

"I'm supposed to do all this for the slip on a Camaro? What do I put in the tank, imagination?"

"The job pays three hundred a week to start. If you turn something sweet it's permanent. There's always work in this business for a reliable mole."

"I thought GM's business was making cars."

"Let the boys on the line do that. My job's to see they're left alone to make them. Yours too, if you take it."

Rick looked at the midget jukebox mounted on the wall of the booth, flipped idly through the selections. Simon and Garfunkel, the Beatles, Petula Clark, Nancy Sinatra, the Righteous Brothers. "Sounds of Silence." "These Boots Are Made For Walkin'." No inspiration there. The waitress cleared away the dishes, placed the bill facedown on the table, and withdrew.

"What if there's nothing to turn?" Rick asked. "I'm no good at building frames."

"Frames are for guys with no patience. There's always the chance they'll fall apart, and then you're worse off than you were before."

"But what if there's nothing?"

Sugar thumped the table with a square-nailed finger. "Everything in this world that walks or flies or swims has got to shit somewhere; it's only a matter of time before they pick the wrong place. Everybody fucks up. A creep like Wendell Porter's got fuck-up written all over him. There's something."

"Have you got the title with you?"

The other man drew a long fold of stiff paper from his inside breast pocket and produced a ballpoint pen. "Do I sign it over?"

"I don't know about canary yellow."

"I'll give you a note to the foreman in the paint shop. It won't cost you a cent."

"Sign."

Sugar wrote his name on the back of the document and gave it to him. "You'll have to work fast. Congress is going to want a rabbit to pull out of its hat before the November elections. Let's make sure this safety thing isn't it."

"Anything else?" Rick put the title in his shirt pocket. Most of it stuck out.

"Just a lift to the bus stop."

Chapter 5

Saturday night on Twelfth Street.

Dorsaled Caddies and orange Cougars and dinged-up Olds 98s with acres of chromed engine grumbling under their bare metal hoods, trailing Smokey Robinson and the Supremes and Otis Redding like bright streamers of pure sound. Coming up on midnight the street was lit like a parade route and smelled of pigs' feet and mustard greens from 24-hour restaurants where griddles hissed and spat hot grease and a hundred lean brothers in dashikis and box-back suits heaped baked yams in front of their dates in tight low-cut minidresses and Afro wigs with the diameters of hula hoops. Working girls herded on the corners displaying their bracelets and legware. Going to a Go-Go.

A block east on Woodrow Wilson, the music of the Miracles drifted through the open window into Quincy Springfield's bedroom, where he unfolded a salmon silk shirt with extra-long collar tabs from a laundry box and inspected it for wrinkles. He was all slabbed muscle from the waist up, with a shotgun pattern of hair on his bluish chest and an old knife scar, healed over white, embroidering a lazy S on the left side of his ribcage. In the mirror over the dresser it reminded him of the musical clef on Sweets's tie in Patsy

Orr's office. He slid the shirt on quickly and fastened the bone buttons. Cover up that cocksucker. Forget Patsy for one night anyway.

As he tucked in the tails he could hear Krystal in the living room, humming along with the music as she painted her nails. They would be salmon tonight, to match his shirt; she had asked what color he was planning to wear. It pissed him off. Lately everything about her pissed him off, from her stack of bleached and straightened hair to her Day-Glo lipstick and white plastic go-go boots and ten-inch miniskirts and pink knitted halter tops, open-weave so her nipples showed, brown sugar against teak skin. Although she claimed otherwise, he had known for some time that she was still tricking. He had never been jealous of a woman a day in his life, but he resented the fact that those who knew they were together would assume he was pimping for her.

Krystal was on her way out.

Using a pic to pump up his Afro, he considered going back to Emma. As far as he knew he was still married to her. Emma and her mahogany African carvings and watercolors of tortured slaves and record albums full of pounding drums and chanting natives. He remembered clearly his last day in the house on Hastings. It had been a particularly trying one when an old customer, insisting he had picked a winning number despite the evidence in his own scrawl, had pulled a piece on Quincy and Lydell Lafayette had laid the man out with a pool cue. Afterward, Quincy had walked into that black history lesson of a living room, stopped, turned around, and walked back out. That was a year ago and he hadn't seen the place since.

Emma and her skinned-back hair and no makeup and sack dresses set off by gobs of African jewelry. She worshipped the primitive everywhere but the bedroom, where if he closed his eyes he might have been fucking Amy Vanderbilt.

No, he wouldn't be going back to Emma.

He put on his gray sharkskin jacket and went into the other room.

Krystal, sitting cross-legged on the sofa in a red satin teddy, had finished her nails and was blowing on them: inch-long pink-orange scimitars all her own that left cat-o'-nine-tail scars on Quincy's back. The spaghetti straps that held up the teddy had slipped off her skinny shoulders and her nipples peeped out through the holes in the lace top. She was a little over five feet tall and weighed ninety-three pounds. The first time Lydell saw her he called her a spinner.

"What the hell's a spinner?" Quincy had asked.

"Stick it in and spin 'er."

Quincy opened the door to the hallway. The smell of hot grease from the restaurant below the apartment grew stronger. Krystal asked him where he was going.

"Work."

"You don't open for two hours."

"Got receipts to count. Yesterday was payday."

"Well, when you open, will you come back and get me?"

"It's just around the corner."

"I could get raped."

He bit down hard on the obvious rejoinder. "I'll send Lydell."

"I don't like Lydell. Can't you come?" Her voice got whiney.

"I can't just drop everything. You can stand Lydell for five minutes."

"Well, what am I supposed to do till two o'clock?"

"Your toes." He banged the door shut behind him.

Yes, on her way out.

The after-hours place Quincy owned with Lafayette—called a "blind pig" in Detroit, after the local speakeasies of Prohibition—was a two-story walk-up over the Jiffee Coin Laundromat & Custom Laundry on Collingwood, where Quincy had his shirts done. The neighborhood, once middle-class white, had begun to blister and peel with the westward spread of the black ghetto from its Hastings Street origins. Old-timers who remembered better days claimed that the decline had started thirty-five years ago when three gangsters were slain in a gun battle in the brick apartment house on the corner of Twelfth. Collingwood, like the streets around it, had since gone to gang hangouts, second-story massage parlors, and blind pigs like Quincy's.

He climbed a staircase whose rubber runner was worn down to bare wood in scaly patches, knocked twice rapidly on an unmarked door at the end of the hall, paused, and knocked again once. A series of locks and chains snapped and jingled on the other side and the door opened.

Very little of the light from inside spilled out into the hallway. The rest was blocked by Congo standing on the other side of the threshold. Congo was shorter than Quincy by several inches but weighed a hundred pounds more, his shoulders sloping down directly from his shaven head with no neck between into a mountain of hard fat and hidden muscle. He wore a black shirt stained lighter under the arms, pink suspenders, and a pair of green pinstripe suitpants that Lydell could have used to cover the Sting Ray. It was believed locally that Congo, whose flat face and truly black skin belonged to an African idol, had been imported from Nigeria; Congo himself never denied it, but then he seldom spoke. In fact, Lydell had hired him off the wrestling circuit, where he'd been billed as Cape Horn, the Wild Man From the Ivory Coast, and rechristened him. The name on his contract with the World Wrestling Guild was Vernon Kress, and he had spent the first twenty-six years of his life in Joplin, Mississippi. He moved out of Quincy's path without a word.

The room, which had been a railroad flat before Quincy and Lydell acquired it and tore down the walls, was as long as a diner and contained a dozen Formica-topped tables and thirty-six tube steel chairs bought used from a failed restaurant. Black shades covered the windows. There was a poolroom in back that doubled as a place to shoot craps and a bar at the far end of the main room with a brass rail and turning stools, an elaborate arrangement in a neighborhood whose establishments mostly got by with just a table for set-ups. Lydell had bought the bar and stools cheap along with the jukebox by the back door off a truck with Kentucky plates, no questions asked. Percy Sledge was singing "When a Man Loves a Woman" on the juke when Quincy entered.

Lydell, in his charcoal suit and hat with the yellow band, was seated on one of the stools, smoking a Kent in a jade holder and counting bills from a pile of wrinkled currency into neat stacks on the bar. His paperweight was a nickel-plated British Bulldog revolver with black electrical tape wound around the grip.

"How we doing?" Quincy took a bottle of 7-UP from the refrigerator behind the bar and pried off the top. The carbonation was the only thing that gave him temporary relief from his chronic heartburn. The heartburn had started the day he began doing business directly with Patsy Orr.

"Six thousand so far." Lydell coughed, tapped ash into a tray rounded over with butts, took another drag, coughed again. "That's in tens and twenties. I'm down to fives and singles now."

"We done worse."

"Not the day after payday we ain't."

"Hard times."

"My ass. Harder the times, the more folks gambles. They're taking it down the road."

"That shit again."

"Word's out, man. We's worse than VD."

"You're dogging your rounds is what it is. You was to pay as much attention to filling that satchel as you do to plugging every leaky cunt between here and Adelaide—"

Lydell was looking up at him with his hound-dog eyes. "Word's *out!*"

"*Your* word."

"Patsy's word, if you only listened. Nobody else is doing bad as us, he said it himself. We ought to get down on our knees and thanks the people still buying numbers from us. They could get their fingers busted just for looking our way."

"Why? It don't matter who takes the bets; Patsy gets his cut."

"His cut."

"We don't take more than nobody else."

Lydell started coughing again, removed the butt from its holder, and squashed it out. "You won't see it, man. The guineas want Twelfth Street, no middle money to the brothers. They's bleeding us so's we'll sell out cheap."

"Bullshit. They got the rest of Detroit."

"A long time ago they made a mistake and let the brothers buy into the numbers. They was selling booze and girls, they didn't want to count all them pennies. Then booze got legal and the girls wasn't enough, they got into heroin and the track and college ball. They didn't make no partnerships, just boogied in and took over." He fitted a fresh Kent into the holder. "Don't you go jiving yourself with that 'rest of Detroit.' They don't want no 'rests.' That's what makes a Sicilian a Sicilian." He lit the cigarette with his gold-plated Ronson, coughed again.

"Forget the Sicilians. Those coffin nails are going to kill you first."

"Don't change the subject. You ever hear of Big Nabob?"

"Sounds like a hamburger."

"He was just the biggest blackest gangster this here town ever saw. Limos, white girls, fancy threads, he had God in a box. Thought he was bigger than Joey Machine. Now, I know you heard of *him*."

Quincy's knuckles yellowed on the bottle of 7-UP. He took a quick swig and belched bitterly. "Yeah, I heard of him."

"Started skimming, which was okay. We all skims. Only Big Nabob he bragged about it. Hell, why finish the story? Go visit his headstone in Mount Elliott Cemetery. Biggest one there. Gots him a angel on the top and all."

"That was thirty years ago. They don't work that way now."

"Oh, they's quieter. That's why they're bleeding us instead of lead-lining our livers. Don't mean they won't still do that if they gets impatient."

Quincy took off his jacket and draped it on his personal wooden hanger. "Let's get to counting before the customers show up and do it for us."

It came to $8,752, a little less than their best weekday total and a long way behind the Saturday average. Lydell sighed but made no further comment. He snapped a thick rubber band around each stack, stood, and began shoveling the bills into his pigskin satchel. Someone banged on the door, using the secret knock. The hands of the cartoon bear on the Hamm's Land of Sky-Blue Waters clock behind the bar pointed to 1:28.

"Tell 'em to come back in a half hour," Quincy told Congo.

A panel popped out of the door and the bouncer leaped back away from it. No, was thrown; Quincy would remember a distinct piece of a second between the time the blast blew out the panel and he heard the report. He thought a wrecking ball had struck the building. A piece of Congo hit the back wall twenty-two feet away with a wet slap.

A second blast disintegrated the door's centerpiece and the rest of it hinged and parted in the middle as three men battered their way through with bootheels and shotgun butts. Lydell lunged for his Bulldog. The top of the bar exploded. He grunted, pulled back his hand empty, and clasped the other around his wrist. Blood slid between the fingers.

One of the invaders remained by the ruined door while his companions sprinted forward, bounding over Congo's shattered body and clutching pump-action Remingtons with cut-down stocks and the barrels blunted back to the slides. All three wore long winter coats flapping open over dark turtleneck shirts, old jeans, and black army boots. They had on jersey gloves and their faces were covered by ski masks. Quincy thought they must have been sweating like pigs.

The record-changer dropped "The House of the Rising Sun" onto the turntable and the first harsh notes rasped out into the room. The man who had shot the bar racked in a fresh shell and obliterated the front of the juke. The record shrieked and fell silent. Pink and green smoke rolled out of the splintered neon tubes.

Quincy thought that was unnecessary.

The man worked the slide again and pointed the shotgun at Lydell. "Close that bag and toss it over here." His voice was even rougher than the singer's. Quincy was sure he was disguising it.

Lydell, still clutching his wrist, had sunk back onto his stool. Vermilion blood stained both hands and pattered to the floor in large iridescent drops. Quincy reached past him, snapped the satchel shut, and held it out.

"Toss it, I said."

Quincy threw the satchel at the man's feet.

"Check it out."

Although this was directed to his near companion, the man's eyes never left Quincy. They were Arctic blue.

The other man came over and picked up the bag. Parking his shotgun in the crook of his left arm, he thumbed back the latches and pulled it open. Whistled.

"Cash register."

The man with the satchel strode around behind the bar and punched NO SALE on the register. When the drawer licked out he scooped up the rack and dumped its contents—bills, coins, and all—into the satchel. He had trouble closing it.

"You two get on the floor."

Quincy put his hand under Lydell's arm to help him off the stool. Lydell's color was bad and his knees wanted to buckle, but his wrist didn't seem broken. Quincy suspected he had picked up some stray pellets. He helped the stricken man down to the floor and got down on his stomach beside him. The boards smelled of stale beer and Lestoil.

Quincy jumped when the blasts came. A hot rain fell on his back and he thought he'd been hit until he realized the particles belonged to one of the fluorescent light troughs suspended from the ceiling. The trio had opened fire on the fixtures to cover their retreat.

Just like a guinea, Quincy thought, shaking the first of a million glass shards out of his Afro.

Chapter 6

"**H**ello?"

"Al, this is Phil in Chicago."

"How are you?"

"Same. The back, you know. Plus I got some trouble with the Commission."

"What kind of trouble?"

"Just too goddamn many meetings. Sometimes I wish it was like in the old days with Sal. Somebody gave you a pain in the ass, you sent some boys over. You know. Now we have meetings."

"Times change."

"Times change."

Pause.

"So what's what, Phil?"

"It's this Whitey Esposito. He unloads the ore boats at Ford's there, the Rouge plant. They laid him off?"

"He went to you?"

"Don't sweat it, Al. He knows me. I knew his old man."

"He's got a lot of balls. He's off one day, he runs to you."

"Al, the way we look at it down here, even if he's not with us, one of the family, he's a friend of ours."

"I don't give a shit whose friend he is. I got friends was laid off that same job. I'm in the middle of negotiations here. I can't worry about no one man. He could be my brother, I got a whole union to think about."

"Don't get sore. I'm saying friends of ours shouldn't get the same deal as the rank and file."

"That's the way it is, is it?"

"I don't make the rules."

"Phil, I tell you what. I don't run girls, you don't tell me what to do with my steelhaulers." Click and dial tone.

Lew Canada switched off the little recorder. The reels stopped turning. He looked at Ed Wasylyk across the yellow oak table. The sergeant had traded his uniform for a plaid sportcoat, slacks, and a knitted blue shirt with a white racehorse embroidered over the pocket. His pouchy face looked older and less healthy without the starched blues. His hair, a mousy combination of brown and gray, needed trimming. "Who're Al and Phil?" he asked.

"Phil Benito. He's mobbed up down in Chicago, owns a string of laundries and whorehouses there. State Department's in the middle of deportation proceedings against him. For soliciting, although he's responsible for three murders that the Chicago P.D. knows of. He looks after Mafia interests here in the Midwest; that's the Commission he was talking about. Al is Albert Brock. We had a tap on his line for about a month last year. That's when the conversation you just heard took place."

"This the American Steelhaulers Brock?"

"There's another one?"

"You won't hang him with this tape."

"Hell, no. Every little kid in Detroit knows the steelies go hand-in-glove with the Cosa Nostra. We got others would tie Brock up in court till nineteen eighty, if we could only use them."

"Who's stopping you?"

"The Supreme Court, for nine. Thirty years we been tapping

phones, now they say we need a court order, which we can't get without probable cause, which is why we tap phones in the first place. Anyway, Brock pays guys to sit in the dock for him. What we want is bars in his face."

"How come?"

Canada showed his white teeth. He spent almost as much time brushing and flossing as he did in the shower. "You mean besides siphoning off the Steelhaulers' pension fund to keep his *paisano* friends happy?"

"Fuck that. You don't hear the members complaining."

"Albert Brock could rape Ladybird Johnson live on Dean Martin and the rank and file would claim she attacked him," Canada said. "That's because he'd loan his last dime to a steel employee in trouble if it didn't get in the way of contract talks. He knows which side his bread's buttered on and who churned it. And he's the only man who can keep the wops from robbing the union treasury blind while he's national president and make them like it."

"Sounds like a good argument in favor of leaving him where he is."

"Which is what we'd be doing if he stayed smart and kept his nose out of Detroit politics."

"I was wondering when we'd get around to the mayor," Wasylyk said.

"Why'd you think I took you into an interrogation room to discuss this? The walls of my office stop two feet short of the ceiling. That squad room's a direct pipeline to the Eyewitness News Team."

"Cavanagh's got a hard-on about Brock, huh?"

"More like the other way around." Canada leaned forward and laid a hand on the table. His long, clean-pored face, shaved with a scalpel, reminded Wasylyk of the death-mask of some minor eighteenth-century English general he had seen once in the Detroit Institute of Arts. He wondered what the inspector's nationality was. "What I say next stays in this room," Canada said. "Cavanagh's record squeaks: Second term in office, no garbage strikes, he's got the race thing pretty much nailed down. No other big-city mayor can claim anything like it except maybe Daley in Chicago. And Daley doesn't want to be President."

"Jesus. I didn't know he had the bug. I knew he was running for senator."

"He'll crap out. The party nomination will go to Soapy Williams, who raised the Democratic donkey from a pup in this state. Point is it's the mayor's shot at a national profile. Why not President? He's young, Irish, and Catholic, just like JFK. The voters are always hoping lightning will strike twice. He could stir up some dust at the sixty-eight convention if Johnson doesn't run. Hell, even if he does. A lot of people who voted for him two years ago are wishing they hadn't."

"Bobby Kennedy might have a thing or two to say about it."

"That prick."

"So what's the Presidency got to do with Albert Brock? I know *he* ain't running."

"The American Steelhaulers Association is the most powerful labor union in the United States, maybe in the world. Brock controls a third of the blue collar vote in this country. How's it going to look if the mayor of an industrial town like Detroit can't claim a boost from a labor leader in his own backyard?"

"What's Brock got against him?"

"He doesn't like the way Cavanagh handled the contracts with some city employees. We intercepted a memo he sent to the head of the local last year, urging him to advise his people not to vote for re-election. Of course there were others. Labor support for the mayor dropped twelve percent in November."

"He still won."

"He might not have if Brock had brought his opposition out into the open. That memo was meant as a lesson, a little sample of what he could do if Cavanagh doesn't toe the line. A line he has no intention of toeing for Brock or Princess Grace. Like you said, he's got the bug. So we have to do something about Brock before he can get up to speed. The senate primary this fall is history. We're looking two years down the road."

Wasylyk fished a crushed pack of Pall Malls out of his shirt pocket and lit one off a kitchen match he struck on the table. He dragged in a lungful and tossed the curled match into a corner with the others. "I'm a cop, not a fucking press secretary. I thought you were too. I liked you better when I thought you was a sneak for Internal Affairs."

"On the books, the unit was formed two years ago separately from I.A.D. to report directly to the mayor on charges of wrongdoing inside the department. 'Wrongdoing,' that's what politicians call crimes in the eighty percent bracket. We do some of that; Cavanagh knew about those Grecian Gardens payoffs before Vice raided the place last January. What we really are is his private staff. That's another piece of information that doesn't go out that door when you do. The voters wouldn't understand why a man in office in a free country would need secret police."

"I'm one of 'em, I guess. My old man voted for Eugene Debs. So what's the game plan?"

"Trace this Mafia thing to its source. We know Brock's office is into Patsy Orr because of the muscle Patsy's old man Frankie lent Brock twenty years ago when he was running for president of the local. Frankie Orr was a visionary, but he always looked too far ahead. That labor racketeering thing is what got him deported finally. Sal Borneo was supposed to go down for the same thing, but he died. You remember Sal. Frankie married his daughter."

"Can't tell the Sicilians from an A-bomb without a scorecard. That the Sal our boy Phil was yakking about on the tape?"

"Phil goes back a ways," Canada said. "Not many of the old gang left. That's why Frankie's kid Patsy is in charge."

"Patsy the Crip. The old man must've strained him through a sheet."

"Talk is Frankie's still running the show from Messina. Anyway, if we can track one dollar from the Steelhaulers pension fund to Patsy's pocket, we can send Brock up to Jackson for a year, or at least snarl him in the system long enough to forget about making headaches for the mayor. Hell, the exposure alone would play hell with his support at the grass roots."

Wasylyk flicked ash at the table. "Tough case to make. Those Mafia boys got more places to launder cash than Liberace's got teeth."

"I never said the job was easy. You in?"

"What's my part?"

"Nothing you haven't already done enough times to have strong feelings about. Stakeouts, the odd shadow job, some time undercover if it comes to that. It won't. I got a federal judge might come through with an order for a temporary wiretap when the time comes. When it does you'll take your turn on the earphones. You know the drill."

"Doesn't sound a whole hell of a lot different from what I been doing twenty-nine years. I thought detective work was supposed to be glamorous."

"That's the spy game. You've been watching *The Man From U.N.C.L.E.*" The inspector rose and smoothed the crease on his black suitpants. "Hey, it beats boosting disk brakes."

"The brakes pay better."

"Lawyer fees cut into the profits. So you in?"

Wasylyk took one last drag and mashed the butt into an old burnhole in the table. "I got nothing better to do but sit home and watch *Days of Our Lives.*"

"Swell. Come up to seven. I'll introduce you to the squad."

"I'm dead on my feet. What's it, three o'clock?"

"Almost four. You'll have to get used to hookers' hours. *Sub rosa* units work mostly at night."

"Well, the overtime ought to make up for a patrolman's salary."

"What's overtime?"

"Shit. I should've guessed." Wasylyk stood, bones cracking, and watched Canada gathering up the tape recorder. "How come you can get an order for a tap now and you couldn't then?"

"We didn't know then what we know now about this particular judge. Remind me to show you his file sometime."

"How'd you fill it?"

"Tapped his private line." Canada held the interrogation room door.

Chapter 7

The seventh floor of Detroit Police Headquarters at 1300 Beaubien—"1300," as it was known throughout the department—was made up of barnlike rooms lit through opaque glass panels in the high ceilings and had an acoustical linoleum floor and steel mesh over the windows. The windows, taller than a man, looked to Quincy as if they should contain grim saints carved out of slick marble. It was that kind of building, designed in the 1920s by a white architect who had seen *Intolerance* one too many times. Quincy felt cold and exposed and very black sitting in a vinyl chair in front of the white sergeant's desk, one of a dozen or more arranged in two rows, most of them unmanned at 4:00 A.M. His hands were icy when he held them to his cheeks. He diagnosed his condition as shock.

He wondered how Lydell was doing. The cops had let Quincy ride with him in the ambulance to Detroit Receiving, where the patient got into an argument with an emergency room orderly who wanted to cut the ring off the injured hand. It was a big gold ingot with a diamond set in the center, which Lydell liked to tell people had been presented to him as a utility infielder with Milwaukee after the 1957 World Series. Quincy, whose father had left Negro ball to go into bootlegging when the Klan broke his hands, had gotten his friend into the crap game where he'd won the ring. Nobody shot the bones like Lydell. But the dispute had convinced him his friend would come out with all the parts he went in with, and Quincy had agreed to ride down to 1300 in a car from the Tactical Mobile Unit.

The fat sergeant had short pale hair tipped with gray and freckles everywhere, even on the backs of his hands. He typed with one finger, pausing between letters to study the keyboard as if he had never seen the old gray Royal before that morning. Something about him made Quincy think of the locker room at the Y; it drove him crazy until he traced it to his nostrils. Man used Ben-Gay like Krystal used perfume.

"That your real name, Springfield?" he asked finally.

"Just in Detroit. Other places I use Harry Belafonte."

"You watch your mouth, boy. I can ask this same shit down at County with a turnkey's finger up your black ass."

"It's my real name."

"Know the guys that hit you?"

"All I know is they was white."

"You said they had their hands and faces covered."

"Necks too. That's how come I know they was white. Why'd you wear a turtleneck on a warm night in June unless you didn't want people knowing you was white?"

"Maybe they didn't want anyone knowing they were black."

"On Collingwood? Shit."

"You watch your mouth, boy. I won't tell you again."

Quincy said nothing.

"Anything else you remember?" asked the sergeant.

"One who done all the talking had blue eyes."

"I've seen Negroes with blue eyes. You know Johnny Blue? Don't say you don't, 'cause I know he's been to your place."

"Johnny's are pale blue. This one's was deep and chilly. He was white, all right."

"I'll put down you don't know who the guys were." Keys whacked paper.

Quincy, who after his father's death had grown up in a shoebox on Erskine with his mother and shared a bathroom with two other families, thought it was a big room for so few detectives. A thin black man in a white shirt and suitpants with a Smith & Wesson Airweight under his left arm sat reading the *Free Press* city edition two desks down, and two white men with Smitties on their belts were discussing yesterday's Tigers game at the water cooler by the door. Aside from them, Quincy and the sergeant had the place to themselves. A religious program was playing silently on a portable black-and-white TV atop a file cabinet. The horizontal hold was slipping; the minister's head showed at the bottom of the screen with his dark-suited torso at the top. Nobody was watching.

The hallway door opened and two men came in. One was as tall as Quincy but leaner and wore an immaculate black suit that was starting to show its age in the knees and elbows. He had a long, slightly angular face and crisp black hair going gray. The other man was shorter and sloppier-looking in a plaid coat, wrinkled slacks, and blue shirt without a tie. He needed a haircut. They stopped to talk to the two cops at the water cooler. The man in the plaid coat shook their hands.

The fat sergeant was snapping his fingers at Quincy. "Stay off the clouds, boy. This ain't no liquor beef I'm asking you about."

"Three 'boys' is all you get," Quincy said, and swung at him from his chair.

But he'd been hustled, taken in by the sergeant's inanimate-looking bulk. The sergeant gave the rickety typewriter stand a shove and the Royal landed in Quincy's lap. It threw off his aim, and the fat man ducked under the fist, cross-drew the revolver on his belt, and laid the four-inch barrel against Quincy's right temple in a backhand sweep. The room pirouetted and the ceiling came down on top of him.

For an instant he teetered on the edge of unconsciousness, then pulled back, dizzy and nauseated. He was on his back on the floor, still sitting in the chair, with a paralyzing weight on his chest. It was the typewriter, lying upside-down with the carriage return lever gouging his shoulder. The ceiling rocked itself to a standstill. Six pairs of legs stood around him in a semicircle, tapering up to belt buckles and bellies, mountains with tiny heads carved on their peaks. It was like looking up at Mt. Rushmore through the small end of a telescope.

"What happened?" It was the mountain in black talking. Quincy recognized him now as one of the two men who had entered the room moments ago. He picked out the three detectives and the plaid-coated newcomer and the fat sergeant in his white shirtsleeves, freckled fists balled at his sides. The revolver was clenched in one of them but not pointed at anything.

"Puke took a cut at me." The sergeant holstered his gun and kicked Quincy hard in the ribs. The pain lanced up to his temple. "You're busted, jig. Climb out from under that machine before I add stealing office equipment to assaulting an officer."

"What's he doing here?" asked the man in the black suit.

"Name's Springfield. Some guys hit his blind pig on Collingwood this morning. Offed the bouncer and rabbited with what was in the register. He says. His partner's at Receiving, caught some shotgun spray."

"What time?"

"About one-thirty. They were getting set to open."

"That's Homicide's squeal. How'd you wind up with it?"

"Coopersmith was dragging his ass off a double shift. I didn't have anything better on so I took over the paperwork. Nigger killings off Twelfth Street aren't exactly commissioner's priority. Come on, Beulah. 'Ngowa. I go off duty in four hours."

Quincy had managed to heave the Royal over onto its rubber feet. Now he got his knees under him and jacked himself up using the fallen chair as a lever. The room did a slow Twist. His head was going *bloing-bloing*.

The angular-faced man in the black suit studied him. The upper third of the man's head seemed to be resting on the single black lintel of his eyebrows. He looked clean for a cop. "Did he hit you?" he asked the sergeant.

"I talked him out of it."

The man in the plaid coat was amused. "You should talk to Castro."

"Tank him for disorderly."

"He took a cut at me, Inspector."

"Next time let him connect."

Quincy said, "Give me my call first. I got to call the hospital."

"Sergeant Esther didn't hit you that hard."

"Not me. Lydell."

"Lydell?"

The sergeant said, "That's the partner. I don't know where their mammies get those names."

"You'll get your call when you make up your mind to quit bullshitting," the inspector told Quincy. "Nobody robs a pig *before* it opens. Not for what's in the till."

The Wayne County Jail was clean as lock-ups went, no bugs and they lent him a broom once a day to sweep the cell and cleanser to scrub the little sink and toilet. The blue coveralls were as comfortable as pajamas. He had no cellmate. It was a quiet place to stretch out on the shallow mattress and listen to the pulpy mass heal over his right ear, the traumatized skin crackling as it dried and shrank. The throbbing had receded to a warm buzz. He would miss it when it was gone.

He stopped thinking about the injury after two sheriff's men dragged a Negro in coveralls into the cell kitty-corner from his and dumped him on the cot. The man's eyes were swollen shut and his lips were puffed. He lay motionless on his ruined face after they slammed the cell door and didn't stir hours later when they came with supper. Quincy wondered if he was dead and how long they'd let him stink before they hauled out the carcass.

The next morning, Quincy's second at County, he woke up and looked across at a pair of cinnamon-colored hands dangling between the bars of the man's cell. Quincy got up and leaned his face against his own cell door. The man's face had broken out in yellow blistery streaks and the blood on his split lip had dried to a black thread, but Quincy could see something glittering in the slits of his eyes. He was short and slender, with straight glossy black hair that would have reminded Quincy of Johnny Mathis if the man's face didn't make him think of Quasimodo.

The man was saying something now. He had to try a second time to make it come out like words. "Got a cigarette, brother?"

"Don't use 'em," Quincy said.

"That's okay. I'm too pooped to puff anyway."

"Whitey do your face?"

"I ran into a door. It was marked POLICE. I couldn't see on account of the flashing red light." He started to smile and winced. Fresh blood glittered on his chin.

Despite the distortion, the man's voice had a roundness and depth that suggested practice. Quincy wondered if he was some kind of preacher. "What'd you do, brother?"

"Broke a window."

"Liquor store?"

"Restaurant."

"How come?"

"They wouldn't serve me, so I threw a chair through the front window. Waiters did this." He gestured toward his face.

"Had a date, huh."

"No, it was just me."

"Brother, you're crazy."

"I heard that before."

"What'd they hang on you?"

"Assault and battery of five waiters. I didn't hear the other charges; they were beating on me with sticks at the time. What'd *you* do?"

"Slugged me a cop."

"Yeah? Who for?"

Quincy felt himself grinning. "I hear you."

They were silent for a moment.

"When do they feed you here?" the man asked.

"You missed supper. Breakfast's coming."

"How do you know? You got a watch?"

"No, I can hear the trays."

Silence again.

"You a preacher?" Quincy asked.

"I'm a singer."

"No shit, where? Church?"

"Used to. Guess I will again. I cut twelve sides for Barry Gordy, but he didn't renew my contract. He said my English was too good."

"Whyn't you do something about it?"

"Tried. Can't. I've got a BA from Wayne State and I can't shake it."

"So you bust windows in restaurants."

The other man turned his better eye Quincy's way. "Where'd you study psychology?"

"Twelfth Street."

A big deputy came down the hall and stopped in front of Quincy's cell. He wasn't carrying a tray. "Springfield?"

"Where'd he go if I ain't him?"

The deputy unlocked the door and opened it. "You get your phone call now."

In the corridor between the cells, Quincy asked the man with the swollen face what he called himself.

"Mahomet."

Chapter 8

There was no telephone.

The room the deputy took him to and left him in was twice the size of Quincy's cell, with two laminated tables surrounded by vinyl chairs and three machines against the wall selling coffee, sandwiches, and cigarettes. Copies of *Argosy, True,* and last week's *Life* littered the tables. The inspector from yesterday stood by the cigarette machine. He had on the same black suit without even a rumor of lint and a red tie on a white shirt. He placed a quarter against the slot in the machine. "What brand?"

"Don't smoke," Quincy said.

The inspector made a noise in the back of his throat and pocketed the coin. "Me too. Have a seat."

"Cop said I was getting my phone call."

"I can save you a dime. They kicked your friend Lafayette out of Receiving yesterday. All he had were splinters in his wrist and hand, from where the shotgun blast hit the bar. Thirty minutes in and out. He'll be writing down numbers left-handed for a day or so, but he's fine."

"You could be lying."

"It's a fair bet. I lie a little every day. You can call and find out for yourself after you leave here." He waved a hand. "This is the guards' lounge, like it?"

"Beats where I been."

"You ought to try a bamboo stockade on Rabaul."

"Where's that, downriver?"

"It was in New Guinea. Still is, probably. I don't plan to go back and check. Battery acid?" The inspector slotted a dime into the coffee machine.

"Yeah, okay." In the cells it was milk; Quincy had decided the county didn't want its inmates staying awake. He slid out a chair and sat down. The slippery seat felt good. He'd memorized all the slats in his cot.

He wondered about Rabaul.

The other man bought coffee for himself too and carried the waxed cups over to the table and set them down. Before sitting he unbuttoned his coat and tugged up the knees of his trousers. Quincy could count his pores, man was that clean. He made Quincy, who hadn't shaved since day before yesterday, feel even grubbier.

"My name's Canada. I apologize for Sergeant Esther. The department dumped him on me six weeks ago and I don't like him any better than you do. But he does his job."

"Done one on me."

"You were begging for it. I'm talking about that racist shit. This department's in enough trouble without it."

"That's what I heard." In January, a gambling raid on the Grecian Gardens restaurant a block from 1300 had turned up a "Christmas list" of recorded payoffs to high-ranking police officials to ignore gambling in the Greektown area. A number of the officials named had since announced early retirement.

"Scandals come and go like buses," Canada said. "The population of Detroit is better than forty percent black. If we don't improve relations with the Negro community we could have another Watts on our hands. I told Esther if he mouths off like that again I'll get his fat butt suspended."

"Don't make no difference to me. Man's got enough trouble getting by on his own without worrying about everybody else that's his color. Do I get to make my call or what?"

"You really don't believe me. About your partner being okay."

"I believe you. Now I don't got to think about Lydell I can use a lawyer."

"I'd have thought he'd show up with one himself before this," Canada said. "Friend like that."

"Lydell looks out for himself."

"Who looks out for Quincy?"

A deputy with a Wyatt Earp moustache entered the room, bought a pack of Kools, and left. Quincy sipped coffee; battery acid was a fair description. "You got a wife, Inspector?"

"I did for a while."

"She call you Inspector or what?"

"She called me Lew when she wasn't throwing things at me. It's my first name. That's what you wanted to know, right?"

"Okay. I thought as long as you knew mine."

Canada rotated his cup between his palms. So far he hadn't drunk from it. "I did some homework on you while you were in the tank. Your old man used to leg liquor from Ontario back in the dry time. The Machine mob killed him."

"Strung him up by his wrists in the Ferry Warehouse and barbecued him with blowtorches, my ma said. I never knew him."

"He ran with Jack Dance. Jack the Ripper, the papers called him. I was just a kid when they gunned him and two of his boys in an apartment on Collingwood. Just down the street from your place now."

"That so?"

"It can't be easy working with the Italians, knowing they killed your father."

He'd been wondering how they were going to come around to it. "Like I said, I didn't know him. And I don't work with no Italians.

Me and Lydell sell drinks after hours. What you going to do, throw me in jail for it?"

"Settle down. You've got a lot of anger in you, you know it? Can't be the jail time; you've got two priors for liquor violations, so this is old stuff to you." Canada drank from his cup finally. "Someone knocked over a policy operation on Clairmount an hour before your joint was hit. Same M.O., three guys in ski masks with shotguns. Nobody was killed there, so it didn't come across the police blotter. You numbers people aren't much for hollering cop."

Quincy said nothing.

"The street talk is someone's crunching down on the West Side: Policy, dope, fencing. Especially policy, which means whoever it is is targeting the Negro rackets. Only thing around with that kind of muscle is the Mafia. Getting on with Patsy, are you?"

"Patsy who?"

Canada sat back. "I'm not Vice. I don't give a shit about numbers and who's selling who a snort after the bars close. I'm just trying to avoid a war. Is Patsy Orr turning up the heat or what?"

"Arrest the three guys. War's over then."

"Assuming they're not all out in Vegas by now, what good's that? He'll just hire three more. Next time maybe they'll get smart and take you out instead of your bouncer."

"What you want, Canada? You got your street skinny. You don't need me."

The inspector slid a copy of *True* out of the clutter of magazines on the table and laid it in front of Quincy. The cover was a color photograph of a square-built man standing on an asphalt lot with his back to a row of gleaming diesel tractor-trailers parked facing the camera, Macks and Whites and Kenworths with square grilles and shiny stacks. The man, in his fifties, had on a navy blue suit and patent-leather shoes and stood with his elbows turned out slightly and his hands hovering in front of his thighs in an unconscious weightlifter's stance. His hair was short and spiky, dark on top and graying on the sides so that his temples looked shaved, and there was about his scowling face and thick frame—not going to fat so much as retreating before it slowly, fighting it at every step—that echoed the bottled thunder of the towering rigs at his back. The legend on the cover read:

BROCK!

The Steel Behind the Steelhaulers

EXCERPT FROM A SENSATIONAL NEW BOOK

"Ever see him?" Canada asked.

"On TV, sure. He invented unions."

"I mean in person. Maybe you saw him in Patsy's office a time or two."

"I never been."

"The express elevator to Patsy's floor only makes one stop. I've had a man watching the elevator for two months. Your description shows up on the list six times. I can haul him down here for a positive ID."

"Bullshit." But he'd hesitated, and had seen the other man flick his tongue at the flutter of doubt and wobble it around.

"Okay, it's not an express. Point is you'd have to have been to the Penobscot Building to know it. Anyway, Brock's too sharp to pay a call on a *paisan*." Canada took a crumpled envelope out of the side pocket of his coat and laid it on top of Brock's face.

"What's that, breakfast?" Quincy didn't touch it.

"Wallet, change, keys. Make sure everything's there and give me back the receipt. You can change into your street clothes in Admissions. I never filed charges."

Quincy looked inside the envelope and dumped out its contents. He counted the bills in the wallet, groped for and handed over the twist of paper he'd gotten for his valuables, and put everything in his jumpsuit pockets. He rose. Canada wasn't watching. "Aren't you going to ask why I put you in lock-up?"

"My ma taught me never to ask the Man for nothing." He started for the door.

"How's your side?"

Quincy slowed. "Which side?"

"The one they took thirty-two stitches in at Receiving last spring. You walked into a blade at the Chit Chat Lounge?"

"Hurts when it rains." He hovered inside the door.

"You've got balls, Quincy. It's one thing to spit over the brink when you don't know what it's like to have your blood filling your shoes, something else when you do. Once is lucky. Twice doesn't happen. Not in Motown."

Quincy returned to the table. "You got family, Inspector?"

"One uncle in a nursing home in Stockbridge."

"Nice place?"

"It's okay. The doors to the rooms are painted different colors so the patients won't get lost."

"My ma caught clap from her customers. When she couldn't feed herself no more the Welfare folks stuck her in Ypsi State. Up there they keep them doped so they're less trouble and tie them to their beds so they don't fall out. She strangled herself with the ties, they said. They wasn't sure just how."

"I'm sorry."

"I dream about it sometimes. Dying like that."

"I get you."

Quincy made another try at leaving, then went back.

"You got a brother locked up for trashing a restaurant," he said. "Calls himself Mahomet?"

"Never heard of him."

"Well, what's bail on a thing like that?"

"Up to the judge." Canada filled his mouth with coffee and held it for a moment, then swallowed. "If nobody files for personal injury, say five hundred."

"I'm short fifty. I'll be back with the rest."

"He a friend of yours?"

"I just like to hear him talk."

"Lucky for him those three guys didn't take your wallet."

"Guess they was in a hurry after they blowed down Congo."

"Speaking of Kress, who's going to claim the body? Doesn't look like he had any relatives."

"I'll send Lydell. He hired him." Quincy was leaving now.

"While you're at it, tell him the police in Toledo want to talk to him about some bad checks he passed down there a couple of years back."

In Admissions they'd hung his silk shirt and sharkskin jacket on wire hangers in a cabinet with a lot of other clothes that had never been hung anywhere before. Quincy would've told the deputies to burn them and worn the jumpsuit home if it didn't mean being seen in his neighborhood in county blue. He changed, caught a cab to Wilson, and went up to the apartment for a shower and fresh threads. Krystal was still asleep at 9:00 A.M., spreadeagled buck naked on her back on top of the covers with her hair in her face and snoring like an Evinrude. He could never look at her pointy little tits and visible ribs without feeling like a child molester. He thought he'd give her a couple of hundred when she woke up and send her packing.

Scoured and shaved, he put on an emerald shirt with gold cufflinks and a pair of brown pinstripe pants and used the telephone in the living room to call Lydell. He had to shout the name several times before the old woman who answered told him to hang on a minute. Lydell lived rent-free in a house on Palmer with the old woman, who was deaf as a brick; Quincy had once made the mistake of asking him what he did to earn his bed and board.

"Put it this way," he'd answered. "I'd jerk off in my hand and throw it in there if it means clean sheets and plenty of hot water."

After five minutes during which Quincy listened to distant house-sounds and a television recipe for creamed chicken, Lydell came on the line. The telephone was a wall unit in a narrow hallway. "Quincy, my man. You out?"

"I just found out you left Receiving," Quincy said. "What you been doing to cut me loose?"

"I was working on it, man. I can't go in no police station. I got troubles that direction."

"Fuck that. Ain't no Detroit cop going to wet his pants over what goes on in no Toledo."

"Toledo? Shit, I done forgot about Toledo." He spoke quickly. "So you go over the wall or what?"

"Tell you later. What's happening at the place?"

"Ain't nothing happening. Police stuck one of them yellow seals on the door. What's left of it."

"They padlock it?"

"Ain't nothing to padlock. You seen what them three done to it. Ain't you going to ask me about my hand?"

"I heard you got some splinters."

"Splinters, that's what they said? Shiiit. Damn near blowed it clean off. Man, I hates shotguns. They got no sense of fine judgment."

"Think it was Sicilians?"

"Who else?"

"I didn't ask you for no questions," Quincy spat. "We got to be sure."

"We can always ask 'em."

"Who, Patsy?"

"We can start with this guinea he's sending, whatsizname, Gallante. He called while you was in the can. Wants to meet us tomorrow at the Civic League." A grin crept into Lydell's voice. "Sounds like he knew when the cops was going to kick you before the cops did."

Chapter 9

Four barrels made all the difference.

Bob Hertler's GTO, hobbled by a carburetor designed for a family car, had been like a mountain cat stuck with iron shoes. Now, sailing east on Jefferson along the river, playing the pedal to catch all the lights green, Rick felt the Z-28 filling its lungs with clean damp air, Pure premium-leaded hammering in its veins. The pavement skinned underneath like Teflon.

It had taken thirty minutes for the paint crew at the Chevrolet assembly plant in Westland to spray silver over the original yellow, heat-dry and buff it; another ten to put the two thick black racing stripes on the long hood. The bucket seats were upholstered in black Naugahyde, and Rick himself had replaced the lambswool steering wheel cover with perforated leather. The leather smell joined the air off the river and made Rick think of new shoes and fresh-cut grass and the last day of school. For once he felt as young as he looked. He flipped the radio on and punched up WKNR. The Beach Boys were just finishing "Little Deuce Coupe." He laughed. The announcer came on and identified the frequency: 1300. It reminded Rick of police headquarters and he sobered.

He fished the fold of notepaper out of the pocket of his one good dress shirt and checked the number. He had a 10:30 A.M. appointment with a Miss Kohler at an address on Whittier, base of operations for the Porter Group, or Wendell's Wonders, as a sardonic press had dubbed the organization of headline-rakers, Chicken Littles, and general pains in the butt of the American automotive industry. Rick knew the Miss Kohlers of this world, rodentlike creatures in University of Michigan sweatshirts with granny glasses and pencils in their hair. Unpaid volunteers were like professional virgins, standing sentry over treasures of questionable value.

The place wasn't what he'd expected. Porter's television image, tousled hair and unpressed Ivy League suits, bespoke an office and anteroom in a building with a wheezy elevator or a converted warehouse overlooking a broken streetlamp. Either the image or the address was wrong. Set back from the street with a sign on the lawn bearing only the letters PG, the house was a Colonial of turn-of-the-century vintage, painted rose and white, with gables and shutters and flower boxes under the windows. A huge eucalyptus, shipped in by some long-dead lumber baron or stove manufacturer, overhung the roof. The place had all the fussed-over detail of an infirm child's dollhouse. Rick took the composition driveway to a little square lot behind the house and parked between a late-model Mercedes and a VW Beetle with mismatched fenders. He figured the VW belonged to Miss Kohler.

A three-by-five card wedged into a corner of the window in the front door urged him in ballpoint pen to please enter. When he closed the door behind him a little brass bell looped over the doorknob jangled.

"One minute," said a woman's voice from the back.

The entryway, ten feet by twelve with a staircase leading to the second story, was painted bright yellow, the shade he had just banished from the Camaro, and contained a potted fern, three-drawer file cabinet with a five-volume set of engineering manuals standing on top of it, and a small desk holding up a splash of nasturtiums in a ceramic vase, a low sleek Smith-Corona electric with a powder-blue shell, and a black telephone with a banana-shaped caddy attached to the receiver. The plastic nameplate on one corner read ENID KOH-LER. Rick considered the first name and added ten years to his image of Miss Kohler.

The telephone rang and a tall brunette in a red knitted dress cinched with a wide black belt clicked in on high heels through an open door in back, laid a sheaf of blank forms on the desk, un-screwed a diamond from her left earlobe, and picked up the receiver. She was in her late twenties and had the long straight black hair and high coloring of a gypsy. "This is Miss Kohler," she told the person on the other end.

The Mercedes. Not the VW.

"No, Mr. Porter is in Washington. We don't expect him back until tomorrow afternoon."

Rick studied her hands. No ring.

"May I help you?"

She'd hung up and was looking at him. She had brown eyes.

"Rick Amery," he said. "I'm a little early."

She took inventory. He'd dressed carefully for his role as a volunteer: blue suit and brown wingtips, freshly polished. His lapels and black knitted tie were a little narrow for the current fashion, but that was all right; dorky lobbyists didn't go broke on Carnaby Street. He couldn't tell if she approved.

"Fill out this application, please." She handed him a form and a Bic pen and pointed to a kidney-shaped school desk in the corner.

He used his real name but put his age down as thirty. When he came to *Reason for applying for this position*, he hesitated, then wrote, *Hoping for a career in politics*. He'd decided he couldn't sustain the altruist dodge he'd been tinkering with all morning. Out of the corner of his eye he watched Enid Kohler screw her earring back on, roll a sheet into the typewriter, turn it on, and begin tapping. She was competent, but no keyboard whiz. He was sure she'd never seen the inside of a secretarial school.

A man fifteen years Rick's junior came down the stairs on the trot, walked past Rick without a glance in his direction, and stopped by the desk. He was willowy, dressed in a denim workshirt with the sleeves rolled above his elbows and faded jeans stuffed into the fringed tops of brown suede boots. His hair was black and curled over his collar. *VW?* Rick thought. Enid stopped typing and looked up.

"I just got off the phone with the state police," he said. "They're dragging their feet on those accident projections."

"They can't refuse to give them to you. They're public record."

"You know the bureaucracy."

"I also know how many people General Motors employs in this state and how many of them vote," she said. "Keep trying. Tell them we'll get a court order if we have to."

"If we can find a judge who doesn't like his job."

"Excuse me."

They looked at Rick, who had approached the desk with his completed form.

"I'll take that." Enid plucked the sheet out of his hand and laid it on a shallow stack. "Thank you very much, Mr. Avery. We'll call you."

"Amery. I couldn't help overhearing. State cops giving you grief?"

"Nothing we don't experience every day in one form or another," she said. "If you join the Porter Group, you'll always know which way you're going. Straight uphill."

"May I?" He put a hand on her telephone pad.

She nodded, watching him. He picked it up, scribbled a telephone number on the top sheet, tore it off, and held it out toward the long-haired young man. "That's the state police commander's home number. It's unlisted. It helps to talk to the boss."

The young man looked at the number and grinned.

Enid Kohler sat back. The dress clung to the long firm line of her right thigh. He decided she played tennis. "I'm impressed, Mr. Amery. What's your source?"

"Reliable."

"You sound like a newspaperman."

"I was with the *Times* two years until it folded." His subscription had been about to expire anyway. Under cover he told the truth whenever it was convenient.

She looked at his application. "It says here you're a mechanic."

"I got tired of journalism. With a wrench you can see what progress you're making."

The long-haired young man laughed shortly. "Brother, did you come to the wrong shop."

"Give that number a try," Enid told him.

"Yes, *ma'am*." He clicked his heels. "We still on for lunch?"

"Unless the commander invites you over to his place."

He laughed again and thrust his hand at Rick. "Leon Schenck. Call me Lee."

"Rick Amery." Rick shook it. No calluses to go with the laborer's attire.

"Hire this guy." Lee went upstairs.

"Nice kid," Rick said.

"He's twenty. Around here that's adult." She took inventory again. "You don't look like a politician, Mr. Amery."

"Rick. I'm not."

Her eyebrows went up. He was glad to see she didn't pluck them. "On your application—"

"You don't have to be a politician to be in politics. Behind the scenes is good enough for me. Public office doesn't interest me so much as the process of putting someone there. Isn't Lee a little young for you?"

"You've got a lot to learn about diplomacy if politics is what you want," she said after a moment. "But let's see if we can put your mechanical aptitude to work. How are you on pretext and subterfuge?"

He hesitated. "I've been dating since I was twelve."

"It's a start. This is a listing of towing services in the metropolitan area." She opened a drawer and handed him a sheaf neatly razored from the Yellow Pages. "Find out how many GM cars have been towed in for safety-related repairs over the past twenty-four months. Get the nature of the repairs. Concentrate on models made after nineteen sixty-three. Use whatever story you want, only don't represent yourself as a police officer. That's illegal."

"Shouldn't I be calling the dealerships? Those are warranty jobs."

"The dealerships are on to us. When the towing services catch on we'll have to go someplace else, maybe newspaper files. Wendell was getting his information directly from the General Motors Building in the beginning, when he was writing *Hell on Wheels* and nobody knew him from Hubert Humphrey. Now they call security when he walks past on the other side of Grand."

"Wendell, is it?"

She colored a little. He liked women who blushed. "We're very informal here, Rick. In lieu of salaries we get to call the boss by his first name. You'll find a telephone in the next room." She tilted her head toward the door in back.

"Why GM?" he asked. "Ford and Chrysler use the same standards."

" 'Cut off the head and the arms wither.' Wendell says it so often he ought to have a sampler made for the wall of his office."

"You do needlepoint?"

A muscle worked in her jaw. She jerked a thumb over her shoulder. "In there."

He kicked himself all the way through the door. He was out of practice, letting his opinions show when he was supposed to be Silly Putty for the molding. He'd lost Enid Kohler for the time being.

The room had been a parlor, and Edwardian touches remained in the floral wallpaper and a bow-window looking out on a bird feeder in the yard. The card-table and kitchen-chair furnishings were strictly Johnsonian.

"Hi, I'm Pammie. Wendell's the only one around here who wears a tie."

The girl seated at the table sorting three-by-five cards into a recipe box fit his early expectations of Wendell's Wonders. She wore a gray short-sleeved sweatshirt over white shorts that left her fat thighs exposed and she twinkled at him myopically over the tops of slanty glasses with a Band-Aid on the left bow. She had acne and her brown hair was gathered with a rubber band into a frayed stalk on top of her head like Alice the Goon's. *VW*, Rick thought.

"Sorry." He undid his collar button and loosened the tie. "I'm Rick."

"I know. I heard. Welcome aboard. That telephone should be cooled down enough by now."

Pammie was perhaps nineteen. As he took a seat and reached for the instrument, he hoped his bones didn't creak too loudly.

He worked his way through the listings in order, taking notes on a legal pad Pammie slid his way and scratching out each number when someone answered. Letting a little Oklahoma creep into his voice, he identified himself as an independent surveyor employed by AAA.

Pammie giggled after he hung up the first time. "You're good."

"It's the twang," he said. "People think hicks are too stupid to be pulling anything."

"What if a hick answers?"

"Then I talk like a Yankee." He imitated JFK.

She giggled again. "Now you sound like Wendell."

It was slow work. At the end of twenty minutes he'd made only three calls and filled a dozen pages with notes in his personal short-hand. It was surprising how many General Motors cars had had safety equipment problems. Pammie, reading and culling old cards from the file box and adding new ones, soon stopped listening. Rick was about to place another call when the telephone rang. Line 2 lit up. He heard Enid answering in the next room.

"Oh, hello, Wendell. How's the weather?"

Rick glanced at Pammie, studying a card. He picked up the receiver and punched 2.

". . . same as yours. I'm at Metro Airport. The meeting was canceled."

Rick recognized the voice from television press conferences, the Harvard accent softly reminiscent of Kennedy's.

"That's the second time," Enid said.

"I know. They're ducking me. Can you meet me at American? We'll have lunch at the Hilton."

"Is that wise?" Her tone was barely above a whisper.

"I'm tired of being wise. It hasn't gotten me anywhere. Are you free?"

"Yes."

"Don't tell the others I'm here yet. Nothing gets done when everyone's depressed."

Rick waited until they both hung up before he punched Line 1. He was busy dialing the next number when Enid leaned in through the door. "Pammie, can you watch the phone? I have to go out."

"I thought you and Lee were going to lunch."

"Damn." She glanced at a tiny gold watch on her wrist. "Apologize, okay? Tell him I'll explain later." She clattered away without a glance at Rick. Thirty seconds later the Mercedes swept past the window, startling a bluejay off the feeder.

Rick broke the connection on a busy signal. That explained Miss Kohler. This was going to be easier than he thought.

Chapter 10

"**W**hen you said Kresge, I was expecting a stool between Hardware and Lingerie," Lee said.

Rick and the long-haired young man were sitting under the skylight in the Kresge Court Cafeteria, bathed in greenish light filtered through the orchids and ferns that grew in fuzzy profusion between the wrought iron tables. He had brought Lee there because the odds of running into any of his former police department colleagues in the lower court of the Detroit Institute of Arts were too small to measure. They finished their meals and listened to Frankie Avalon crooning over the speakers.

Rick said, "It's good plain food but they make it look like an oil painting. You didn't look the diner type." Which was a lie; Lee Schenck looked as if he spent more time in diners than canned soup.

"It's nice, but I could've caught a burger someplace. I'm not really into food anyway. Lunch is like an oasis, you know? In the working day."

"Thanks for joining me," Rick said. "I hate eating out by myself. People look at you."

"I say let 'em look. Each to his own thing."

Rick couldn't tell if this guy was for real. He had the hair and the prole look, but looks were easy. He himself had ditched the jacket and tie back at the office. They had started to get in the way.

They split the check—Rick had learned early that picking it up only put others on their guard—and walked down Woodward, taking their time rounding the corner to where Rick had parked on John R. The late-June day was warming up for a two o'clock scorcher, but memories of the Michigan winter were still fresh and the sidewalks teemed with strollers drawing out their lunch breaks. A white Lincoln convertible with Oriental-looking headlights cruised past with its top down and Mitch Ryder screaming unintelligible lyrics from the radio. Lee jerked his long loose body with the beat.

"Almost bikini weather," Rick said. "We'll have to wangle lunch on Belle Isle then."

"If I'm not overseas."

He glanced at Lee. "Vietnam?"

"Peace Corps."

"No kidding, how long you been?"

"I just got accepted last month. I'm waiting for my assignment."

"What country you hoping for?"

"I studied Spanish six years. I'll probably get Nairobi." He laughed his short laugh.

"They say it looks good on the résumé."

"I'm not doing it for me."

Rick decided he was for real.

"So the Porter Group is just a temporary stop."

"More than that," Lee said. "It's a chance to do something important while I'm waiting for the big one to come through. Safe cars are worth fighting for, right?"

"I guess."

"Oh, yeah, I forgot. You're the next Hubert Humphrey. Pammie told me."

"Pammie seems to be the office intercom system."

"She's a groovy kid. I like everyone at PG. They're not into that middle-class *schtik*. It's like I'm part of a big family."

"You an orphan?"

"Let's just say my folks and I have agreed to ignore each other. What about you, married?"

"I tried living with someone once. We kind of came to the same agreement." Rick fished his keys out of his pocket. "Sorry you got stood up."

"Yeah, well, Enid's dedicated."

"You two been going out long?"

"I wish. We just work together. Sometimes we graze at the same table. She says I'm a sweet boy."

"Bitch."

"Yeah. Nice wheels." Lee got into the Camaro on the passenger's side. "You ought to see the accident stats on GM's sports models."

"I got an earful of them this morning." Rick slid under the wheel.

"I'm into bikes myself. I had a Harley until the bank took it away."

"Now, *they're* dangerous."

"Yeah, but they're supposed to be."

Rick started the car. He thought he heard a lifter. He'd pop the hood later and take a look. "Enid's a good-looking woman." He checked the mirrors and pulled out behind a DSR bus.

Lee laughed. "Ursula Andress is a good-looking woman. Enid's the best argument against anti-Semitism I know. You better forget her."

Jewish. He'd been betting on something more exotic, like Egyptian. "She taken?"

"Married. To the Porter Group."

"Got a thing for old Wendell, huh?"

"You guys in suits." Lee shook his head. "It's a new generation, man. Everybody isn't just looking out for themselves any more."

"Yeah, I've heard Peter, Paul and Mary."

"Even if she *was* warm for Wendell's form she wouldn't stand a chance. He's been with the Arctic Princess since before I was born. That's Mrs. Porter. Caroline, the future first female justice of the Supreme Court."

"Not popular, I guess."

"She's a lawyer, what's else to say? Capitalist dinosaurs, that whole lot. But she keeps us out of jail. You new guys sure ask a lot of questions."

Rick backed off. He was getting his range now.

They discovered they were both Tigers fans and discussed Al Kaline and whether Charlie Dressen would recover enough from his heart attack to resume his management duties before the end of the season. Lee thought Mickey Lolich should be traded before he cooled off. "Guy's twenty-six," he said. "Over the hill."

Rick stopped at the light on Adams. A Negro built like Rosey Grier, wearing a dashiki and dark glasses and an enormous Afro, was seated Indian fashion at the base of the Edison fountain, plucking a sitar for a small audience. A Maxwell House can stood on the grass nearby with a sign taped to it reading REMEMBER BLOODY SUNDAY—GIVE TO THE NAACP. Rick thought, but couldn't recall what Bloody Sunday was all about. He bet himself that Lee could. He'd have the date.

"I never realized so much of this work was done on the telephone."

"We stuff envelopes too, a shitload of envelopes. What did you think, we go into plants dressed as the help with spy cameras in our shoes?"

"Something like that."

"You bought the GM line. They'd like people to think we're a bunch of crackpots who break into files and go through the garbage at the proving grounds. Wendell says consumer advocacy is in the same position unions were in thirty years ago. Pushing for seat belts makes us Communists or something."

Wendell says. Leary says. Tommy and Dick say. Che said. Talk about buying someone's line. The whole fucking generation was a Chatty Cathy doll filled with other people's words. Rick felt as if he'd aged forty years since morning.

"It'd throw a lot of people out of work for a long time," he said. "All those new safety features."

"Not so long, just during retooling. How much work you think gets done by people killed or crippled in accidents?"

"Did Wendell say that too?"

Lee lifted his chin. "He's a great man. You'll see when you meet him."

Did it again.

The light changed. They crossed the intersection. The man with the sitar was playing for himself now; his listeners had drifted off.

"Don't go stiff on me, Lee. I'm on your side."

The young man exhaled and ran his fingers through his hair. "Sorry. These rednecks who put their goddamn jobs ahead of people's lives get me uptight. Sometimes I think I might as well be talking to my folks."

"Thanks for the indoctrination. I'm just the new kid in town."

"You ain't heard nothing till you talk to Wendell. When he gets back, ask him to show you his slides. Better yet, get him to take you to the Farm."

"Where's that?"

"It's up in Macomb County. I can't describe it. You'll have to see it for yourself."

They swung left on Jefferson. The sun had turned the surface of the river into a sheet of white metal. The Windsor skyline was fuzzy in the glare. "Is Enid uptight?" Rick asked.

"Most women with her bucks, when they get involved in a cause they just throw money at it. The Porter Group's into her for ten thousand and she still spends sixty hours a week at the office. Practically runs the place."

"Ten thousand?"

"What I heard."

"Who's she related to, Horace Dodge?"

"All I know is she inherited more than I'll ever see. Hey, the game's started." Lee turned on the radio and found WJR. McLain was starting against Baltimore. The rest of the way back to the office their conversation centered on the game. Afterward Rick couldn't remember who was ahead.

Chapter 11

Patsy Orr was uncomfortable, and only part of it involved having to support himself on one of his aluminum canes in a hot public booth while he waited for the clumsy Puerto Rican exchange to complete a simple connection.

"Pasquale, you there?"

"Yes, Dad." All his muscles tensed, including the atrophied ones in his stricken legs. When he'd first learned that his contact with Frankie Orr would be reduced to conversations on the telephone, he'd hoped he would be less intimidated, but it was as if the old man could compress all the awesome qualities of his blade-straight, burnished old age into his gliding whisper of a voice. Despite its lack of timbre it had a virility at sixty-four that Patsy, who had been mortified once to hear his own thin tones played back in open court from a tape recording made from a wiretap, could never hope to acquire. He pictured himself in thirty years with a querulous cackle.

"There's a boatload of transistor radios sitting on a dock in Mexico waiting for a deposit," Frankie said. "What about it?"

"I sent you a check yesterday."

"Me? Jesus Christ, you were supposed to send it direct to General Díaz in Caracas. You know what happens to radios when they sit around in that climate? I've got people in Miami who aren't interested in buying hot paperweights."

"You didn't tell me to send it there."

"Have I got to tell you to go to the toilet? You're a *capo*, Pasquale, not some *insensato* street soldier needs a map to find his dick."

Patsy reflected that his father had picked up a lot of the *linguaggio* during his sojourn in Sicily.

"Well, let's just hope one of these spick assholes doesn't cop the check and buy himself a fiesta." Ice cubes collided on Frankie's end. Before deportation, his American doctors had warned him against drinking, but it wouldn't be ginger ale in the glass. "Account's getting low, by the way. I need another eighty grand."

"It'll take me a week or so to shake that much loose."

The drinking sounds were amplified by the receiver. "What are you selling there, subscriptions to *Grit*?"

"I got a lot of capital tied up in this policy move. DiJesus and his outfit don't work cheap."

"I don't like the way that out-of-town ape operates. You can't just run around killing niggers these days like there's a bounty on them. What about Gallante?"

"He starts today. Hammer and anvil, Dad, just like you taught me. Gallante's the anvil."

"Keep me up on it. And tell DiJesus not to go so hard on the coloreds. We get Cronkite down here. I know what's going on in Alabama and Mississippi. Heat like that is bad for business."

Sweets, wearing a neat homburg square on top of his pointed head, trundled over to the booth. He had seen his employer was tiring. Patsy put some backbone into his voice. "How they treating you there?"

"Okay, I guess. I have to drink this piss-poor Scotch because you can't get decent wine here. I should've stayed in Messina."

"You can go back." He tried not to sound eager. The calls from Sicily had been fewer and less regular.

"No, I might still get the chance to jump to Florida. Christ, I was in diapers when your grandparents took me away from the Old Country. New York and Detroit's home." More clinking sounds. "Have Albert get in touch with me. Tell him the usual way."

"Brock's my department." He sensed Sweets looking at him.

"Talk to you day after tomorrow, same time. Remember what I said about DiJesus." The connection broke.

Sweets pulled back the door of the booth while Patsy was cuffing his wrist to his other cane. "Back to the office, Mr. Orr?"

"The Detroit Club."

The bodyguard helped him into the back of the black Lincoln Continental parked by the curb and climbed in next to the driver, who turned off the radio in the middle of an interview with Charles De Gaulle and started the car. It skinned out between passing cars with an inch to spare on each bumper. Patsy had hired Carlo out of a Miami hospital following his recovery from injuries received in a six-car pile-up at Daytona.

Across the street, cramped over his equipment in the back of a Michigan Bell service truck, Ed Wasylyk wondered why gang guys always rode around in black cars. He took a picture of it through the glass peephole, then rewound the tape on the big reel-to-reel Panasonic recorder a few notches and played it back. He hoped he hadn't lost anything when he repositioned the sonic gun aimed at the booth. All this *Star Trek* shit was getting on his nerves.

"Back to the office, Mr. Orr?"

"The Detroit Club."

Not far enough. He rewound some more.

"Brock's my department."

He backed the rest of the tape onto the feed reel, removed it, fixed a strip of masking tape to the hub, and wrote the date and time on the strip. Then he put the reel with the others in one of the shallow drawers built into the back of the truck.

Only Patsy Orr's side of the telephone conversation was on tape. The other half would have required a tap, which was six kinds of legal hell if Patsy's or Brock's attorneys suspected the police were bugging a public telephone. What Wasylyk had recorded was inconclusive even if it were admissable in court without a judge's signature. But Canada would want to hear it.

The headquarters of the United Civil League for Community Action was much less impressive than the name and occupied two large rooms above the Economy Printing Company in a charred two-story brick building at Twelfth and Clairmount. The League, established in the wake of stunning civil rights victories in the Deep South, was pledged to fight for equal housing and employment opportunities among Detroit's huge Negro population. But the door to its offices at the top of a narrow blistered stairwell, steel-reinforced and equipped with a peephole that opened and shut, looked a lot like the entrance to a blind pig. Which is what it was after the legitimate bars closed at two in the morning.

But at three in the afternoon nobody was on peephole duty and the doorknob turned without resistance in Quincy Springfield's hand. He went in followed by Lydell Lafayette. The large barroom, looking naked and indecent in the slanty sunlight coming in through the windows with tadpoles of dust swimming around in it, was deserted but for an elderly Negro reading a tip sheet at one of the tables. Wreaths of blue cigar smoke coiled around his helmet of silver hair and drifted toward the ceiling, where they were chopped to pieces by the fan.

"Meeting two guys, Henry," Quincy told the old man. "They here yet?"

Henry turned a page and blew a ring without looking up. "White guys?"

"Yeah."

"Stuck 'em out back. Hee-hee."

They started that way. Henry said, "Anybody got six-two-two, Lydell?"

"Not today."

The old man reached into his workpants, came up with two

creased and stained bills, and gave them to Lydell, who pocketed them and recorded the transaction in his vinyl-bound notebook. "Somebody's birthday?"

"Two somebodies. My daughter had twins last week."

"Congratulations."

He waved the cigar. "She shucks 'em out like Chrysler. I don't hit soon, that asshole she's with'll dump 'em all on me and take off for California."

"Well, good luck."

"If I hit, I'll buy the sumbitch a lifetime supply of Trojans."

The adjoining room was slightly smaller and stacked high with whiskey cartons that blocked most of the light from the windows. A shaded bulb hanging from the ceiling illuminated a patch of plank floor occupied by a brown freckled desk and five chairs, only two of which matched. In the small hours the desk and chairs were shoved back and the patch of floor used to shoot craps. Devlin, Patsy Orr's bullet-shaped bookkeeper, sat behind the desk with his fingers laced on his stomach like a polyester Buddha. He remained seated as the pair approached. The other man rose to face them.

"Mike Gallante," Devlin said, "this is Quincy Springfield and— I'm not good with names. . . ."

"Lafayette, like the street." Lydell offered his left hand. His right arm rested in a sling he had fashioned from a black silk scarf. A white bandage extended from under his French cuff to his fingers. The World Series ring twinkled on his third finger, symbol of a contest won at Detroit Receiving if not in a baseball stadium.

The man who had risen took the hand. "How's the arm?"

"I'm just glad I still gots it. It was touch and go there for a while."

Gallante's smile was polite. He was almost as tall as Quincy, with thinning black hair combed flat to his scalp, a square jaw, and a pillar of a neck like the man in the Arrow ads. He wore a gray lightweight suit tailored to his broad shoulders and narrow waist and a blue silk tie on a blue-and-white striped shirt that made him look cool, the only man to manage that in the stuffy back room; Quincy felt adhesive in his rose-colored shirtsleeves, and globules of sweat were breaking over Devlin's too-tight collar. The place smelled of ferment. A brown leather case containing eyeglasses rested behind the display handkerchief in Gallante's suitcoat pocket.

"It must have been a terrifying experience," he said.

"Man don't think terrifying at a time like that." Lydell preened, fanning himself with his hat. "Man takes *steps*. Or he ain't a man."

"What steps did Springfield take?" Devlin was looking at Quincy.

Quincy looked back. "Springfield don't get himself killed for no money."

"Exactly. Where's the profit?" Gallante spread his hands. "Can we sit?"

When they were all seated, Gallante crossed his legs, showing a silk sock in a suede shoe. "It was my suggestion we meet here, in your neighborhood," he told Quincy. "People become guarded when they're out of their element, hard to read. I like to know the men I'm doing business with."

"What kind of business we doing?" Quincy asked.

"The money-making kind. Next to whiskey, the policy business is the most stable one around. People play the numbers when they're flush and have the cash to spare and they play them when things are tight and they want to get ahead. But like any other business it has to stay current. It's still being run in this town the way it was when Joey Machine was in charge. Where would Ford be if it were still offering the same models it had for sale in nineteen thirty-five?"

"Cars change, numbers don't," Lydell put in. "What's wrong with the way the business is run?"

"To begin with, you Detroiters still base the winning number on the last three digits in the daily report from the Federal Reserve."

Quincy said, "What's wrong with that? It can't be fixed."

"That's what's wrong with it. Back East they use the last three digits in the payout from the seventh race at Hialeagh."

"Can't fix that neither," Lydell said.

"Wrong. Say it's Saturday, the heaviest day for betting, and a lot of the bets are on the same number or close to the same number; these things happen, especially around a holiday like the Fourth of July, when everyone plays seven-seventy-six. I call a bookie just before the seventh race and get the odds on every horse at the gate. I do some arithmetic and if it looks like the total will run in the seven hundred range I place some bets, changing both the odds and the payout."

Quincy searched Gallante's self-satisfied features. "You'd need a computer to do that."

"Math is Mike's specialty," Devlin said. "He won a national contest when he was a kid. President Roosevelt shook his hand and gave him a plaque."

"I was ten. He asked me if I cared to join his Brain Trust. I asked him what the job paid."

Lydell said, "Shiiit."

"Go ahead, Springfield, fire off a list of numbers, as many as you want. The boy with the sling can write them down. He'll add, subtract, multiply, and divide them in his head and give you the right answer before your boy carries the first one. I've seen him do it a dozen times. He never misses."

"My name's Lafayette."

"We'll do parlor tricks when we all have more time," Gallante said. "What do you think of the idea?"

Quincy said, "You fix the game, you lose customers."

"They'll never know it's fixed. The payoff amount is published in a hundred newspapers for anyone to read. Of course there will be winners. We want winners so they can flash their rolls and strut around in their new suits and give the rest of the neighborhood a reason to play next week. By choosing *which* number wins, we'll always be twelve lengths out in front."

Quincy touched Lydell's knee as the latter was struggling to open a pack of Kents one-handed. He was having enough trouble thinking in that stuffy room without smoke. "I don't run the numbers in this town. Patsy's the man you want to talk to."

"I already have. He's telling all his bosses to inform their customers of the change, beginning next month. This is your notice."

"So why make the pitch to me?"

"It's just a sample of the ideas I plan to bring to your operation here on Twelfth. I'm aware of the difficulties you've been having lately."

"Our difficulties got ski masks and sawed-offs," Lydell said. "You got any ideas who they was, Mr. Idea Man?"

"Patsy's working on it. He takes care of his people."

Devlin yawned bitterly.

Gallante went on. "Meanwhile you need security. Bouncers like your man Congo are for showing drunks the door. The man I have in mind will oversee a whole new system." He glanced at a watch strapped to the underside of his wrist and looked at the bookkeeper. "He's late."

"He'll be here."

"My clientele spend all day taking orders from the Man," Quincy said. "They don't want no white gorillas breathing down their backs when they're drinking and gambling."

"Harry works the shadows." The stagnant air stirred; someone had opened the door from the bar. Gallante stood. "Quincy Springfield, Lydell Lafayette, this is Harry DiJesus. Harry flew in from Vegas this morning."

Quincy got out of his chair and pulled his shirt away from his back. The man who had just entered strode between the stacked cartons into the patch of electric light, looking straight at him. White man, a little shorter than Quincy, muscular under his green silk sport shirt and tan flannel slacks, with a gold chain around his tanned throat. Collar-length blond hair and the chilliest blue eyes Quincy had ever seen.

Chapter 12

In his seventh-floor office, Lew Canada broke the seal on a gray cardboard envelope bearing the return address of the FBI's Detroit bureau, pulled out a green-bar computer sheet twenty-two inches long and folded in the middle, and whistled.

The office was an extension of the man, scoured and free of clutter. The papers on the desk were sorted in neat stacks and the walls were naked but for a bulletin board with mug shots and newspaper clippings tacked to it and a twelve-by-twenty horizontal glass frame containing a coppertone photograph of sixteen young men in jumpsuits posed casually with their weapons in front of a C-47 transport plane.

Sergeant Esther, who had delivered the envelope to Canada's desk, said, "Something?"

"Printout on that DiJesus name Wasylyk got from Patsy Orr yesterday. Take a hinge." Canada held it out. The sergeant took it.

Harold DiJesus, a/k/a Harry DiJesus, Harry Jesus, Jesus H., and D. J. Harold, was born in Brooklyn, New York, 5/11/35, arrested in Manhattan 10/6/47 for aggravated assault, convicted, and sent to the New York State Reformatory at Elmira for six years. Since then he had been arrested fourteen times on charges ranging from simple assault to homicide. His last conviction in 1958, for assault with intent to commit great bodily harm, had gotten him twenty-four months in Sing-Sing. Since his release he had been picked up three times by the Clark County Sheriff's Department in Las Vegas, Nevada, for assault with a deadly weapon and once for homicide in the commission of a felony. Charges were dropped in all four cases. A mug shot and description were on their way under separate cover.

"Nice Italian boy." Esther laid the sheet on the desk.

"Says there he was questioned in the Anastasia homicide," Canada said. "When the mob sends you to Vegas it means someone likes your work. What did we do to attract such an important visitor to our fair city. Anything yet on Gallante?"

"I just got off the phone with the feds. They got several Gallantes on file, all bad news. They're sending 'em over."

"I got a hunch our Gallante isn't any of them. What'd Patsy say on the tape, Gallante's the anvil? Wish we had the other side of that conversation."

"We're kind of getting away from Albert Brock."

"Patsy mentioned him." The inspector sorted through the papers on his desk and pulled the transcript of the tape Wasylyk had made. " 'Brock's my department.' "

"Hell, that's good enough for me. Let's run down and pick him up."

"Don't be a smartass. Sounds like Frankie's got something on with Brock and Patsy was giving him lip about it. I'm waiting on a call I made to the authorities in Messina, Sicily. Trying to find out what Frankie's been up to lately, who he's been seeing." He gnawed his lip over the transcript. " 'I got a lot of capital tied up in this policy move. DiJesus and his outfit don't work cheap.' What policy move?"

"The nigger. Whatsizname, Springfield. That wasn't any amateur knockover at his pig."

"Put someone on him, a colored officer. Borrow one from General Service. Not one of those United Negro College Fund types; someone who looks like he belongs on Twelfth Street. And call the Clark

County Sheriff's Department in Vegas. Get the details on that Di-Jesus bust for felony homicide."

"Yessir."

When Esther left, Canada leaned back to rest his head on the swivel. He looked at the group photograph on the wall. The blat of the twin engines, the flap and pop of the chute and the wind whistling through the lines. A heavy machine gun pounding on the other side of a hill. Mortar shells shrilling among the palms. Morning drill outside the stockade, the orders barked in guttural Japanese. The way you knew an officer was approaching your hut by the sound of his monkey-stick swishing against his jodhpurs. The shit-hole in the dirt floor.

After a while, when you had been there long enough that any information you might have would be of no use to them, the beatings became routine, a way of breaking up the day during the long spell of inaction that plagued troops everywhere. You understood them then, the orange sons of bitches, and that was the worst torture of all, because the last thing you wanted to do was understand them. . . .

The telephone rang.

What was a telephone doing in a stockade?

When at last Canada answered it, he was reaching across twenty years and half a world, so that when his fingers closed on the solid surface of the black receiver the contact was like an arc to the present.

"Hello?"

"This is the overseas operator. Your call to Messina, Sicily is waiting."

After the call he went out into the squad room, threw a handful of change into the tray by the electric percolator, and poured a slug of black coffee into his personal cup. It was the night of July first and a window fan was sucking in air from the street that had the temperature and consistency of saliva. The pot had barely been touched. Like the British Army in India, Canada believed that drinking hot beverages kept one cool in the hottest climate. Right or not, he was the only man in the room who hadn't sweated through his shirt. The fluttering black-and-white TV was playing a CBS Special on Vietnam. He stared for a moment at footage of a firefight in the jungle, then switched channels. Johnny Carson was interviewing Bing Crosby.

Sergeant Esther hung up his telephone with a report like a pistol shot and beamed at the inspector. He looked like a fat freckled boy.

"I'll guess," Canada said. "Same M.O. in Vegas."

"Ski masks and shotguns. DiJesus and two guys hit a licensed whorehouse at the end of the Strip and blew down a customer when he tried to play Batman. Two hookers hit by the spray. One of them lost an arm, guess she's giving her hand-jobs lefty now. Place wasn't mobbed up, sheriff's boys say."

"Bet it is now."

"They picked up DiJesus on an anonymous tip. None of the witnesses ID'd and he walked."

"Greedy little Patsy. The fat slice off the black game's not enough for him. He wants the whole loaf and he's importing out-of-town talent to get it. He must have a hard-on to impress the old man."

"Clark County suspects DiJesus in six hits in Vegas alone. The scroat had his own little Murder, Incorporated out there, didn't hardly take a hand himself except in special cases. Want me to put out an APB?"

"No, we'll let him rattle around for a while."

"He'll hit Springfield's operation again."

"Springfield didn't want to help us when we asked for it. Putting him in the can for twenty-four hours didn't change his mind. Maybe a little banging between Patsy's hammer and anvil is just what he needs."

"DiJesus won't fuck around next time," Esther said. "He's not the type to stay satisfied with blowing down bouncers and johns."

"So next time Homicide can tag him twice. Don't forget, it's Brock we want. You get in touch with General Service yet?"

"Next item on the list." The sergeant lifted his receiver and started dialing.

Crosby was singing "The Second Time Around." On still days on Rabaul, the radio in the commandant's office could be heard in the stockade. Every third song was a Crosby recording. Canada turned off the set.

"I just heard back from Sicily, by the way."

Esther was waiting for someone to pick up the telephone on the other end. "Frankie been out playing boccie with the boys like a good little deported guinea?"

"Took me twenty minutes to pry a straight answer out of what they call law over there; they've got that language barrier thing down cold. It seems that nobody in Messina has seen anything of *Don Francisco* in more than a month. Story's the same in Palermo and Catania."

Esther cradled the receiver. "Think he's back home?"

"I don't think even the sacred law of *omerta* could keep the lid on a secret like that. But I think he's close."

"Cuba?"

"It worked for Luciano, but that was before Castro. If Frankie's there it means he's getting on better with that cigar-rolling son of a bitch than anyone else except Brezhnev. Do we know the number of that booth Patsy's been using?"

"I'll send a car."

"No, use someone in plainclothes. I don't want Patsy looking out his window and seeing a blue-and-white parked by his outside line."

"I'll go myself."

"While you're there, call the phone company. Get a record of all the incoming long-distance calls placed to that number over the past two weeks. There can't be that many. Not many people call a booth."

Esther made a note on his telephone pad. "What do you want first, that or the shadow from General Service?"

"General Service," Canada said. "Ask for the best colored undercover they've got. Steal him if they won't give him to you. Maybe we'll get lucky and DiJesus will ice Springfield right in front of him."

Chapter 13

"**E**nid tells me you're doing a fine job."

Rick got up from the card table to shake Wendell Porter's hand. It was a long bony hand attached to a lot of shirtcuff; the sleeves of his three-button gray herringbone jacket were the least bit too short for him. He was taller than he looked on television, and up close Rick could see that the charmingly disheveled appearance of his dark tousled hair was more barber's artifice than Ivy League carelessness. He had thick black eyebrows and deep vertical creases in his face that washed out under studio lights, making him look younger onscreen. Rick knew he was in his middle forties. The famous Harvard accent was less pronounced in person.

"I just make calls, ask questions, and write down the answers," Rick said. "It's pretty hard to screw that up."

"You'd be surprised." Porter glanced at Pammie, immersed in a telephone interview, and leaned closer to Rick. "It isn't easy getting people who know what they're doing when you don't pay. Actually, though, I was referring to that phone number you gave Lee Schenck. Enid says Commander Whozis was a fount of accident information."

"Some of them drop their guards when they go home."

"It's handy to have someone around who understands the policeman's mind."

Rick wondered what that meant.

"What time is it?" Porter asked.

Rick looked at his watch. "Almost eleven."

"I'm due up at the Farm at noon. Would you care to come along? Pammie can manage here. Enid says Lee told her you asked about it."

This was going too well. He was still turning over the policeman comment.

"I'd be honored, Mr. Porter."

"Wendell."

They stopped in the entryway, where Enid looked up from her typing. Today she was wearing a blue silk blouse and a paisley scarf secured with a gold pin. Her hair was up. Rick could see blue highlights in it.

"We're going up there now," Porter said. "If Washington calls, tell them I'll get back to them. Let them stew."

"Think they'll call?"

"Probably not."

"Want me to prepare a press release about the no-show yesterday?"

"Not this time. Half the media is convinced I'm one of these conspiracy freaks now. Let's wait a little before we convince the other half. Oh, and call Caroline and ask her if we're still on for dinner. I haven't touched bases with her since I got back."

"Aye, aye, sir."

Rick fell in behind Porter's lanky stride. So far, a cool "Good morning" was all he had been able to get out of Enid since yesterday's jackass comment about her doing needlepoint for Wendell.

Porter's car was a maroon Volvo sports coupe, six years old but in excellent condition. It was equipped with seat belts, the first Rick had ever seen except on airplanes. Porter gave him an approving glance when he hooked his up without waiting to be asked, secured his own, and they pulled out of the little lot. Rick was surprised when the safety lobbyist sped up to catch the light at Jefferson and changed lanes to pass an Olds 88 lumbering along at just below the limit; he'd been prepared for a demonstration in geriatric roads-manship. The most persistent rumor about Porter said he didn't have a driver's license, had in fact never learned to drive. Rick now made his mind a blank page on the subject of Wendell Porter.

"Enid says you worked for the *Times*," Porter said. "I used to have friends there. Maybe we know some of the same people."

"I doubt it, sir. Wendell. I was a leg man for one of the columnists. I didn't spend much time in the offices."

"Which columnist did you work for?"

"Jake Greenburg."

"Jake died, I heard."

"I heard that too."

"Drank himself under. Godawful way to go."

"I heard cancer," Rick said. "Jake was a teetotaler when I knew him."

"Guess I have him mixed up with someone else."

As Porter worked the clutch and brake, Rick noticed his expensive oxblood loafers were scuffed and run down slightly at the heels. Everything about the man's carefully rumpled aspect made him think of those tables people bought brand new in department stores and clobbered with chains and hammers to make them look like something from a junk shop.

"I haven't been very subtle, have I?" Porter said then. "I'm sorry if I sound like I'm giving you the third degree. You're older than the average Porter Group volunteer and I'm a little paranoid. I'm pretty sure the automobile people have detectives on me."

"I'm thirty."

"I'd have thought older. Not that you look it; you could pass for twenty or less. It's more of an attitude thing. Maybe it's just my gray hairs showing. Young people are so much more mature than they were when I was one of them."

"A lot of people think they're slipping. Smashing the windows of recruitment centers and all."

"At least they give a damn about something. If they didn't, I'd be a group of one." They wound up the ramp of the northbound Chrysler, past Receiving Hospital and a billboard advertising the 1966 Rambler.

"Small as it is, the group makes a lot of noise," Rick said.

"We employ professional lobbyists in Washington, and my wife handles the legal side through her firm. But dedicated young people like Enid and Lee and Pammie supply the blood. With a few exceptions they're not around long, but while they're here, look out."

"Burnout factor that high?"

"Youth wants change now and when it doesn't come right away they lose interest. Staffing's my biggest headache, that and trying to sprinkle salt on the tails of certain politicians."

"Enid one of the exceptions?"

Porter throttled around two trucks hauling separate halves of a mobile home up the slow lane. "Enid's special. I honestly don't know what PG would have done without her these past three years."

"That's a long time between paychecks."

"Enid needs a paycheck like I need a Swiss bank account. Her father owned the land that Southfield stands on today."

"What made her choose PG?"

"Why don't you ask her?"

"She doesn't care much for me."

"She can be distant sometimes. Don't let it throw you."

Detroit leveled out into the neighborhoods, rows of low houses gridded between broad flat streets laid out like perpendicular raceways, a motorists' town. In Hamtramck they got off on Caniff, passed shops and bakeries bearing signs with Ukrainian and Polish names, and took Mount Road straight up through the enormous suburb of Warren. North of Twelve Mile Road the General Motors Technical Center sprawled for blocks, looking like a well-tended college campus. Its brick buildings housed the automotive Goliath's Engineering, Research, Styling, and Manufacturing departments.

"Indian country," Porter mused. "Whenever I drive past the place I think I know how a northern Negro must feel passing through Mississippi. I'm half surprised a mob of thirty-year men doesn't block the road and pull me out of the car and string me up for treason. I worked for GM two years."

"I didn't know that."

"It was on the line, in the Westland assembly plant. I hung doors on Chevies. The job saw me through two years at the University of Michigan."

"I thought you were from back East."

"I was born and raised in Boston. Then my father moved the family out to Ypsilanti and invested everything he owned in Tucker."

"Um."

"I was studying law at the U of M. When Tucker went belly up it was either drop out of school or finance my own education. If it weren't for GM and a Harvard scholarship I'd probably be checking cars in and out of a parking lot somewhere. On the other hand, if it weren't for GM, Tucker wouldn't have been hounded out of the automobile business in the first place. You could say I had an ambivalent youth."

"So that's what turned you against them?"

"Personal vengeance is expensive and not all that satisfying. My father believed in Pres Tucker. So did I. He cared about the people who would ride in his cars. Seat belts, disk brakes all around, padded dash, pop-out windshield. I saw one of his cars roll over on the test track. The driver walked away without a scratch."

"He was probably wearing a helmet."

"A helmet doesn't protect your arms and legs and spine. It won't do you much good when you catapult through a fixed windshield because there's nothing to stop you when the car stops suddenly."

Rick said nothing. He'd already alienated one important source by speaking his mind.

"Not everyone can look back at a specific incident in his life and identify it as the turning point," Porter said. "Watching that test driver climb out of that car with nothing worse than a bad case of nerves was mine. Until then I'd been planning to go into corporate law. I switched to civil liability. I'm not the lawyer Caroline is, but I won two important cases of negligence against dealerships after their faulty servicing led to accidents. That was good enough for a while. Then it occurred to me that I could be a lot more effective by preventing the accidents from happening in the first place. That's when I became a lobbyist."

"Tough decision. Economically speaking."

"Not so tough. I gave up my shot at real money when I turned my back on corporate. Also I had the good fortune to marry well. The pro-industry press has made a lot of that, but when I met Caroline she was fresh out of law school with an office over a credit orthodontist's and one client."

"You?"

Porter nodded. He'd stopped to let a redhead in a sundress walk her dog across the street. "I won't quote Lincoln at you on the subject of lawyers who represent themselves. She's built a large and successful firm on her efforts on behalf of the Porter Group and the Porter Group's raked in an impressive number of national headlines over her victories in court."

"Sounds like the perfect union."

"Yes, it does." Porter was silent after that. Rick registered the silence and stored it away.

"Sounds like you're having trouble in Washington, though."

"It's hard to organize a senate subcommittee on auto safety when the senator's always busy somewhere else. The automotive industry employs a lot of people, and a lot of them vote. I suppose it's naive to expect a politician not to act like a politician, but I can't get it through their heads that victims of fatal accidents *can't* vote."

"Maybe if you didn't harp so much about seat belts. They're kind of radical compared to the other things, disk brakes and padded dashes."

"Brakes stop cars, not people. And if you have a seat belt you don't need a padded dash."

"I can't help thinking about all those people you hear about who survive terrible accidents because they're thrown clear."

"You hear about them because it almost never happens. Most injuries occur after the initial impact, when the victims are still bouncing." Porter glanced sidelong at his passenger. "I can tell you're not convinced."

They were out in the country now, rolling down a straight two-lane blacktop with barns and fields on both sides. Rick wondered how far they were going and what they'd find when they got there.

"There's no arguing with statistics," he said. "We've gotten along for almost seventy years without strapping ourselves to our cars. What's next, training wheels?"

"My friend, you'd be right at home with those officers who denied parachutes to our flyers in World War One because they thought having them would inhibit their courage in combat. Changing your mind will be my good deed for today."

Rick didn't like the sound of that.

Chapter 14

Lydell lit a Kent one-handed—he was getting the hang of it—and coughed. "Fucking cops."

The police seal was gone from the smashed door of the blind pig and he and Quincy had entered to find that the law had added refinements to the damage caused by the three men in ski masks. Flies and flashbulbs clotted the smear on the floor where Congo's body had fallen and the squashed carcasses of Camels and Chesterfields lay in scorched depressions amid the broken glass from the jukebox. White fingerprint powder blurred the dark surfaces, black the light. The bar and tables were rookeries of crumpled waxed paper, some of the crumples containing the metamorphosed remains of half-eaten sandwiches. The room stank of ferment.

Quincy crunched over the debris, leaned in through the door of the little unisex bathroom, where a cigar floated on top of the yellow water in the toilet, and twisted the handle. The water gasped and gushed.

"Wisht we could flush the whole place," said Lydell.

"Get somebody in to clean up. We open tomorrow morning same time as always."

"Shouldn't you better ask Mr. Gallante about that?"

"He don't own the pig."

"Yet."

Quincy touched the blasted section of bar. "Find Curtis Odie and get him to plane this down and chunk in a new piece. He's a rough carpenter. I don't want nobody else bitching about splinters."

"Wasn't splinters done this to my arm, I said. They plucked out eleven double-ought slugs. Lead poisoning alone could of croaked me."

"Closest you ever been to croaking is them weeds you smoke."

"Bullshit. Kills germs. I read it in *Confidential*." Lydell coughed and flicked ash at the floor. "You sure this cat DiJesus was one of 'em?"

"Sure enough. God don't give even white men eyes like them that often."

"Well, we just going to let him walk in and wrap the place up for the wops?"

"You got another idea?"

"I still got my Bulldog. Them blue eyes don't see backwards."

"He's just a screwdriver. Break one, they got more."

"Dude didn't say one word that whole time," Lydell said. "I don't trust a man don't talk. That's the reason I don't have a mutt. Who knows what they're thinking, they don't say it? Rip your face off soon as lick it."

"That ain't no way to talk about women."

Both men turned. Krystal had come in the open door. She had pink ribbons tied in her stack of straw-colored hair and six shades of violet on her eyelids. Her dress, electric purple with flowers exploding all over it, started just above her nipples and ran out of material at her crotch. She was wearing five-inch platform sandals and half a pound of copper bracelets. When she walked she made more noise than a junkwagon.

"Whooee," she said, looking around. "Sorry I missed the part-*y*."

Neither Quincy nor Lydell paid her any attention. They were looking at the man who had entered behind her, a cinnamon-

colored Negro with straight black hair smoothed back like porcupine quills and dark glasses with plain black rims like Little Stevie
Wonder wore. He had on a hip-length brown leather jacket with
wide lapels, bell-bottoms, and high-heeled brown boots with
buckles. Even in the heels he wasn't medium height. His black shirt
was unbuttoned, showing a V of absolutely hairless skin down to his
belt buckle. He stopped in the middle of the room and took off the
glasses. Both eyes were puffy and ringed with mustard-colored
bruises.

"Looks like the cops helped themselves to your likker." Behind the
bar, Krystal took a square bottle of gin off one of the nearly empty
shelves, filled a rock glass almost to the rim, and colored the clear
liquid with Rose's Lime Juice from a bottle in the refrigerator. "Law
'n' order." She drank.

"Something stuck on your heel." Lydell was still watching the
stranger.

"Oh, that's Mahomet. You boys got any ice?" She opened the
refrigerator again.

Quincy remembered him now. "I bailed you out," he said. "I
didn't buy you."

"I owe you, man."

The rich baritone was always a surprise coming out of that slender
little body.

"He come to the apartment looking for you," Krystal said. "I was
on my way here, so I brung him along."

Lydell said, "The Klan comes looking for him, you bring them
along too?"

She laughed into her glass. "He ain't Klan."

"I don't like to see a brother getting beat on," Quincy said. I'd of
done the same for a alley cat. But I wouldn't take him home."

"I thought maybe I could sing in your place till I paid you back."

A choking fit cut off Lydell's laughter. Quincy pounded him on
the back until he resumed breathing, then took the cigarette from
between the fingers of his partner's good hand and extinguished it

in the ashtray on the bar, previously the only butt-free two square inches in the room. He shoved the jade holder into the side pocket of Lydell's coat. "Don't need no singers nor acrobats neither," he said. "Try the Baptists."

"I don't owe them."

"Missing a bargain, bro." Lydell leaned on the bar, his chest sucking and blowing out like a bellows. "Dress this boy in a white suit like Cab Calloway, hire somebody to come in and play the accordeen. Charge twice't as much for drinks during the floor show. That's how the Cotton Club got started."

"Shut up and breathe."

Krystal said, "C'mon, sugar, hire him. Krystal likes the way he talks. Just like Sidney Poitier."

He hated it when she puckered up and talked like Betty Boop.

"Told you my English was too good," Mahomet said miserably.

Quincy said, "You want to work it off, there's a broom in back. I got no use for no singers."

Mahomet brightened. "Can I sing while I'm sweeping?"

"Sure. How about a little 'Swing Low, Sweet Chariot' while you're mopping up Congo's guts?"

Mahomet glanced down at the feasting flies without emotion and started toward the poolroom. As he passed Lydell, the man with his arm in a sling placed his good hand on Mahomet's arm. "Ain't you hot in all that leather?"

"It's okay. I don't wear underwear."

Lydell let go quickly.

When he emerged from the back room carrying a broom and dustpan, the newcomer had removed his leather jacket. The cuffs of his black sleeves were fastened with four mother-of-pearl buttons apiece. He hummed as he swept, low and melodic.

Lydell caught Quincy's eye and went into the poolroom. Quincy pointed at Krystal, freshening her glass from the square bottle. "Don't drink up the inventory."

"Yes, boss."

The poolroom was in better condition than the bar. Quincy blew ashes off the green felt on the table and transferred a Dixie cup two-thirds full of cold coffee from a corner pocket to the wastebasket. Lydell was seated on his favorite stool next to the cues. He had been sitting there when he broke one of them over the head of the disappointed gambler who had threatened Quincy with a Saturday Night Special. He had Mahomet's leather jacket across his lap and was going through the pockets.

"Anything?" Quincy selected a cue and set up a combination shot.

"Tap City. Beats me how a man can wear threads like these here and not have nothing in his pockets but lint." He leaned over and hung it on the peg. "What kind of a name is Mahomet anyways?"

"Black Muslim. Malcolm X, remember? They blowed him down last year."

"No, that'd be Muhammad."

"Maybe he just likes it, then. Maybe it's his name." Quincy made the shot.

"Think he's a spy?"

"Can't figure what he'd find out that Patsy don't already know. Or won't when he hears from Gallante and DiJesus."

"I mean the cops."

"Too small. Five-nine's the minimum." He set up another shot and missed.

"Well, I don't like him hanging around. He talks funny."

"He went to school."

"You and me went to school."

"He finished." He sank it on the second try.

"Plus I don't like a man dresses better'n me."

"Forget him."

"Okay, let's talk about the guineas. We going to let Mr. Bigass Deal Gallante and Harry Blue Eyes squeeze our balls till they pop or what?"

"Shit. Scratched." Quincy returned the stick to the rack. "You pick up Congo's body at the morgue like I told you?"

"Oh, yeah, he's out watching the Sting Ray. What am I supposed to do with him when I gots him, take him out dancing?"

"Most stiffs get funerals."

"Who'd come?"

"We'll invite Joe Petite and Sebastian Bright. They'll bring their people and we'll bring ours."

"They didn't even know Congo. They got their own games to run."

"And Gidgy."

"All that pusher knows is horse."

"We all got something in common. We're colored and we deal with Patsy Orr or we don't deal at all. And together we got more guns and blades than the fucking National Guard."

Lydell's grin was a long time coming. He fished the holder out of his pocket and lit up, forgetting and taking his bandaged arm from its sling. "Think they'll go for it?"

"They come from the streets just like us. They'll take any excuse to dress up and show off their cars and their fine ladies. We'll bust the bank on flowers and a coffin for Congo. We'll make it so big they don't dare stay home. What's the name of that reverend at Second Baptist, Otis something?"

"Otis R. R. Idaho. They built the place around him."

"Whips up the hellfire, does he?"

"Whips it up and makes it do the Watusi, they say. I missed a sermon or two myself."

"We'll do it out of his church and the burying in Mount Elliott Cemetery. Make for a nice long funeral route."

"Too bad we can't take it right past the Penobscot," Lydell said, "rub Patsy the Crip's nose in it."

"He'll get a whiff anyways. We'll use a white hearse. If we can't find one we'll buy one and paint it. This is one planting they'll be talking about when they elect Sammy Davis Junior President."

"Congo'd be proud."

"We'll hold the wake here afterwards. The best booze, the best food. The griddle in every rib joint on Twelfth Street'll be sizzling just for us. When we got everyone together, all the bad brothers in town, we'll have us a pow-wow."

"They shake our hands and thanks us for the eats and be on their way."

"Maybe. Or maybe they see when one of us is in hot shit, the rest better grab towels."

Lydell coughed, hacked, and spat into a cuspidor the size of a loving cup. He dragged his charcoal sleeve across his lips. "Suppose Patsy don't like it and sends DiJesus and his boys to pay their respects?"

"I hope to Christ he does," Quincy said. "It'll save us a ton of words."

"Cool it." Lydell was looking past him.

Quincy turned. Mahomet was standing in the doorway, holding his broom like one half of *American Gothic*. "We got a scrub brush? For cleaning up guts."

"Try the toilet."

Mahomet started to withdraw.

"Second."

He stopped. Quincy looked at him a moment. "Ever sing at a funeral?"

Chapter 15

The Farm was a farm.

No different from the others they'd passed, a flat forty acres surrounded by barbed wire with a small white farmhouse and two large barns built of corrugated steel in the shape of airplane hangars. A gate fashioned from an iron pipe hinged to a fence post barred the gravel driveway. Wendell Porter got out of the car, opened the padlock with a key attached to his ring, and swung the pipe out of the way. After he drove through he went back and closed and locked it.

He parked in front of the house and got out. Rick unbuckled himself and followed. They mounted a wooden porch containing a big orange cat curled up in a dilapidated wicker chair and went through the screen door without knocking. The smell of the interior, old damp wood and meals cooked and consumed and forgotten, reminded Rick of Mrs. Hertler's kitchen.

The room was in fact a large kitchen, with brown mottled linoleum on the floor and an old-fashioned pump-up gas stove and electric refrigerator with a cylinder on top and a sink whose white enamel was flaking away from the black cast iron beneath. A black steel desk that belonged in a service station stood incongruously just inside the entrance, behind which a gray-haired man sat with one foot up on the typewriter leaf watching Tom and Jerry on a set with rabbit ears. The man wore a short-sleeved white shirt with a blue necktie and dark work pants, but his footwear, a white sock and high black lace-up shoe, was a dead giveaway. He was a security guard.

"Think he's ever going to catch that mouse, Fred?"

"I keep hoping, but he ain't in thirty years. 'Morning, Mr. Porter." Fred put his foot on the floor and handed Porter a clipboard with a ballpoint pen tied to it.

Porter signed the attached sheet. "This is Rick Amery. The Porter Group just increased by one."

Fred regarded Rick from behind square-rimmed glasses, then reached into a bowl on the desk and held out a blank white button the size of a nickel. "Pin this on. Don't take it off while you're on the grounds. And sign in."

Rick obeyed and was surprised to see Porter select a button for himself and pin it to his lapel. Porter smiled at his reaction.

"White on Tuesdays, Thursdays, and Saturdays. Blue the rest of the week. The guards have orders to eject anyone not wearing the right button, me included. GM might send in a double."

"You believe that?"

"What I believe makes no difference. Fred was with security at the Ford Willow Run plant for twenty-seven years. We all dance to his tune."

"Henry the First used to try to sneak past me there; he liked his jokes. I caught him every time and didn't it piss him off." Fred got up and turned off the TV in the middle of a commercial for something called a Frisbee. A square Colt Army rode in his belt holster with its barrel in his right hip pocket. "Henry Deuce gave me a watch last year and showed me the door. That was the first and last time I ever seen him."

"Is he a volunteer?" Rick followed Porter down a narrow hallway behind the kitchen and out a side door.

"No. Everyone at the Farm is on salary."

They took a path worn down to bare earth to the nearer of the two hangarlike structures. As they drew close, Rick saw that the building was at least twice the size of a normal barn. It could have sheltered a 747.

"I have Caroline to thank for the house and property," Porter said. "One of her clients, a developer, got in a financial crunch and couldn't meet her fee. He'd been planning to build a shopping center. We paid up the taxes and here we are."

"Where are we?"

"On the boundary between theory and proof." The consumer advocate opened a door next to the big closed bay and held it. Rick went inside.

He wasn't prepared for the assault on his senses that followed.

The interior was the size of a football field, bounded on four sides by cork paneling and the complex girdered structure of the roof forty feet overhead, where a series of suspended fans turned under louvered vents shaped like gables. The floor was asphalt over cement. Sandbags stacked in a solid lace pattern like tires encircled the center, creating an oval one hundred yards long by sixty yards wide. There a driver in a silver firesuit and red crash helmet was threading a brick-colored Chevrolet Impala convertible through an obstacle course of yellow hazard cones. The roar of the big 409 engine in the enclosed area was horrendous.

"Slip these on," shouted Porter, handing him a pair of noise-suppressing earphones from a table full of them. He put on another pair.

"Ventilation's our biggest problem," he went on at the top of his lungs. "The fans don't quite do it, and we can't open the doors without bringing in the whole neighborhood to investigate the noise. Fifteen minutes out of every hour is as long as I dare expose anyone to the fumes, and the shifts are rotated so that nobody's here two days in a row."

Rick nodded. The screech of the Impala's brakes as the driver negotiated the turns came unadulterated through the suppressors. He had knocked over about a third of the cones.

They weren't the only witnesses to the exercise. A man in shirt-sleeves and earphones stood with his back to them taking notes on a clipboard, and a motion picture camera attached to a steel tripod recorded everything under arc lights as bright as the sun. A big man in slacks and a loose blue zip-front Windbreaker spotted the new-comers and came their way. He was wearing earphones and Rick was certain the jacket concealed a handgun. Just then the man with the clipboard raised his hand to signal the driver, who cut the ignition and coasted to a stop six feet short of him.

Silence rang.

The earphones came off. Porter introduced Rick to the guard, whose name was Arthur. He was in his late thirties with black hair thinning on top and shallow gray eyes. He nodded at Rick and stepped past him to shoot back the heavy bolt that secured the bay doors. The air sweetened noticeably when he pushed them open.

Porter and Rick went over to where the man with the clipboard was talking with the driver, who had removed his helmet to reveal a shock of curly blond hair on a Nordic head.

"Hal Bledsoe, Günter Damm, Rick Amery," Porter said. "I hired Hal away from Production and Design at AMC."

Rick shook the round-faced Bledsoe's pudgy hand and grasped the bronze one offered by the driver. "I thought I recognized you," Rick said. "You ran in the Vegas Grand Prix a couple of years back."

"You were there?" Damm spoke with a soft German accent.

"No, I caught it on the tube."

"Günter doubled for Elvis in *Viva, Las Vegas*," Porter said. "He doesn't like to talk about it."

Damm's aristocratic face became animated. "He signed my driv-ing gloves. He said I could have a speaking part in his next picture, but I broke my leg at Monte Carlo and missed the shooting. *Roust-about*. He sent me an autographed poster."

"But he doesn't like to talk about it." Bledsoe was grinning.

"How'd we do?" Porter asked.

Bledsoe handed him the clipboard. "We're running out of cones."

Porter skimmed the top sheet and the one underneath. "Nothing we didn't expect. That's just too much car for those nine-and-a-half-inch drums. How'd we do for stopping distance?"

"That's next."

He gave back the clipboard and pointed at Damm's helmet. "May I borrow it?"

The German hesitated, then held it out. "You paid for it."

Porter handed Bledsoe his earphones and put on the helmet. When he'd adjusted the chinstrap, he looked like an investment broker for the Detroit Lions. He smiled at Rick. "Feeling adventurous?"

"Always do on Saturday."

"There's another helmet on the table."

It was silver-colored fiberglass and a snug fit. Rick emptied his pockets onto the table and took off the white button. When he rejoined the others, Porter was climbing into the driver's seat of the Impala. Arthur the security guard was clearing the yellow cones from the track.

"Wendell, is this smart?" Bledsoe asked.

"If I were smart I'd be defending corporate vice presidents from charges of income tax evasion. Mount up, Tonto."

The car had no radio or heater. The dash was upholstered with molded foam rubber three inches thick.

"The industry can't claim my tests aren't fair. I'm not prepared to sacrifice my drivers just to prove a point." Porter cinched Rick's seat belt tight enough to cut off his circulation and buckled his own. "The whole country's on a speed binge. The auto companies cut back on safety so they have more money to spend on horsepower. When this model was introduced, it had eleven-inch brake drums. Now it's one and one-half inches less safe than it was last year."

"What are we going to do?"

"Leave that to me. All you have to do is hang on." He turned the key.

Porter's lead foot, hinted at on the way there, found freedom on the unobstructed track. He drove the length of the oval marked off by the sandbags, executed a sliding turn, and roared back the way they'd come, accelerating steadily.

"Detroit's not evil," he said, "just blind, deaf, and a little stupid. Safe cars are like sensible shoes, harder to sell than the flashy pumps that pinch your toes and ruin your arches. In order to avoid sinking capital into something it can't advertise, the industry set out to hoodwink the American consumer into accepting collisions that maim and kill as an inevitability of life on the open road. It succeeded so well it's become a victim of its own con. The statistics you and Lee and Pammie collect are an important weapon against Madison Avenue brainwashing. Hard results here are another." He fishtailed the other way and braked abruptly. Rick waited for his vitals to catch up.

The exhaust bubbled. Porter gripped the wheel at ten to two and gunned the engine twice. The vibration numbed the soles of Rick's feet and buzzed in his fillings.

"Try not to swallow your tongue." Porter shoved the pedal to the firewall.

Mortal wails and the prickling stench of scorched rubber. The Impala leaned forward, pawed the ground, and lunged. Something cracked behind Rick's head and the stacked sandbags on both sides of the car turned into colorless ribbons of speed. The end of the oval track sprang up like something in the pocket of a catapult.

"Stay loose!" Porter jammed on the brakes.

More wailing and toxic smoke. The inside of the car tore loose of the chassis and Rick left his body. Hovering among the girders under the roof, feeling the breeze of the fans blowing down his collar, he looked down and saw his body leave the seat and splash through the windshield in agonizingly slow motion, like a shootout in an Italian western. Then, as if a switch had been thrown, he was back inside his body. The body was inside the car, clamped in place by the belt across his lap. The car had stopped. His view through the wind-shield was blocked by a sandbag lying on top of the hood. The glass had spidered. The engine had stalled and the only sound was the hissing of the broken radiator.

"Are you all right?"

He looked at Porter. The long seamed face under the ridiculous red helmet was a map of concern.

"Ask my stomach when you see it."

The hissing didn't belong to the radiator. The sandbag had sprung a leak and the grains were spilling down the air vent in a brazen stream.

"I'd say you're all right." Porter removed his helmet and ran his fingers through his anarchic hair. "What's the damage, Hal?"

They were surrounded now. Bledsoe and Günter Damm clawed open both doors; the one on Rick's side squawked against a cocked fender. Arthur, whose Windbreaker had ridden up to expose a cedar-handled Ruger in a belt clip, seized the leaky sandbag and dragged it off the hood. The sheet metal had accordioned back almost as far as the shattered windshield.

"The hell with the car." Bledsoe's round features were as pale as the sheet on his clipboard, which he was still clutching. "You okay?"

"I'm fine. I told you it was too much car for those skimpy drums. Make sure you measure the skid marks. I want the stopping distance down to the inch."

"Jesus Christ, Wendell. Promise me you won't do that again."

"No promises." He undid his seat belt and turned to Rick. " 'What's next, training wheels?' I believe that's what you said."

Rick unclamped his fingers from the dash. He had torn two large gouges in the foam rubber.

Porter turned Rick's wrist so he could read his watch.

"Quarter to one. I have an appointment in Rochester in forty-five minutes. Günter will drive you back to the office. You'll have to ask him about the time Elvis let him drive his custom Cadillac."

Rick said, "I think I'll walk."

Chapter 16

Lew Canada, who had small use for irony, never dwelled long on the fact that he had received his most valuable lesson in life from the first man he'd ever wanted to kill.

One day Major Duveen, a game-legged, cigar-mashing veteran of Chennault's Flying Tigers who had bullied, humiliated, and excoriated the men of Canada's company from ground school through combat training and their first jumps, called them into the mess hall to see a newsreel of the Bataan Death March that had not been edited for showing in theaters and stopped the projector on a frame showing a Japanese officer on horseback. The officer had just finished walking his horse over the body of an American GI who had collapsed from exhaustion and thirst and was turning in his saddle to inspect the result.

"Take a long look," Duveen said. "Next time you see some little monkey-faced Jap in a Hollywood movie, and until you see one on your own, I want you cunts to remember what the sonsabitches look like. We weren't thrown out of Corregidor by any army of gardeners in thick glasses. Before we're through here you'll be able to look at a pile of shit in the jungle and tell me in two seconds if it came through a good Yankee colon or some Jap bastard's yellow ass."

As it turned out, Duveen was forcibly retired for breaking both his riding crop and a nineteen-year-old lieutenant's eardrum before they got around to studying the differences between American and Japanese shit; but long after Canada had learned to transfer his hatred of the major to the enemy, he had remembered that freeze-frame and the speech that went with it. He had taken the memory with him after his liberation from the POW camp in Rabaul, and back in Detroit his ability to read the enemy (both on the street and among his fellow officers) had seen him from a scout car to plain-clothes and finally to the command of a special division the rest of the department knew nothing about. He would still be tempted to kill Duveen if the two met on the street, but he liked to think that before he did he would have the good manners to thank the major for his advice.

Now, staring at the group photograph on the wall of his office, Canada was struck by the thought that he had lost sight of that Japanese officer. Albert Brock, his Jap bastard of the moment, had been in the public eye so long he had fooled himself into thinking he knew the labor leader. In fact he was hardly better informed than the guy on the loading dock who came home every night and had supper and read his newspaper and fell asleep in front of Huntley and Brinkley.

He pulled his personal file on Brock from the deep drawer of his desk—in this frame of mind, a disappointing collection of tran-scripts from tapes, affidavits signed by people who knew even less about its subject than Canada, photographs and newspaper clip-pings going back to 1938, when Brock was elected president of the Detroit Steelhaulers local—and read it all again from start to finish. It left him unenlightened.

Lieutenant Boyle, Canada's second whip on the mayor's squad, was under suspension pending an investigation into why his name had appeared on the infamous "Christmas list" seized in the raid on the gambling operation at the Grecian Gardens. With the imminent early retirement of District Inspector Peter R. Soncrant, who had also been mentioned, that brought the number of high-level vacancies in the department to eight since the probe began. Boyle, like Sergeant Esther, had been a gift from Police Commissioner Girardin and just the sort of choice one might expect from a former newspaperman who had only learned of the squad's existence three months after it was formed. The sergeant at least had worked out, and Canada placed him in charge when he left.

The Doubleday Book Shop was on the ground floor of the Penobscot Building on Griswold, a graduated limestone pile the inspector detested, if only because Patsy Orr directed his father's criminal empire from his office on the forty-third floor; which reminded him that Ma Bell was still dragging her feet on that list of long-distance calls placed to the booth across the street. At least it was Saturday, and unless Patsy was a workaholic—not a common complaint among mafiosi—Canada was spared the sensation that Patsy was standing on top of his head.

He found the book he was looking for in the Local Interest section between a Detroit restaurant guide and Wendell Porter's *Hell On Wheels*. A thick volume with a white pictorial cover showing Albert Brock standing alone on a speaker's platform with laced fingers held high over his head in a victory salute, its blurbs promised a personal look at the labor chief's life even if its title, *BROCK! The Steel Behind the Steelhaulers,* was unencouraging from a muckraking point of view. Canada had been wondering about the book ever since he had discovered it excerpted in last month's issue of *True.* He bought it and took it back to the office.

"Anything yet from the phone company?" he asked Esther, who was filling a paper cone with water from the cooler. The sergeant took in more liquids than any man Canada had ever known, and sweated out two quarts for every pint.

He shook his head and drank. "They only move fast when they tot up my wife's bill."

"See if you can light a fire under them."

"Taking up reading, Inspector?"

He showed Esther the cover.

"We could write a book of our own by this time," the sergeant said.

"Make a damn short read if we did."

But the book wasn't much better than the file. Brock had been brought up in Ecorse, not the most honest two square miles in North America, the son of the owner of a small cartage firm that in twenty years managed to increase its fleet from one horse-drawn wagon to three secondhand Mack trucks, one of which was always parked over the grease pit in the garage. He had driven for a time for his father, then when the company went bankrupt, bought a rig on time and hired out as an independent. The 1929 stock market crash ended that. Later he hauled steel for the Ford River Rouge plant, which earned him a draft deferment after Pearl Harbor when the company switched its emphasis from automobiles to Liberty ships and B-17 Flying Fortresses at Willow Run. His involvement in the labor movement, beginning in the Depression when he took his lumps from strikebreakers, came to a head in 1938 when, running from the lowly position of shop steward, he was elected president of Local 406 of the American Steelhaulers Association in an upset victory over the two-term incumbent. It was a short hop from there to the national presidency, which at last count he had held for sixteen years and four terms. In that time he had established locals in forty-eight cities and expanded the union's scope beyond truck drivers and dock laborers to include police officers, clerical workers, and migrant farmers. All this was public knowledge.

What wasn't widely known, and what this most laudatory of authorized biographies had missed completely, was the union's mob connections. It had been muscle provided by Frankie Orr rather than any personal popularity on Brock's part that had catapulted him from blue-collar obscurity to the front office in Detroit, the hub of the organization. The methods were as old as the blackjack and fully as effective: a threat in this shop steward's ear, a few dozen extra ballots in that box, a gentle reminder in the counting rooms that certain bookmakers were waiting to collect on busted sure things and longshots that came up short at the finish. It made no difference that four years later Brock's sweeping reforms in the local had carried him into a legitimate landslide victory at the national level; a deal was a deal. The pension fund was made to order for laundering money skimmed off the tables in Frankie's casinos in Vegas, and for two and a half decades now the washing machines had been running non-stop at Steelhaulers.

Skimming through the book, reading the testimonials of statesmen and sanitation workers, housewives and holy men—one thing about Brock, he never forgot his apprenticeship among the rank and file—Canada got the impression that most of the material had been handed to the author by Brock himself, or at least by his people. There was, however, one new piece of information, and if for no other reason than that it was a fresh straw to snatch at in a sodden stack, the inspector decided to follow it up.

The biographer's name was Clinton Baedecker. There was a photograph of him on the back panel of the jacket—a rawboned, deeply tanned man in his late thirties, roughhousing with his two small towheaded daughters on someone's lawn—and a brief note that said the author made his home in Detroit. Canada pulled down the city directory and slid his reading glasses down the *B*'s, but Baedecker's name didn't appear there. Nor was he listed in any of the suburban directories. He called Information and was told the number was unlisted.

"My name is Canada," he said. "I'm an inspector with the Detroit Police Department. I need that number. This is a police emergency."

"I'm sorry, Inspector. You have to file a request in writing."

He depressed the plunger, got the 1300 switchboard, and asked for Stationary Traffic. He introduced himself all over again for the bored-sounding female clerk who answered.

"Baedecker, Clinton." He spelled both names. "He must have drawn a parking ticket sometime during the past two years. I'm after a telephone number."

"We wouldn't have that even if a ticket was issued."

"An address would do."

"You'd have to call the Secretary of State's office. It's not our job to match license numbers to addresses and telephones. You might try the Traffic Court Bureau."

He got a male clerk there, who kept him waiting five minutes while he went through the records. "A Clinton Baedecker appeared before the magistrate to oppose a ticket for careless driving on October fourth, nineteen sixty-five. Officer who issued the ticket didn't appear and the case was dismissed."

"Did he give a telephone number?"

"Yes." He read it.

Baedecker answered on the third ring. He had a light voice for such a rugged-looking man. When Canada introduced himself he laughed shortly. "Word sure gets around. Who told you I'm researching a book about the Detroit police?"

"Nobody. I'm reading your book on Albert Brock and have a question."

"Is this police business?"

"Yes."

A match scratched on Baedecker's end. "Go ahead, Inspector."

"In Chapter Three you mentioned Brock's involvement in a strike at an automobile plant in nineteen thirty-one. I wasn't aware he ever worked for an auto company."

"It was after the bank repossessed his first truck and before he went to work hauling steel. The plant was in Dearborn, where they made hood latches for Chrysler."

"What were the circumstances of the strike?"

"A pregnant female worker was fired for fainting on the job. Brock and the others shut down their machines and refused to let anybody in or out. The Dearborn police showed up with professional strike-breakers. There was a brawl, but nobody was seriously hurt. Chrysler fired the strikers and replaced them. That wasn't too difficult with a Depression on."

"Doesn't sound like much of a strike."

"I only mentioned it because it was Brock's first exposure to the labor movement and because it predated the strike at the Kelsey-Hayes Wheel Company by five years. Most histories identify that as the beginning of the movement locally."

"What was your source?"

Baedecker exhaled; blowing smoke. "How's the Grecian Gardens investigation coming along?"

"The commissioner's planning on calling a press conference next week. I'll get you an invitation."

"Well, it's a start. I came across the story when I was going through some old newspapers at the library. It wasn't in the *Times*, *News*, or *Free Press*. The *Banner* used it for filler. DEARBORN POLICE QUELL COMMUNIST RIOT, the headline ran."

"I never heard of the *Banner*."

"You wouldn't. It went out with the rest of the tabloids when times got hard. Brock had referred to the plant in passing during one of our early interviews. He was too busy to see me, so I got what details there are from one of his old cronies. I understand the reporter who covered the story is still living. Connie Minor is the name."

"A woman?"

"No, he had a column in the paper with a picture."

"Where can I reach him?"

"Search me. I didn't try. Like you said, it wasn't much of a strike." Baedecker blew out again. "How's chances of my getting a look at that Christmas list?"

Canada said he'd see what he could do, thanked him, and hung up. So far the Supreme Court hadn't ruled on the constitutionality of lying to a writer.

Chapter 17

Elrod Brown was built like Chilly Willy and dressed like a black caricature of a white undertaker. His black suit and gray cotton gloves with matching spats came straight out of the mortician's catalogue. (Lydell swore the silver rims of his eyeglasses had come from his customers' fillings.) He spoke with a pronounced lisp, and his infrequent laughter, intended to be obsequious, was uncomfortably close to a giggle. Following Brown through the big display room behind the main parlor, listening to the relative merits of options and standard equipment, box springs, and aerodynamic engineering, Quincy felt as if he were shopping for a new car instead of just a box to put Congo in and cover up with dirt.

The fat man stopped and slapped the curved lid of a casket the color and general shape of a Luden's cough drop. "This is the top of the Eternity line," he said. "Solid bronze. Guaranteed not to collapse or leak for a thousand years."

Lydell said, "Who we see if it falls apart in nine hunnert and ninety-nine?"

"Pop the hood," Quincy said. "Let's see what she's got."

Brown lifted the lid. Lydell said mm-*mm*! and stroked the white satin lining. "This is nicer than my apartment."

"Marcus Garvey was laid to rest in a casket just like this one." The mortician giggled.

Quincy asked how much.

"Six thousand dollars. Now, that's the manufacturer's suggested retail price. I can let you have it—"

"Ain't you got nothing more expensive?"

Brown lowered the lid. His hand shook a little. "This is the Jeroboam. The Nebuchadnezzar is the same model with fourteen-karat gold fittings and an Italian silk lining. Eighty-five fifty."

"We'll take it. How much does that come to with the flowers and the white hearse and limos?"

"Don't forget the choir," Lydell said.

Brown scribbled some figures in a leather-bound notebook. "Eleven thousand five hundred. A fifteen percent deposit is customary."

"Pay the man, Lydell."

He took a roll of bills out of his pocket. "Hundreds okay?"

"Body's at the Wayne County Morgue," Quincy said. "Vernon Kress is the name. You pick up?"

"Pick up? Oh, sure." The mortician watched the bills piling up on his outstretched palms. "When do you want to hold the services?"

"Tomorrow."

"Tomorrow is Independence Day."

"It is for Congo."

"That isn't much time. They have to ship the casket from Lansing, and, er, I understand the remains are not in the best repair. They may require extensive reconstruction."

"For eleven and a half grand you can let bids," Quincy said. "C'mon, Lydell. We're late for church."

Quincy drove the Sting Ray. Lydell no longer wore a sling, but the pain pills the doctors had prescribed for him at Receiving made him too giddy for Quincy's taste as a passenger, especially since he washed them down with rye. It was a blistering, tar-smelling Sunday morning and the top was down. The radio in a pink-and-black DeSoto cruising along next to them carried details of John Kennedy, Jr.'s recovery from first- and second-degree burns suffered when he fell into a bed of hot coals during a trip to Hawaii with his mother. A plastic surgeon who had treated the late President's five-year-old son in the Honolulu home of Henry J. Kaiser reported that reconstructive surgery would not be necessary.

"Poor little fucker," Lydell said. "Gots his lily-white butt blistered at a luau, and here you and me's worried about someone blowing our heads off. Makes you ashamed."

"His old man got *his* blowed off, don't forget. You never heard John-John piss and moan. He saluted at the funeral." Quincy nicked a red light at Fourteenth and flipped the bird at a trucker who leaned on his air horn.

"Bet it didn't cost half as much as Congo's."

"I thought about renting a black horse. You know, with the boots stuck backwards in the stirrups? But I didn't want to look like a copycat."

"It's too much bread to spread on the dead. You going to do the same for me next time DiJesus comes around dressed like John Clawed Killy?"

"He behaved himself this morning."

In fact Gallante's man had not showed his face in the blind pig at all during business hours, stationing himself downstairs instead to scrutinize the customers on their way up. No one complained. Gallante had reported shortly after dawn to count the policy receipts, with DiJesus looking on. They had done a little better than the week before. Quincy was pretty sure conditions would continue to improve now that the Sicilians were in residence.

Lydell assumed Elrod Brown's lisp. "This here's the Jeroboam. The Nebuchadnezzar comes with bucket seats and air conditioning. You believe that shit?"

"I liked the His 'n' Her Sweetheart Burial Plot. With the stone shaped like a big old heart."

"Shiiit. When my time comes you can stick me in a bag and leave me out by the curb." Lydell leaned forward out of the slipstream and lit a Kent.

Quincy considered the subject. "Not me. I want a Viking funeral. Like in *Beau Geste*. Float me out in the middle of Lake St. Clair and set me on fire. Right in front of the Detroit Yacht Club."

"I don't know what you see in them crummy old movies, bro."

"Endings," Quincy said.

The Second Baptist Church, at Monroe and Beaubien, was the oldest of its kind in Detroit, purchased from the Lutherans in 1857 and serving the needs of a Negro congregation organized in 1836. At eighty-six, the Reverend Otis R. R. Idaho had been its pastor for almost fifty years, longer than any other minister in the city. They found him standing on the chair behind his desk in his walnut-paneled study in the basement, pounding a nail into the only section of wall not already covered by a photograph in a frame. He was still wearing his white surplice from the morning services over gray pinstripe pants and white scuffed sneakers.

"Have a seat, children," he said without turning.

Lydell sat down, stretched out his legs, and closed his eyes; the secondary reaction to the pills and liquor was setting in. Quincy wandered around the room looking at pictures. The minister was in all of them, shaking hands with local and visiting luminaries from Soupy Sales to Martin Luther King. Many of them were auto-graphed. George Washington Carver had a large sprawling hand.

"A sinful vanity." Idaho, who seemed to be able to see backwards, for he still hadn't turned, finished pounding and hung a recent likeness of himself posing with the Supremes. "We're all equal under Christ, but since the day Teddy Roosevelt pressed a nickel into my hand for opening the door for him at the Detroit Opera House in nineteen sixteen . . ." He trailed off. Half a century up North had taken none of the molasses out of his deep Mississippi drawl.

Quincy said, "I know what you mean. I seen Cootie Williams once at the state fair."

The minister used the tail of his surplice to wipe a smudge off the glass and climbed down. His height surprised Quincy, who would have found himself looking up at him before Idaho's shoulders had begun to stoop, and his grip on Quincy's hand was firm despite the fact that all his bones showed under a thin sheeting of flesh. His ears stuck out on stalks from his head with its fringe of white hair. The cord of a hearing aid snaked down inside his clerical collar. Quincy thought he looked like Mahatma Gandhi.

"Your friend looks done in," Idaho said.

Lydell was asleep with his ankles crossed and his hands folded on his stomach.

"He had a rough week."

"You ought to send him home from the blind pig once in a while."

"You know about us?"

"I baptized half the population of Twelfth Street. They tell me things they wouldn't tell their brothers and sisters."

"I'm surprised you agreed to see us," Quincy said.

"A professional sinner may reclaim his soul as well as an amateur. Besides, I play three-one-nine once a year. That's the date I was ordained. Sit down, son."

Quincy waited for the old man to lower himself into his chair before he took a seat. "Thanks for seeing us on short notice."

"Death is difficult to reschedule. Was Brother Kress a Baptist?"

"I don't know."

"Did he request a Baptist ceremony?"

"Not that I know of."

"Did he attend services here?"

"I don't think so."

Idaho examined the hammer he had used to hang the picture and set it aside. "I assumed you were close. Not many employers would arrange a funeral for a worker. Your particular business is not known for its generosities."

"Well, he didn't have any people."

"Interesting. One wonders who will come."

Quincy changed the subject. He had started all wrong, anticipating the usual octogenarian density. He would have liked to see the minister shoot craps against Lydell.

"You said on the phone tomorrow would be okay for the service. I want to go over the arrangements with you, see if they're okay."

"Have you arranged dancing?"

"No."

"Then I'm sure they'll be fine." Idaho glanced at Lydell. "Your friend looks done in."

Quincy hesitated. "He's on medication. What's the usual donation?"

"Three hundred dollars." The minister uncovered a full set of false teeth. "It's an old church. Old churches need new roofs. The last one came courtesy of a fellow who called himself Big Nabob. That would be before your time."

"I heard about him. Joey Machine killed him."

"I never saw such a fine funeral. People today have no imagination. Your friend looks done in."

This time Quincy let it slide. Idaho's brain seemed to have picked up a scratch or two like an old record. "There'll be a choir and a lead singer. His name's Mahomet."

Idaho reached up under his surplice. His hearing aid released a high-pitched squeal. Quincy flinched. He wondered how it sounded in the minister's ear.

"Sorry. The batteries are going. What is the singer's name?"

"Mahomet."

"It wasn't the batteries," Idaho said. "No."

"No what?"

"No Mahomet. I won't have that man in my church."

"It's God's house."

"God doesn't have to kick the radiator when the pipes clog."

"If it's his name—"

"I wouldn't have him if his name were St. Thomas Aquinas. The last time he appeared here I almost had a riot in the congregation."

"What'd he do?"

"He interrupted his own interpretation of 'Praise God From Whom All Blessings Flow' to deliver an oration on the dignity of man. Specifically the black man. By the time he was finished he had the entire attendance ready to march on the City-County Building."

"He's big on dignity," Quincy averred. "When I met him—"

"There is a time and place for that sort of thing. I submit that regular Sunday services at the Second Baptist Church do not answer. No Mahomet." He placed his palms on the desk. "You'd better take your friend home now. He looks done in."

"What about a donation of five hundred?"

Idaho had started to rise. He paused halfway out of the chair with his sharp elbows bent above his head, looking like a daddy longlegs. "You'll see he confines his vocal exercises to the hymnal?"

"I'll shoot him in the head if I got to."

"Don't hit the big crucifix." The minister stood.

Chapter 18

Rick liked the new apartment on Watson, but he missed the personal touch he had enjoyed at his last place of residence.

At $130 per month, the new place—three rooms with bath on the fifth floor of a turn-of-the-century brick building overlooking Woodward—fell easily within reach of his new salary, and the additional room had reunited him with some items he had placed in storage when he broke up with Charlotte; but the anonymity of apartment living took some getting used to after eleven months in the little bedroom over Mrs. Hertler's kitchen.

Not that he spent much time on the fifth floor. After sleeping in late this Sunday, he had thrown on a T-shirt and jeans, eaten two quick scrambled eggs over *Dick Tracy*, and come down to the sun-plastered square of asphalt next to the building to inspect the lifter he had heard under the hood of the Z-28 earlier in the week. He had identified and corrected the problem in five minutes with a tooth-brush and a capful of gasoline, then as long as he was there he went ahead and changed the points and drained the crankcase. Now, four hours later, he was stretched out under the car replacing the rusty bolts that held the crossover in place with a stainless steel set purchased from the hardware store on the corner. The radio was tuned to CKLW, where the disk jockey was playing the Beatles' *Revolver* album in its entirety. Rick would have switched stations if his hands weren't full. "We had a pretty good thing going in rock 'n' roll until the Brits came in and screwed it up," he'd once told Charlotte. She was a fan, and that had been the beginning of the end.

"If I didn't recognize the car, I'd still know it's you by those kids' shoes you wear."

He looked at a pair of white plastic wingtips standing in front of the car. "Hello, Dan. Get WJR on, will you? Lolich is pitching."

Dan Sugar walked around to the driver's side. The radio went off. "Later. I was thinking maybe you lost my telephone number."

"I've been going to call. Goddamnit!" The wrench slipped and he knocked the top off a knuckle. A trickle of blood tunneled through the dirt and grease on the back of his hand.

"What do you think of Porter? I know you met, on account of one of my boys saw you leave the office together yesterday."

Rick sucked the knuckle. "Who was he watching, me or Porter?"

"Hey, I plug the holes. That's why I got sixteen people under me, seventeen counting you. So is he a flake or what?"

"He's not any part of a flake. I haven't got a handle on him yet, but I know that much. And you can forget that stuff about him not knowing anything about cars. He's either the best driver I ever saw or the luckiest."

"Where'd he take you?"

"To a farm."

"You mean like with cows and turnips? What's the matter, the fresh produce at the A & P ain't good enough for the Boy Wonder? It ain't safe enough for him, maybe."

Rick tightened the last bolt and wriggled out from under the car. Sugar had on white flared slacks to go with the shoes, a yellow bowling shirt with *Dan* stitched over the pocket in green script—the tail out to cover his gun—and a pair of wraparound sunglasses that made him look like Gort the robot in *The Day the Earth Stood Still*. His big raw face was cherry red in the sunlight.

"He's got his own proving ground up in Macomb County." Rick wiped his hands off on a streaked yellow chamois. The knuckle was still seeping. "His security's a joke, but the tests he runs there are your real threat. Everything else is just numbers."

"Yeah, yeah, that's for the boys in Legal. What about Porter, his slip showing yet?"

"I'm pretty sure he's not running a white slavery racket on Whittier, but I've only been working there two days. Jesus Christ, Dan."

"How long's it take to get the scent? You're a little rusty, maybe."

"Undercover isn't like Nescafé. You have to bring people along. That doesn't happen overnight."

"We ain't got much longer than overnight. Washington wants a goat before November and we're it unless we can discredit Porter first. This *I Led Three Lives* shit don't cut it."

Rick wiped a spot of grease off the Camaro's fender and slammed down the hood. "I already blew off one source for pushing too hard. I can get it for you fast or I can get it for you good. Take your pick."

"Just get it. You let me worry about making it good." Sugar produced a spiral notebook from his hip pocket and leafed through it. "What about this broad works for him, this Kohler dame? I hear she's a looker, anything in that?"

"That's the source I blew off. I'm working on it."

"He spends more time at the office than he does with his wife, the high-class lawyer. I bet them desks see more action than the beds at Howard Johnson's."

"It's promising, but don't count on it. He's pretty caught up in his work."

"Maybe he's queer."

"You're wasting my day off, Dan."

"Yeah, we shouldn't be seen together out in the open anyway." He ran a finger along the Camaro's silver finish. "Nice. I kind of liked the yellow."

"I can tell by your shirt."

"Spiffy, ain't it? I had it custom done in this little place in Hamtramck. I'm thinking of starting up a team at GM, call ourselves the Security Sleuths. You can join after you finish this job."

"What's your average?"

"I don't get you."

"Do you bowl?"

"Never tried. Can't be too hard, with so many Polacks doing it."

Rick gathered up his tools. "I'll call when I have something."

"Call anyway," Sugar said. "You give me a toothpick, I'll build a cabin."

After he'd gone, Rick went upstairs, took a shower, and put a Band-Aid on his injured knuckle, which had begun to throb. He changed into a clean shirt and sweatpants, punched a hole in a can of Schlitz, and watched two innings of the baseball game on TV. When Kaline grounded into a double play to retire the Tigers in the seventh his mind wandered.

Everything in this world that walks or flies or swims has got to shit somewhere; it's only a matter of time before they pick the wrong place. Everybody fucks up.

Where do the Wendell Porters of this world go to fuck up?

Maybe they don't have to go anywhere. Maybe somebody fucks up for them.

He had a sudden thirst for knowledge.

It was the way of these infrequent attacks that they occurred invariably on Sundays and holidays, when the library was closed.

He watched the game a few minutes longer, then turned off the set and went into the bedroom, where he pulled a faded Stroh's beer case from the back of the closet.

It contained most of the magazines he had held on to over the past several years—mostly *Motor Trend* and *Popular Mechanics*—along with the inevitable dross that got swept up in any unorganized collection: a *Newsweek* with Khrushchev on the cover, several *Photoplays*, the special *Life* JFK issue following the assassination, and some *Cosmopolitans*. Those and the movie magazines had belonged to

Charlotte. He sat cross-legged on the floor among the torn and creased covers and sorted through the *Cosmopolitan*s.

It was funny how things stuck in your head, particularly when you kept coming across the same magazine when you were looking for something else. Each time he had planned to throw out the women's publications, and each time after he'd found what he'd wanted he had returned the stack to the box.

He found it now, a single line on the cover among that month's features—the month being March 1964—checked the table of contents, and turned to the article. The page opposite the title was a full-length black-and-white photograph of a woman in a tailored dress carrying a thick briefcase down the ramp from a commercial jetliner. Her face was turned slightly away from the camera, presenting a clean-edged profile, long of neck with blond hair up, that recalled Princess Grace. The title was *"The Queen of Torts."*

The article that followed, written in a breathless style by a female journalist clearly in awe of her subject, recounted a day in the life of Caroline Porter, with a brief introduction tracing her rapid rise from storefront lawyer to canny counsel to the Porter Group. Her landmark case, in which she had successfully defended her husband from a charge of industrial espionage brought by General Motors's battery of male attorneys, received only a line. The writer was far more concerned with Mrs. Porter's mannish fashions and trademark pearl earrings, the only jewelry she ever wore aside from her wedding band.

Although it was useless for Rick's purposes, he read the piece twice before reinterring the magazine with the others in the beer case and shoving the case back inside the closet. Tomorrow when the library opened he would read more.

Caroline Porter.

Enid Kohler.

Say what one liked about Wendell Porter, he had a knack for surrounding himself with beautiful capable women.

Chapter 19

"I wasn't saying it just to be saying it," Krystal said. "It was nice. I mean, really nice."

Quincy said, "Nobody's arguing, okay?"

"I remember when they put my mother under, it was like your generic, all-purpose, one-size-fits-all funeral. Preacher kept getting her name wrong. I didn't give a shit, I mean she threw me out when I was fourteen, said if I was going to pedal my ass all over town I might as well do it for a living. I only went because my brothers said if I didn't they'd hang out in front of my apartment and throw the johns down the stairs and because I wanted to make sure that old woman was dead. It was the only time I ever seen a smile on her face. Didn't they do a good job on Vernon? He looked nice." She'd been calling him Vernon ever since they'd begun the arrangements. In life it was always Congo, when she'd addressed him at all.

"He looked deader'n Bojangles," Lydell said.

They were riding in one of the two white Cadillac limousines Quincy had hired for the procession; ahead of them, following the hearse, was the limousine carrying the Reverend Idaho, and behind them an assortment of Lincolns, Corvettes, Thunderbirds, Chevies, and Theron "Gidgy" Gidrey's black-and-green Excalibur, was strung out for eleven blocks doing fifteen miles an hour on the way to Mt. Elliott Cemetery. Krystal, touching up her face with a compact shaped like a clamshell, had on a black minidress with sequined lace across the bodice, black fishnet stockings, and silver sandals with leather straps cross-hatching her calves like Richard Burton wore in *Cleopatra*. Quincy wore black sharkskin with his only white shirt and no necktie and Lydell had exchanged his yellow tie and hatband for respectful black. Quincy's window was down and East Lafayette smelled of hot asphalt and spent cordite from exploded firecrackers. He had to remind himself it was the Fourth of July.

They passed a parked panel truck bearing the WWJ Channel 4 logo. A few yards away a silver-haired man in a blue blazer stood on the sidewalk with his back to them, facing a TV camera. He was holding a microphone.

"That Ven Marshall?" Lydell leaned forward and cranked down his tinted window.

"Probably just some reporter. Them anchormen don't go outside for nothing."

"I was on TV once," Krystal said.

"Think Patsy's watching?" asked Lydell.

"Somebody'll tell him about it if he don't see it."

"I waved when I was getting into the wagon. Only they cut out the wave when they showed it."

"Hope you're right," Lydell said. "I hate to think of spending all that bread on just Congo."

"I was in a movie once, but the cops burned the negative."

Quincy said, "The reverend surprised me. I didn't think he could hop around like that."

"He sure gives hell hell," Lydell said. "Where's Mahomet? I thought he was riding with us."

"He took a bus back to Collingwood. Said he don't like to see folks put in the ground."

"Man can sing. What's that he sang?"

" 'Freedom Road.' "

"Beats them low notes to death. Makes Lou Rawls sound like Little Anthony."

"Man can sing," Quincy agreed. Before the service he had taken Mahomet aside and told him he'd personally break his dick off if anything but lyrics came out of his mouth. He had had an anxious moment when Mahomet got up in front of the choir and cleared his throat, but when Quincy rolled up his funeral program and bent it in half, the singer got the message, and the next three minutes were the sweetest Quincy had ever spent in a place where he didn't want to be. Mahomet was good, phenomenally good; the timbre of his voice was like the reverberation of a great bell, and the emotion behind it held the tragic richness of wine put down when "Freedom Road" was new.

There had been a brief tingling silence between the end of the last, incredibly attenuated note and Idaho's approach to the pulpit, like a stone hanging at the top of its high arc before plummeting anticlimactically to earth. Perhaps because of it, the minister had started slowly and worked his way up, droning at first, then shortening his vowels and chopping his consonants, to a tent-fire pitch, ending with:

" 'And now also the axe is laid unto the root of the trees; therefore every tree which bringeth not forth good fruit is hewn down, and cast into the fire!' "

Mahomet had then joined with the choir to sing "Praise Ye the Lord," but although it stirred the people in the pews, many of whom joined in, clapping and swaying, it was that first quiet solo that had stayed with Quincy. It made him think for the first time of what Congo had lost, and of what all those who shared his color had lost since the first slaver set anchor off a barbaric shore. He thought then that he understood Emma and her tribal artifacts a little better, without wanting to see any of them again.

The graveside service was brief, with Idaho reading quietly from Matthew under a canvas with folding chairs set out for Quincy and his party while the other mourners stood in their dark clothes and jewelry. The pallbearers were Quincy, Lydell, Joe Petite, and Sebas-

tian Bright from the East Side, and two of their collectors. Despite
his name, Petite, a former Detroit Piston, was nearly seven feet tall,
with wrists and ankles that stuck out of the suits he bought by the
yard. Bright, shorter by almost a foot and a half, was two hundred
pounds of hard fat with a glossy shaved head and a gold tooth in
front; today he had foregone his trademark fawn suits for sober
black flannel.

The casket, whose brushed bronze finish shone softly in the sun,
descended into the vault with a hydraulic hum. When it came to rest,
Idaho tossed the first handful of earth onto the lid. Quincy bent to
scoop up a handful, paused, dropped it into the grave, and walked
away. When Lydell joined him, dusting off his palms, Quincy
stopped and pointed his chin in the direction of Mt. Elliott Street,
where a man in a black tank top and faded Levi's was leaning back
against a sky-blue Cobra with his arms crossed, showing his biceps.
The sun flared off a gold chain around his neck.

"My, oh, my," said Lydell. "Mistuh DiJesus he sho' nuff do likes to
see his customers all de way into de ground, don't he? Think Patsy
sent him?"

"You don't send guys like him anyplace. They just show up."

"Man knows his wheels."

Krystal caught up with them. "What you all looking at?"

Quincy told her. She shielded her eyes with her hand. "He don't
look like such hot shit to me."

"He killed Congo."

"Man's got balls," Lydell said. "Fuzz here and everything."

Quincy said, "They ain't looking for him. If they tossed him right
now, he'd be cleaner than you."

"Town's full of dudes like that, showing off their big muscles,"
Krystal said. "Ain't a stiff wad in the bunch."

Lydell poked a Kent into his holder. "What you figure he wants?"

"A look at the meat." Quincy resumed walking. "Let's go back to
Collingwood."

Gidgy's Excalibur, bottle-green with black fenders and running boards, was parked in front of the blind pig when they got there. Loosely patterned on the 1930 Mercedes, the car had a flat rag top, wire wheels, a long medieval-looking hood secured with a leather strap, and chromed exhaust pipes bending down from holes in the hood.

"How'd he get here ahead of us?" Lydell stood on the curb while Quincy tipped the driver of the limousine. They'd let Krystal out in front of the apartment building on Woodrow Wilson to change.

"Gidgy never stays for graveside," Quincy said. "He only bought the car for Sundays and funeral processions."

"Looks like something the house nigger drives the rich old white lady in to Mah-Jongg. Them dope fiends got no taste."

"Twenty grand worth of car, bro. They only sell a hundred and fifty a year."

Lydell coughed. "Maybe Johnson's right. They's hope for this here Great Society after all."

Upstairs, Mahomet was pouring clear liquid from a cocktail shaker into a glass on the table where Gidgy sat. The singer had taken off the black coat he'd worn to the funeral and tied on an apron that covered him almost to his patent-leather boots. As always he wore elevator heels.

"Thanks for coming, Gidge." Quincy shook the hand of the man seated. It was like flipping a limp tow rope.

"I was just telling your man here he's wasting his time tending bar. He's good enough to sing with the Temptations." Gidgy had on a box-back jacket that sheathed him past his hips and a red-and-green-striped bow tie on a Madras shirt. The brim of his white Panama and the smoked lenses of his old-fashioned round spectacles shielded his weak eyes from the unaccustomed glare of daytime. His long, could-be-forty, could-be-sixty face was like dark oiled wood, and his mouth was where smiles went to die. A gold earring the size of a Lifesaver glinted on his right lobe. A joint smoldered in a corner of his mouth like a conventional cigarette. From time to time he tilted his head to one side to release the acrid smoke trapped under his hat.

"I tried it," Mahomet said. "Quincy knows all about it."

Quincy lifted Gidgy's glass and sniffed at it. "He can't mix drinks neither. How much vermouth you put in that shaker?" he asked Mahomet.

"About a cup."

Lydell said, "Jee-sus. We been working on the same bottle since we opened."

"The man asked for a martini. Was I going to tell him I never made one?"

"Mahomet's new," Quincy said. "You hungry?" He nodded toward the spread on the bar. Krystal had overseen that part, little thin sandwiches and cocktail wienies among the ribs and collards. The room smelled like a barbecue.

"Maybe I get the munchies later. The rest coming?"

"Hope so. We can't get all that into the fridge."

"It was a nice one," Gidgy said. "I only been to one better."

"Big Nabob?"

"I ain't that old. Buried my brother in fifty-nine. Well, my half brother, but I sprung for both halves. He tried to fly off a roof."

Lydell was making a sandwich of ribs on pumpernickel. "Thought you boys never used the stuff you sell."

"You mean to tell me you never played a number?"

"Not since I been in the business. It's like cooking for yourself. Where's the surprise?" He took a bite.

"Surprises is all I sell."

After a few minutes the others began to arrive, first in singles and small groups, then in a steady stream until the bar and poolroom were filled with happy mourners juggling drinks and paper plates heaped with food. Quincy demoted Mahomet to waiter and for a time he and Lydell were too busy behind the bar to hold a conversation with anyone. Along with Joe Petite and Sebastian Bright and their people, the guests included longtime customers of both the blind pig and Quincy and Lydell's policy business and other Twelfth Street-area entrepreneurs. Beatrice Blackwood, at fifty-two a handsome, fine-featured Jamaican who operated the Indio Spa on Bethune (No Asian Girls), arrived on the arm of her glowering, dashiki-clad houseman Kindu Kinshasha, who had fought heavyweight under the name Marcus Tyler. By the time Krystal showed up in a purple dress trimmed with black feather boas, the effect was lost in the crowd. She had Lydell float a twist of lemon in a tumbler full of gin and went off in a corner to sulk and soak.

"Anything for you, my man?" Lydell squirted seltzer into a glass of Scotch for Kindu Kinshasha to take back to his mistress.

"I don't drink."

"Religion?"

"Ulcer."

Lydell handed him the glass. "I heard you fought Clay."

"You heard wrong."

"Beatrice told me you sparred with him when he was nineteen, twenty."

"You don't *fight* Clay. You try to get out of the ring alive." He turned back into the crowd.

"It ain't my argument," Sebastian Bright was telling Quincy over a bottle of Budweiser. His shaven scalp and the gold tooth in the fixed smile sent off semaphores of reflected light.

"Cops told me the same three hit one of your places on Clairmount the night we got it," Quincy said.

"You talking to cops now?"

"They was talking to me. You fixing to just let the Sicilians walk in and take over like the last thirty years never happened?"

"I don't know it was Sicilians. *You* said that. I figure it was just some brothers trying to get ahead. I find them I cut their nuts off, but I understand why they done what they done. I ain't looking for no war I can't win."

"You don't fight, you already lost it."

Sebastian laid a pudgy hand on Quincy's wrist. His smile was set in concrete. "You throw a good wake, and I'm sorry about your boy. But you go stirring up shit with the Man, somebody gonna take you out. Maybe one of us."

Quincy said, "Old Patsy cranks the organ, you just shake that tin cup, huh?"

The gold tooth disappeared. "I was running policy slips for Machine before you sat on your first pot. I seen that stairwell he got shot up in with his bodyguard right after they drug out the bodies. Looked like somebody went and dumped a tub of guts down the steps. Patsy's old man Frankie done that, or had it done, which is the same thing. So when Patsy says, 'Nigger, git,' I dips my head and says, 'Yes, suh,' and shuffles on out de do'. I got this far playing the percentages. You want to lay it all down on a longshot, you just go right ahead. I'll throw dirt down your hole."

The wake had been going two hours when four new guests entered, single file because the doorway was barely wide enough for one. They stood just inside, two Negroes in their middle years and two in their twenties, looking around. Their loud sportcoats and open-necked shirts, strained at the shoulders and too short in the arms, stood out against all that funeral black like Easter eggs in an alley. Quincy went over to them.

"You're Springfield?" The speaker, built along Quincy's lines but longer in the arms, simian, took his hand in a knuckle-demolishing grip. His graying hair, strung through beads that rattled when he moved his head, hung to his shoulders, thrusting the Neanderthal bone structure of his face into frightening relief. He made Quincy feel fey. "They mentioned you on the Six O'Clock News. That's some send-off you gave Vernon."

"You relatives?" There was a certain similarity of build.

"No. Hell, no. We wrestled with him. You seen me on Channel Nine maybe, right after Mitch Miller."

"I work nights."

"I'm Mighty Joe Young, the Gorilla from Manila. These here is my son and my nephew, they're the Bongo Brothers, Boone and Bosco.

They bend crowbars and shit over each other's heads to warm up the crowd."

"Bet it works." Having just reclaimed his hand from Mighty Joe Young's, Quincy merely nodded at the two younger men, who looked enough alike to be twins, second carbons of their father and uncle with less spectacular facial framework and tightly curled hair cut close to their scalps.

"And this is Anthony Battle."

Quincy looked at the last man, a Joe Young contemporary with an advanced forehead and hostile eyes in a medium-dark face without expression. "Just Anthony Battle? What's your gimmick?"

"I wrestle."

"Anthony should of been world heavyweight champion. He's the only man to take a cocoa-butt from Bobo Brazil and laugh at him."

"What happened?"

"It was during a press conference," Battle said.

"Oh."

Mighty Joe Young explained. "The World Wrestling Guild owns all the contracts. The championship belt looks best on Bobo, so they bought the reporters to keep the story out of print."

Lydell had joined them. "Think you can get me a date with Amazonia the Python Queen?"

"She's married," Mighty Joe Young said. "To the Guild treasurer."

Quincy said, "Sorry you couldn't make the funeral."

"I read about this Congo getting killed, but I didn't know it was Vernon till tonight when I seen the procession on TV. Old Cape Horn had a headlock on every one of us at one time or another. We come to pay our respects."

"Vernon's friends are welcome. What you all drinking?"

"It's not us and the Sicilians. It's the white man kicking us back down to the bottom."

Mahomet's deep voice, raised at the bar, flattened the murmuring in the room. Heads turned. The singer was standing in front of Joe

Petite, looking almost straight up at the former basketball center towering over him by nearly two feet.

"You think we push liquor after hours and sell numbers because we want to?" he went on. "We do it because the white man has kept us out of everything legal. Now, just when we're starting to build ourselves up in the last place that's open, he's saying coloreds need not apply. He killed one of us like he was stepping on a bug, or did you forget you're here swilling and stuffing your face because of him? You'd be standing in his blood right now if I didn't clean it up day before yesterday."

There was a little silence before the tall man set his glass down on the bar and turned to go; it was an eerie vacuum in that room filled with people, and Quincy thought of the tingling moment that had followed "Freedom Road" in church. Petite paused when he reached Quincy.

"It was a real fine day, brother, but your help needs a muzzle." He left.

The crowd started to thin out after that. Sebastian Bright shook Quincy's hand, showed his gold tooth, and went out without a word. Beatrice Blackwood kissed Quincy on the cheek, said, "It was lovely, dear. Stop in any time for a body shampoo and a massage, no charge", and left with Kindu Kinshasha. On his way out, Gidgy told Quincy he was expecting a shipment of Mexican that he'd cut him a deal on if he was interested.

Mahomet came over. His face was tragic. "Sorry, boss."

"It was a good speech, man. Martin ought to know about you."

"Twelve thou, with the booze and eats. 'It was a real fine day, brother.' Shiiit." Lydell subsided into a coughing fit. Quincy pounded him until he stopped.

Mighty Joe Young held out a card between two fingers the size of frankfurters. "This is my agent's number. He'll know where to reach me anytime you want me." The others followed him out.

"We can always have him put a half nelson on Patsy," said Lydell, gasping for breath.

When the last guest had departed, Quincy sent Lydell and Mahomet home and scraped Krystal out of the corner where she sat
spraddle-legged on the floor with her glass in her purple lap. Hours
later in the apartment, still half-asleep and smelling of junipers, she
found him in the dark and made him hard and climbed aboard. The
telephone rang.

"Quincy, this is Sebastian Bright."

"Yeah, Sebastian." He put a hand on Krystal's back, interrupting
her rhythm.

"I got the people if you can get the guns."

He sat up, dislodging her. The luminous dial on the alarm clock
read 3:10. "What happened to playing the percentages?"

"Fuck the percentages. They hit Joe Petite's place tonight behind
the barbershop. Joe was dead a long time before he got to the floor."

Chapter 20

"It's funny how the second- and third-rate speaks all hung on to become restaurants and such while all the best ones got torn down or turned into laundromats. I interviewed Chaplin here when he was in town researching *Modern Times*, and the service isn't any better now than it was then. How'd you track me down?"

His companion's racing-changes between subjects made Canada struggle to catch up. He swallowed a mouthful of corned beef and rye and chased it with beer from a thick mug. "I called the Detroit Press Club. They told me you spend a lot of time here."

Here was a busy restaurant in the warehouse district, a cave of a place cut into the side of a soot-stained brick building that was new when Detroit was the stove-making capital of the world, before Henry Ford saw his first piston. The walls were plastered with black-and-white pictures of federals with axes staving in kegs and cases of bottles, and the tables all had shelves under the leaves for stashing the evidence whenever the cop on the beat strolled past a window—a pretty conceit, as if the cop wouldn't stop in to wet his own whistle. On a stage the size of a speaker's platform, a girl in a turtleneck sweater and jeans with straight blonde hair to her waist sat on a high stool strumming a guitar and warbling a song about the Civil War. Consistency of theme was apparently not a priority.

"I keep up my membership, God knows why. I haven't been near a typewriter in twenty years."

Connie Minor, baptized Constantine, was a round little man with fine white hair brushed back over pink scalp and bright, intelligent eyes in a red face that made him appear jovial; an impression that faded within five minutes of meeting him. He tasted his chowder, recoiled, and poured ice water from his glass into the bowl. He wasn't drinking. A coin-size medallion on a silver chain around his neck announced for the benefit of paramedics that he was diabetic.

"Before looking you up I read some of your columns in old issues of the *Banner* at the library," Canada said. "They hold up better than anything else in the paper. Why'd you quit journalism?"

"I quit it the way Batista quit Cuba. While I was busy getting in tight with the Purple Gang and that crowd, the news business was developing a social conscience. I never did. I thought it was tough enough getting along as an individual without having to drag the whole human race with you. Still do, which is why Cronkite never calls. Oh, I bumped along for a while, did some vacation columns for the *News* and *Times* and a couple of radio scripts for *The Lone Ranger* when I really got desperate. I even wrote a book. I don't imagine you read it. It was about Jack Dance."

The Brock book was the first one the inspector had found time to read in years. "Was he as kill-drunk as they say?"

"Jack? He played cops and robbers his whole life. He thought everyone got up and brushed the dirt off after the shooting was over and went home."

"What do you do now?"

"Sell power lawn mowers. Want one?"

"I don't have a lawn."

"That's what everyone says. I sure do stink."

Canada drank some beer. "Can we talk about Albert Brock?"

"You bought the soup."

"Do you know Clinton Baedecker? He wrote a book about him."

"I read it. It's a joke. No, we haven't met." He blew on a spoonful. "What's wrong with it?"

He returned the spoon to the bowl. "Cold. I shouldn't have added the water."

"I meant the book."

"I know." He pushed the bowl away. "There are two million Steelhaulers in this country. A million and a half of them would carry Brock on their shoulders to the Cape of Good Hope and back if he asked them to. The rest are too young to remember what the union was like before he took over and cleaned house. A million of them easy would buy a book about Brock if it was properly respectful. *Dr. Zhivago* didn't sell a million copies. Baedecker isn't in the business to go broke."

"Are you saying the book is a whitewash?"

"Come on, Inspector. You read it."

"I read it as a cop. I'm asking your opinion as a journalist. Or as someone who sells power mowers."

"There isn't a thing in it you couldn't get out of press releases from Brock's office. Son of a poor trucker makes good through pluck and luck; that's not a biography, it's an episode of *Leave it to Beaver*. The first Greek laborer who refused to add another brick to the Parthenon until he got a second handful of grain hired someone with a broken nose to protect him from the broken noses the contractor hired to change his mind. To hear Baedecker tell it, you'd think Brock never shook a hand that ever held a blackjack."

"He didn't have any broken noses to back him up at that plant in Dearborn."

Minor's smile almost managed jovial. "You *did* read the book. The *Reader's Digest* cut out that part."

"Baedecker told me the strike didn't amount to much."

"Not if you don't count several broken heads, courtesy of Sal Borneo and the Dearborn police. I was there. Were you ever hit by a leather sap?"

Rabaul sprang forward, clearer than memory. "No. Not by a sap."

"It's not much more fun to look at. Borneo's thugs went through those auto workers like salt through a hired girl. Jack Dance was one of them."

"What about Brock?"

"He fought his way clear. I caught up with him in a blind pig around the corner and interviewed him there."

"I read your piece."

"Not my piece. My editor spiked the piece I wrote and ran four inches about a commie uprising. If I ever had a chance to cultivate Brock as a source I lost it that day. I had a feeling about him, too. It sounds like hindsight now, but if you were to ask me at the time which one of the people I saw that day would still be talked about thirty-five years later—Well, hell. I picked Seabiscuit too and didn't put any money down." He sipped at his water.

"Borneo was boss of the local Mafia then?"

"They called it the Unione Siciliana in those days. Maybe they still do. But yeah. Joey Machine pretty much had to cooperate with Sal, and even Jack Dance listened to him now and again when Jack wasn't chipping away at the Machine mob, which was pretty near all the time. Those were wild days. A bunch of us prided ourselves on knowing who was fighting who and who was neutral from one week to the next. These days, gang-watching is about as exciting as matching socks."

"You'd be surprised." Canada sat back, playing with his mug. "When did Borneo switch his support from management to labor?"

"Just before the press did. That'd be about the time Harry Bennett opened fire on strikers with machine guns at the Ford plant. The Mafia always was sensitive to public opinion; also the smell of money. There was getting to be a lot of it in the union kitties. Anyway, Borneo wasn't making many decisions by then. He was under federal indictment for interstate labor racketeering and had suffered his first stroke. Someone else was calling the shots."

"Frankie Orr."

Minor looked away, at the girl, who was now singing "Blowin' in the Wind." "Frankie married Borneo's daughter. I don't know why he bothered. The old man knew what he was doing when he brought him in from New York."

"You met him?"

"Just once." He returned his gaze to Canada. "I was sitting as close to him as I am to you when he slit a man's throat with the same knife he used to cut his steak."

The inspector said nothing.

"It was in a private dining room at the old Griswold House. I don't remember the man's name. He was just some flunky who'd got on the wrong side of Frankie's wallet. I remember he was eating rack of lamb, because it was floating in blood before he finished thrashing around. I haven't been able to look at a plate of mutton since. Yeah, I met Frankie." He drained his water glass and swallowed.

"Did you write about it?"

"In the book, finally. He'd been deported by then. I always had this idea that if I could write about it I could forget it. It didn't work. Maybe that's why I quit writing. What good is it if it's not therapeutic?"

Canada said, "He's back. Frankie is."

Minor watched him. He went on.

"Patsy's been spending a lot of time lately in a telephone booth across the street from the Penobscot Building. When we found out Frankie had disappeared from Sicily we asked Ma Bell for a record of long-distance calls placed to that number. It came through this morning. He's in Puerto Rico, a place called the Pinzón Hotel in San Juan."

"It'll be the best one in town. Frankie was never one for rustic charm. Have you told the feds?"

"We're sitting on it for now. They'd just yank him back and we'd have to start all over again. You don't seem surprised he left."

"I'm surprised he stayed as long as he did. Napoleon was on Elba only ten months, and he didn't have TWA. When do you expect him back in Detroit?"

"Not right away. He's working something, and whatever it is he won't risk blowing it by calling attention to himself. Puerto Rico is American soil. He'll be content there for a while."

"Somebody knocked over a Negro policy operation last night on the East Side. That's three recently, with two deaths. Think it's connected?" He smiled at the inspector's reaction. "I don't write any more, but I read. A story like that has a comfortable, old-timey, Joey Machine School feel. The Orr style wasn't all that different, for all the manicures and European tailoring."

"It isn't big enough. He already owns every game in town. Assuming they aren't just independent heists, we think Patsy's just showing off for the old man."

"Patsy never got over starting out in an incubator," Minor said. "You know something you're not telling, but that's okay. Why'd you tell me about Frankie when even the feds don't know he's back?"

"Because you haven't told me everything you know about Orr and Albert Brock. And because all this you've been saying about not being a newshound any more is just so much bullshit. Were you in the service?"

"Four-F, both wars." He touched the medallion at his throat.

"I was a Japanese POW for sixteen months. There was a mirror on the wall of the officer's toilet where they took me twice a week for interrogation. The look on my face in that mirror while they were booting me around is the same one you've been wearing since I got here."

Minor rested his forearms on the table. His left hand wore a University of Detroit class ring with most of the embossed letters worn off. "I spoke to Brock only that one time, after the Dearborn strike," he said. "But I've been following his career. Call it guilt for that piece of crap the *Banner* ran instead of the story I wrote, but he made an impression on me. He handed out leaflets for Walter Reuther for a while, but the UAW wasn't big enough for both of them and he took what he learned with him when he went back into trucking. Like most pioneers he was a realist. He knew that high-minded idealism is no defense against brass knuckles. Thugs are cheap. He passed the hat, upped the ante, and hired some torpedoes right out from under the van lines and auto plants. A good ten percent of those heroic proles you see battling it out with strike-breakers in the old pictures are professional goons. In the process Brock had to have rubbed elbows with Frankie more than once. They were partners long before Frankie backed him for president of the local, probably even before Frankie's father-in-law Sal switched sides. At one time, Borneo strongarms were fighting each other and collecting two paychecks. That's something you won't read in the history of the American labor movement."

"Nor in Baedecker. How come you know so much, or are you going to pull out that old saw about protecting your sources?"

"Sources that need protection are generally unreliable. Whores are best. When they talk at all, they don't lie; no reason to, they screw you for a living. I don't look it now, but I used to know my way around the upstairs joints."

"No wife to slow you down, huh."

"Now you're getting personal."

It was said casually enough, but Canada was aware he'd stepped over some invisible threshold. He backed up. "What else did you hear?"

"The rest is rumor. Maybe a couple of union men martyred to the cause were actually eliminated from inside the ranks for reasons best known to Brock, meaning they were stealing from the strike fund or spying for the other side. A dispatcher named Pike vanished on a deer hunting trip several years ago, along with evidence tying Brock's campaign committee to a series of hijackings in Ohio when the boss was up for re-election and the treasury was low. Even if you could prove murder you wouldn't be able to trace anything back to him. If Frankie were that sloppy he'd have gotten life in Jackson instead of a one-way ticket to Palermo."

"Theoretically that last one would be Patsy's red wagon, not Frankie's. There's only so much you can do from across the ocean."

"Where were you in nineteen forty when Stalin had Trotsky killed in Mexico?"

"Rumors don't spend," Canada said after a moment. "I need something I can show the mayor."

"What do you want to do, topple Brock or scare him off?"

"He doesn't scare."

"I'd hate to see him fall," Minor said. "Whatever he's done he's done for the union. The Steelhaulers know that, and it's why they keep voting for him in spite of the occasional attempt by some full-of-himself politician to discredit him. You don't claw your way to the top of an organization like that without getting blood and dirt under your nails, and only one man in a million can play ball with the Sicilians without giving them the field. Whoever follows him might as well hand them the key to the front door, because we only get one Brock to a generation, and the next one won't have his luck."

Canada smiled. "For a hard-nosed old bloodhound you sound an awful lot like a convert."

"We graduated from the same class. The current breed of journalist spends more time combing his hair than grubbing around after a lead, and the next generation of union executive will come straight out of business school without knowing a clutch from a catfish. If us dinosaurs don't stand up for each other, who will?"

"Does that mean you won't help me?"

Minor produced a ballpoint pen and wrote a name and a telephone number on his paper napkin, which he slid across to the inspector. "Hang on to it. When I was young we didn't give out ladies' numbers."

"Who is she?"

"Just mention me and tell her what you want. Whether she gives it to you is up to her."

"Is this . . . ?" He left it unfinished.

"Her aunt was. I almost married her."

Their waitress came over for the first time since she had served their meals. Canada paid the bill and the two went out into the brassy afternoon light. The alley that ran past the warehouse, paved with sun-bleached asphalt that had long since begun to degenerate back to the cracked earth beneath, ended at the river. Rusty iron rails crossed it in several places among piles of broken concrete. The riverfront on the other side was more of the same. Windsor always reminded the inspector of a boy constantly correcting his stride to match his father's, even when the father stumbled.

Connie Minor was also looking at the river. "A lot of good whiskey came in over that water, under it too; there's still a tow cable down there someplace. A lot more was just plain moose-sweat. The Canucks caught on early that it didn't have to be good to make a profit."

"Miss those times?"

"Not for a minute. I had them. That's why I cut the kids more slack than most, even with all that's happening in the colleges. If you don't screw up early and often you won't have any stories to tell when you get to be my age."

"I'm fifteen years younger than you and there are some stories I'd just as soon not have to tell."

"That's the hell of it, Inspector," Minor said. "You don't get a choice."

Chapter 21

orgive us our trespasses, the sampler read.

Enid Kohler had put her handbag in its usual drawer in the file cabinet and sat down behind her desk before she saw the package, wrapped in white paper without any writing on it and tied with cord. The wrapping tore away from a polished wooden frame, obviously antique, and the needlepoint sentiment worked into brown burlap with brittle thread that had once been scarlet. It was probably eighty years old.

"The kid in the head shop didn't want to part with it," Rick said. "He had it hanging over the cash register for luck. I had to buy an incense burner and a rock poster with it. Ever hear of a group called the Swinging Blue Jeans?"

She looked at him standing in the doorway to the next room. He had on a polo shirt and chinos, no more Brooks Brothers. "You're early."

"Pammie let me in. She's upstairs. I wanted to make the sampler myself, but I couldn't get the hang of it over the long weekend." He paused. "An oral answer is sufficient."

"What you said made me mad as hell," she said. "I'm not some giggly schoolgirl with a crush on the history teacher."

"No argument. The little wire that connects my mouth to my brain breaks sometimes. I'm sorry."

Her face lost its porcelain cast. In a sleeveless silk blouse and pleated slacks with her black hair loose to her shoulders, she looked no older than twenty. "That would have done all along. You didn't need the visual aid, but it's sweet. You must have looked all over town."

"Let's just say I've seen enough beaded curtains and macramé in the last three days to last me until nineteen eighty."

"Have you had breakfast?"

"Is there someplace nearby?"

"That's right, you never got the tour. This way." She led him past the staircase and down a short hall to a fully furnished kitchen painted in pastel colors and paved with swirly linoleum. Sunlight shot through a window looking out on a jungle of poppies and forsythia. She lifted the lid off a coffee pot on the electric stove, looked inside, and turned on the burner. "Pammie always remembers to change the pot and always forgets to put heat under it. It'll be a few minutes. Juice?"

"Anything but grapefruit."

From the two-toned refrigerator she took a pitcher of orange juice, shook it up, and filled two flowered glasses from the cupboard. They clinked glasses. Sipping, she leaned back against the counter. "What did you think of the Farm?"

"It was a jolt."

She laughed. "Wendell told me what happened. Are you sold on seat belts?"

"I never thought they didn't work. If I had a family I'd probably insist on them."

"Bachelors aren't any more indestructible than family men. You ought to know, you've been gathering statistics."

"Ever read Orwell?"

"You don't have to give up your freedom in return for protection," she said. "You men and your dangerous toys. What's the point in trying to get yourself killed?"

"That's not the object. The object is to see how close you can come without actually doing it."

"That's crazy."

He considered retreating. But he'd established himself as devil's advocate, and to change directions now would be suspicious. That was the part he hadn't missed about undercover, the cakewalk. "Most of us are passengers," he said. "Life's like that. Driving a car is one of the few times when you feel like you're in control."

"Right up until you go flying through the windshield."

"I didn't say you're in control, just that you feel like it."

"Is that why you drive a car with a speedometer that goes up to a hundred and fifty when the speed limit on the expressway is seventy?"

"That Mercedes of yours is no tricycle."

"It was a gift from my father."

He used his tongue to pry a string of orange pulp from between two teeth. He hated fresh-squeezed. "Did he give you the ten thousand you donated to the Porter Group?"

"In a way. It was what his life insurance paid."

He drank his juice, hoping for more pulp; when he was picking his teeth he wasn't talking.

"He ran into a truck making a wide turn at an intersection," she said. "They pronounced him dead on arrival at the hospital. My mother never regained consciousness and died a week later of a cerebral hemorrhage. The car wasn't that badly damaged. They might both have survived if they were wearing seat belts."

"I'm sorry."

"That was three years ago. I didn't need the money from the insurance, so I gave it all to PG. That was before the Farm, before *Hell On Wheels,* when Wendell was unknown outside of speaking engagements at women's clubs. My mother had been quite taken with him when he appeared at hers. Anyway, when he got the check he invited me in to tour the office. It was in an old building in East Detroit then, not nearly as nice as this, and his bookkeeping system was a wreck. I didn't work summers in my father's real estate office without learning something. I offered to help. I'm still helping."

Rick said, "He has a talent for attracting just the people he needs for each job. Hal Bledsoe was with American Motors, Günter Damm raced cars for a living, you helped organize a business—"

"—and you were a newspaperman," she finished. "You have a way of getting information out of people without their noticing. You should have been a detective."

He met it head on. "I hung around them some. It was the job. Things rub off."

The pot had been percolating for some time. She took two mugs down from the cabinet. "How do you take it?"

"Cream no sugar." When she was through with it he looked at the mug she'd handed him. It carried an advertisement for the 1964 Corvair.

She smiled and poured herself a slug of black coffee. "It came free through the mail. You'd be surprised how many lists you wind up on once you begin writing for information. GM's computer hasn't made the connection yet between Wendell and W. G. Porter, Esquire. All our pens say General Motors. Wendell gets a big kick out of using them to sign his press releases."

"He gets a big kick out of the whole thing, doesn't he? I mean he's not your stereotypical bluenose alarmist."

"No one ever said you couldn't be dedicated and enjoy your work at the same time."

"What about his wife? Does she enjoy it?"

If he'd expected her to spill her coffee at the mention of the name she disappointed him. "Caroline's a different breed. Blinders on, look-straight-ahead. She goes for the jugular, whether it's in the courtroom or out in the competitive world in general. It's a good match. Without her, Wendell might get tangled up in his altruism and never get anywhere. She knows the odds and how to meet them."

"Don't get all sloppy-sentimental."

He got it then, a whitening at the edges of her nostrils just before she looked up from her mug and saw he was grinning. The tightness evaporated. "Maybe auto safety isn't quite the holy crusade to her that it is to the rest of us. Maybe she'd be just as aggressive if she were representing a millionaire stockbroker accused of insider trading. I suppose it's foolish not to expect a lawyer to think like a lawyer." She glanced at a tiny jeweled watch. "Eight o'clock whistle, Mr. Flintstone. Time to go to the quarry."

Pammie was licking envelopes at the card table. Today she had on a Minnie Mouse KEEP ON TRUCKIN' T-shirt and her hair was tied into its usual corn-shock with a green ribbon instead of a rubber band. Rick assumed the ribbon was for his benefit. He had it on Lee Schenck's authority that Pammie had a thing for PG's newest volunteer.

"I saw the needlepoint thing," she said. "Pretty smooth."

"Is there anything you don't see?" He sat down and slid the telephone over.

"If I don't know about it, it didn't happen."

He was still working his way down the list of towing services. His mind wasn't on the first two calls; he got a female receptionist who was too wary to give him any useful information or let him speak to anyone else, and whoever answered the telephone the second time hung up before he finished his first question. Pammie watched him cradle the receiver.

"Forgot to sound like a hick," she said.

Actually he felt like one. The old Rick Amery would have zeroed right in on a source like Pammie instead of letting a week slide by while he worked on Lee and Enid. "You like baseball?" he asked.

"My brother said I was the best shortstop in Royal Oak, but I haven't had a glove on in years."

"Tigers are playing a double-header Thursday. If we work hard we can be out of here before the second game. Want to go?"

She uncovered a fortune in braces. "I'll bring my home cap."

His next several calls were more successful, and he filled ten pages with notes. Lee Schenck, wearing a tie-dyed shirt that looked as if he'd used it to mop up an oil spill, leaned in while Rick was in the middle of an interview, waved, and withdrew, presumably to go upstairs to his cubbyhole. It was a few minutes before ten. With the exception of Enid, the office appeared to operate on an organic clock.

A little while later Enid came to the door and waited until Rick hung up.

"I was going to draft Lee for this, but since you asked about Caroline I thought you might want to meet her," she said. "Wendell's being sued again over something he wrote in *Hell On Wheels*. I did some of the research, so she wants to ask me some questions and see the records, about fifteen pounds' worth. You don't wear a truss or anything, do you?"

"Where's the stuff ?" He rose.

"Upstairs. Lee will show you."

Lee, sprawled behind a library table in a back bedroom under a steeply tilted ceiling—which explained his habit of ducking his head whenever he stood up anywhere—was reading a magazine from one of the stacks that occupied most of the floor space. His job was to pore through everything that came out on the automobile industry, including Big Three stock reports, and cull any information PG might find useful. Since he never seemed to write anything down, and since Porter wasn't the kind to retain deadwood with or without a salary, Rick assumed Lee had a photographic memory.

When Rick explained his errand, the long-haired young man pointed the hot rod comic book he was reading at three stuffed accordion files on the table. "Going to see the Arctic Princess, huh?"

"That's the plan." He stacked the files one on top of another and hoisted them. It was closer to twenty pounds than fifteen.

"Don't touch her without insulated gloves."

Enid was waiting at the foot of the stairs. "I've got some paper-work to do on the way over. Mind driving?"

"Not if we take my car."

"Do you have seat belts?"

"I'll drive carefully."

"Drive normally. Men with cars like yours are most dangerous when they're being careful."

Outside he put the files on the backseat and held the passenger's door for her. "Where to?"

"Grosse Pointe, where else?" She sat down and swung her legs inside. He found himself wishing she'd worn a skirt.

Heading east on Jefferson he stopped for the light at Cadieux. A sky-blue Cobra was stopped in the left turn lane with its indicator blinking. Rick grinned and gunned his engine twice. The driver of the Cobra returned the salute. The light changed and they parted company.

"What was that?" Enid was looking at him over a pair of glasses with rose frames.

"Camaraderie of the road."

She resumed reading the sheet in her hand. "Why don't you just drop your pants and use a ruler?"

Harry DiJesus gunned his engine back at the guy in the silver Camaro and swung onto Cadieux. He wanted to pop the clutch, but a Tactical Mobile Unit carrying two officers was coming the other way. They passed him without a second look and stopped at Jefferson. He pointed his finger at the rearview mirror and said, "Pow."

He'd never done a cop and wouldn't unless he had to, but he'd always wondered how it would be. Most of the guys he'd done were stiffs going in, stationary targets who died surprised. He still got a lift from it, but it wasn't lasting as long these days; the first nigger in the after-hours joint had been like a dry fuck, he should've tried to get him to open the door instead of blasting him through it. A cop would be something different. Fellow professional, good reflexes. Like taking on John Wayne in *The Sons of Katie Elder.* He always identified with the gun punks in westerns, calling out the top hands with the big reputations. The writers ought to let one of them win once in a while.

But he'd stopped looking for trouble. Every time he had in the past he'd wound up in jail. Others were less lucky and wound up in a tray at the Clark County Morgue. Most of them got off on their guns, it was the only fuck they knew except for what they paid for. At thirty-one, bronzed and well-muscled in his body shirts and tight jeans, DiJesus had never had to pay for it. Recently he'd let his blond hair grow long like the kids', and the effect on women was more than satisfying. With the gold chains he'd begun wearing in Vegas, it made him look like a surfer.

Vegas was looking better and better. Detroit was a hick town, rolled up the sidewalks at 2:00 A.M. except for the after-hours places, and those were for niggers only. He yawned bitterly. He was having trouble adjusting to sleeping at night and staying up during the day. Back home he rose at sunset in his suite at the Flamingo, ordered breakfast from room service while the rest of the world was sitting down to dinner, and cruised the Strip until dawn, meeting friends and sitting in on games he owned a piece of and once in a while doing someone. That was the rent he paid for the good life.

The shotgun raids were a lift, one of the few things that made Detroit bearable. The tall nigger in the barbershop, now; that was a classic. The boy had been an athlete and still had balls, charging him after the first blast with his right side blown away and nothing in his hands but the telephone receiver he'd been holding when they came through the door. DiJesus had waited until he'd almost reached him with those long arms, then squeezed off again. That blast spun him around and folded him up like a big spider.

DiJesus would be glad when this one was over. He was used to dry heat. The sweaty air here made him feel wrung out and greasy and he was developing a rash on his neck from the ski mask, which had been a better idea in the cool desert nights. His incentive for coming east, a piece of the local numbers, wasn't worth scratching and sweating his way through the long sleepy days. Max and Georgie, his partners in the shotgun raids, could do what they liked with what he was paying them; he himself would be an absentee landlord.

He braked for the light at Mack. It changed and a horn blatted behind him. The dentate grille of a gray 1959 Cadillac—"nigger diesels," he'd heard them called up here—leered at him in the mirror. Behind the windshield, two smaller sets of teeth gleamed just as brightly in black faces under big hats. DiJesus turned in his seat to give them the one-finger salute—remembering even as he did so that he'd seen the same car a block behind him on Jefferson. Something slid out of the window on the passenger's side and the Cobra's rear window disintegrated in a shower of opalescent bits.

Chapter 22

The building was less than five years old, a yellow brick construction designed to continue the pleasing horizontal lines of Grosse Pointe's tiny select business district, and sheltered, along with Caroline Porter Associates, a number of doctors' offices and accounting corporations whose names were embossed on the directory in the glass-and-chromium lobby. The elevator doors sliced open on the third floor directly across from a glass wall with the legal firm's name lettered in gold on the door. When Enid opened and held it for Rick and his burden of files, conditioned air touched his face like spring mist.

A receptionist behind a white desk with thin steel legs repeated their names over a Princess telephone and asked them to have a seat. Rick wondered if her beehive hairstyle violated the city's ordinance against skyscrapers.

He deposited the files on a glass coffee table with copies of the *Saturday Evening Post* fanned across its top and wandered around the reception area while Enid made herself comfortable on the tweed sofa. The walls were paneled in blond wood and decorated with Picasso prints in steel frames; the Blue Period, to match the carpet.

In a little while they were joined by a man Rick's age in blue worsted and glasses with tortoiseshell frames. "How are you, Enid?"

"Busy, as always." She took his hand and rose. "Rick Amery, Ronald Engler. Ronald is Mrs. Porter's assistant."

Rick touched a dry hand without calluses. He wanted to ask Engler if a new carpet meant a change of wardrobe, but chose an inanity instead. The neutral-colored eyes behind the glasses let him go when the hand did and passed to the files. "Is that the stuff ? How did Wendell get all that into three hundred and sixty pages?"

"This is only the portion Caroline asked about," Enid said. "The rest would fill this floor."

"Where does he get his ideas?"

"From the obituaries."

Rick grinned.

"Caroline said to show you right in." Engler had edited out the exchange.

Rick picked up the files and he and Enid followed the assistant down a silent hallway lined with framed certificates of merit from a dozen community organizations, some of whose names were familiar to Rick. At the end Engler tapped lightly on a door made of the same pale wood as the paneling and opened it without waiting for an answer. They walked in past him.

"Thank you, Ronald."

It was a dismissal. Engler backed out, drawing the door shut. The office, a corner room, was roughly the size of the ground floor plan at PG, furnished with antiques and an Oriental rug on a parquet floor, and looked more like a Victorian parlor than a place of business. Windows in adjacent walls, hung with ivory satin drapes tied like funeral bunting, looked out on the business section and a wedge of Lake St. Clair, flaring like bright metal under the climbing sun. The walls were beige and uncluttered, bearing only a framed diploma from the University of Michigan and an eight-by-ten photograph of Caroline Porter shaking hands with John F. Kennedy.

The woman herself was standing behind a maple table arranged with desk items, smiling the smile she had smiled for JFK, showing only a thin line of white teeth between bright red lips. Her blond hair was up in its customary Princess Grace style and she was wearing a gold bolero jacket with blue embroidery over a pale silk blouse with a frothy jabot at her throat. Her skirt was brown broadcloth, snug but not tight. Rick saw no jewelry, not even a wedding band.

"Enid, thank you for coming. I know what your schedule is like."

The voice, a contralto, held the same cordial tone she had used to get rid of her assistant. The *Cosmopolitan* article Rick had read had claimed that when addressing the bench she could go from a throaty purr to the crack of a steel whip instantly.

"Anything to keep Wendell out of court," Enid said. "When he's there he's not helping the Porter Group." She introduced Rick.

A slender hand fluttered in his and was gone. He'd been expecting a firm, manly grip and it caught him off guard; which he supposed was the intention. Gray eyes made contact with a static crackle. "You don't look like the fetch-and-carry type." She inclined her head a fraction of an inch toward the stack of accordion files, which he had deposited on a low tea table in a conversation area consisting of a settee and matching straight chair and rocker, upholstered in petit-point.

Enid said, "Rick's new. He plans to be an expert by the end of the week. Is it all right if he stays?"

The red lips tightened almost imperceptibly. There were deep commas at the corners that could no longer be passed off as dimples. "If he doesn't mind being bored. It's not like *Perry Mason*."

"You're an improvement over Raymond Burr," he said. "I hope that's not out of line."

"Hardly. In any case I'm used to it. There weren't many women in my class in law school, and I've heard all the jokes about briefs. Would anyone like tea or coffee before we get started?"

Rick and Enid declined and they went over to the conversation area. Rick waited until the women were seated, then took the rocking chair. Enid, on the settee, reached for the top file on the stack.

"I'll look at the material later," Caroline said. "I just need to ask a few questions about your methods of obtaining information." In the straight chair, she crossed her legs, exposing a trim calf and ankle encased in nylon. Rick could see his reflection in the toe of her blue pump.

Enid said, "Most of our sources are named in the book. I can't discuss the ones that aren't. That was a condition of the information."

"The attorney-client privilege applies. I need those names."

"Why?"

"General Motors's attorneys are charging libel. That's the one area in American jurisprudence where the accused is required to prove his innocence; in other words, that the claims Wendell made in the book are true. I'll need affidavits."

"That would mean exposing them in open court. Some of them work for GM. They'd lose their jobs."

"It may not come to that. The affidavits would be kept under lock and key and introduced only if every other strategy fails."

"Just giving you the names would be a violation of the promise of anonymity. Even if you got the affidavits, which I doubt you could, we might win acquittal at the expense of never developing another source. PG would be crippled. Which is what GM wants. They couldn't care less who comes out ahead in court."

"*We* aren't being sued for four million dollars. Wendell is. Perhaps if you were named in the suit you wouldn't be quite so protective of others." The whip cracked.

Enid crossed her legs. "Why don't you ask Wendell?"

"I did. He referred me to you. You did enough of the research to qualify for a shared byline; even he doesn't know the names of all your contacts."

"I'm sorry."

The two women watched each other across a silence. Rick wondered what was in it besides secret sources.

Caroline pointed a blue toe at the files. "I assume there are documents in here to support the allegations Wendell made on the pages I quoted to you. Are they originals?"

"Some are. Most we had photocopied. GM would have missed them if we kept them all."

"Were they stolen?"

"Well, nobody sneaked into the General Motors Building at midnight with a flashlight and a crowbar, but technically—yes, they were smuggled out by people without authority to remove them from the building."

"Evidence obtained by illegal means is tainted."

"Only if it was obtained by the police. Consumer groups enjoy certain liberties not available to law enforcement."

"I'm talking about how it will look in court," Caroline said. "A lot depends on which judge we draw. Some of them haven't practiced in a long time and know less about the law than our Perry Mason fan here." She measured him a small amount of her JFK smile; then it went away. "I wish Wendell had let me read the book before it went to press. I could have saved PG a fortune in legal fees."

"By castrating the book?" Enid's tone was mild.

"Castration is a poor choice of terms between us, isn't it?" Caroline consulted a yellow legal tablet. "On eleven May nineteen sixty-four you conducted a telephone interview with an unnamed source connected with General Motors. The subject was the ventilating system on the Corvair. Did you tape the interview?"

Rick didn't hear Enid's answer. Her expression hadn't changed after the castration comment, but an arc of raw hostility had passed between the two women and he had felt it, as if he'd touched a spark plug wire. In its wake he knew a blissful warmth spreading through him, an old familiar sensation, and he remembered what it was he had liked—needed—about going undercover. A suspicion confirmed was like a sexual release.

There were no more such confrontations, however, and his attention drifted. He found himself wondering what Caroline Porter would be like in bed. His experience of these gimlet-eyed career women had taught him that the tailored jackets and below-the-knee skirts usually concealed the sort of underwear you saw in stag films, mainly the S/M kind; before the night was through their lacquered nails had skin and blood under them. Maybe that was what had sent Porter looking. From there Rick thought about how Enid would be in comparison, and in that pleasant frame of mind he waited out the end of the meeting.

"I'll have more questions when I get into the material." Caroline laid aside the legal tablet and stood. "Thanks again for making the time."

Enid rose. The two smiled at each other. Rick got up. This time Caroline's hand lingered a moment before sliding away. "Welcome aboard, Mr. Amery. I'm sorry you had to come on when everything's standing on end."

"I get the impression that's the normal state," he said. "It was a pleasure, Mrs. Porter."

"Caroline."

They were halfway back to the office before Enid spoke. "Now that you've met her, what do you think?"

Rick slowed down to let an empty paper sack blow across the street in front of the Camaro. The wind had come up and a pepper of drops appeared on the windshield, scouting a summer storm. "I think Lee's got a lot to learn about women. She belongs in the Arctic like a chili pepper."

"Lee's only seen her in passing. She almost never comes to the office." She watched the grainy scenery.

"So she's not one of Wendell's Wonders. A gun doesn't care if it's being pointed by a cop or a crook. It just does its job."

"Cops and crooks don't marry their guns."

He decided not to press it. He switched on the radio in the middle of the *Batman* TV theme, punched up another station in a hurry. WJR News was in progress.

". . . as developments continue to unfold in the Detroit Police Department's ongoing investigation of the so-called 'Christmas list.'

On the labor front, Albert Brock, national president of the American Steelhaulers Association, announced his endorsement today of former Michigan Governor G. Mennen 'Soapy' Williams for the Democratic nomination for United States Senator. Citing what he called Detroit Mayor Jerome P. Cavanagh's 'disgraceful labor record'..."

A blue-and-white Tactical Mobile Unit powered past them, its siren drowning out the announcer, before Rick could pull over to make room. It swung onto Cadieux, lights wobbling. Rick turned off the radio. "Politicians. How's Wendell getting on with Washington?"

"Like lead and feathers," Enid said. "I don't suppose you have President Johnson's home number."

"Sorry. What he ought to do is con a congressman onto the Farm, give him a ride on the test track."

"He's not ready to go public with the Farm. He wants to be sure of his results before the local authorities find out about it and shut it down for violation of some ordinance or other. A lot of communities in the area depend on General Motors for jobs. But it's not a bad idea. Don't tell me you're converted." She was looking at him now.

"I don't like seeing some poor schnook getting picked on. Big company like that has better things to do than turn loose its lawyers"—he'd almost said *spies*—"on a guy just because he wrote a book. That's not supposed to be what this country is about."

"A lot of people are saying that kind of thing these days. I think the kids are right about as often as I feel like spanking them. Maybe we ought to stage a sit-in at the Federal Building, get the TV stations involved."

Rick said, "I've got a better idea."

Chapter 23

Duane Coopersmith had been with Detroit Homicide seven years and had the dead face that came with the job, as if someone had tied off all the nerves that controlled the muscles of expression. Lew Canada had never acquired the knack, and after six months of body parts in dumpsters and wives in fuzzy bathrobes with their faces blown off by their husbands and dead naked babies with cigarette burns all over their bodies he had gotten a transfer. Career homicide men were like morticians and proctologists, welcome when they were necessary but not the sort of person you invited to a barbecue. Canada, seated on a corner of Coopersmith's desk on the third floor of 1300, shuffled through the Polaroid photographs the lieutenant had handed him: Eight different angles of the same blue 1966 Cobra with a hole rammed through its rear window and thumb-size punctures in the trunk. "Double-O buck?"

Coopersmith nodded. He had a young face and thin fair hair on top of a high forehead, and could have passed for some kind of scientist but for the nerveless features. "The scroat has good reflexes. If he hadn't ducked we'd still be hosing him off Cadieux. They took another pass on their way around the car but the angle was bad and most of the pellets skidded off the roof."

"Where'd we find the Caddy?"

"Parked on Brush. Steering wheel and door handles wiped clean." He consulted the report on his desk. "Registered to Sylvanus Humbert, eleven sixty-three West Grand River. He didn't even know it was stolen until the uniforms called on him."

"Sure it was stolen?"

"Humbert's sixty-eight, a deacon at New Bethel Baptist. You're the inspector. I don't think he did it."

"Where's DiJesus?"

"Interrogation, making lawyer noises. I was about to kick him when you called. It's not against the law to get shot at, thank God; can you imagine the paperwork? Anyway he's too lively for Homicide."

"Can I talk to him?"

"Sure. Here or in Interrogation?"

"Here. It's less formal." Not by much, he thought; there wasn't a single personal item in Coopersmith's office. Everything about the man was department issue, from his thick-soled Oxfords to the scarlet-backed volumes of the Michigan Penal Code arranged in order on the gray file cabinet behind the desk.

The lieutenant used the intercom and sat back. "I expected a visit from Civil Defense or the commandoes in Motor Traffic. These race things are their meat. What's your squad want with it?"

"I don't think it's race related."

"These days it all comes down to race. NAACP, CORE, ACME, AAUM, AAYM—every colored with an axe to grind and a working knowledge of the alphabet belongs to some rabble-rousing group. Mostly they're fronts for blind pigs and policy operations. It's getting so Vice can't bust one without back-ups from TCU and PREP. More initials; the reports are starting to look like eye charts. It isn't like the old days when it was just Jews against Italians and you booked the ones that were still standing. I've got a sergeant in my detail working on a degree in Sociology at Wayne State. The next generation of Detroit cop is going to be so socially conscious it won't shoot a rat without studying the impact its loss will have on the neighborhood."

"Things change." Canada got off the desk. "They were still talking about the last chief of detectives when I joined plainclothes. His
name was Kozlowski. He was in charge of the old Prohibition Squad
during those good old days you were talking about. I'd trade ten of
that miserable son of a bitch for that social worker sergeant of
yours."

"You still haven't told me why you're interested."

"I haven't, have I?"

The lieutenant waited, then said, "Okay, boss. I's jus' de he'p."

A detective whose name Canada didn't know entered with his
hand under the arm of a man of medium height in a tight blue
T-shirt and Levi's. The man was built like a weightlifter and tanned
like no white man in Detroit that early in the summer. Grains of
pulverized glass glittered in his long blond hair. When he started to
sit down, the detective swept the plastic scoop chair out from under
him. He landed hard on the linoleum floor. "Nobody said sit."

"Help him up," Canada said.

"He's an asshole, Inspector."

Canada looked at Coopersmith, who nodded at the detective.

DiJesus slapped away the proffered hand and sprang to his feet,
using only his legs. He tossed his hair behind his shoulders.

Canada said, "Okay."

Coopersmith and the detective left.

"Hello, Harry. I've been reading about you." The inspector returned the chair to its original position.

DiJesus ignored the invitation and remained standing. "Yeah? I
don't know you from Adam."

"My name's Canada. My friends call me Lew. You can call me
Inspector Canada."

"What I want to call is a lawyer. I been here two hours on no
charges."

"Nobody's charging you. You can leave now if you want."

DiJesus wheeled and opened the door.

"The guys that took a shot at you have had time by now to find out they missed. It wouldn't be the first time someone waited for some-one else to step out the front door here. The steps of a police station are kind of a psychological Demilitarized Zone. You'd be surprised what you can get away with. This isn't Vegas."

He closed the door and sat down. "I wouldn't put it past you cops to do it and lay it off on the jigaboos."

"I thought you didn't see them."

"I saw their car. Who else would drive a big gray piece of shit Cadillac like that?"

"The car was stolen. We found it abandoned downtown."

"Maybe I saw their faces were black. They all look alike, that's why they call each other brother."

Canada reclaimed his seat on the desk. "How are your friends Scavarda and Alonzo?"

"Who?"

"Max Scavarda and George Alonzo. We keep track of the visiting talent. Until the eleventh of last month they were bouncing drunks out the door of the Flamingo Hotel. Now they're registered at the Sheraton-Cadillac here, same floor as you. The Flamingo is your address in Vegas, isn't it?"

"Any law against traveling with friends?"

"We only become interested when they pack ski masks and shot-guns. It wasn't the blacks that made a run at you today. Not the ones you think."

The double-whammy appeared to have no effect on the man in the chair. "The more a cop talks the less sense he makes," he said. "We're here on vacation. Nevada's too hot this time of year. Nobody there even owns a ski mask. I heard about these guys knocking over the nigger joints. Sounds to me like you're sore at them for doing your job better than you."

"They're plenty sore at you. But that wasn't them who shot up your car."

"We got coons in Vegas. I guess I know one when I see him."

Canada flicked a shred of lint off the knee of his black trousers;

now they were spotless. "You heavyweights are stupid. It's no wonder you never get anywhere in the outfit. If Twelfth Street Negroes are planning to take out a mob guy they aren't going to lift a car with Soul Brother written all over it. Nobody was out to kill you today, shithead. They just wanted to make you piss your pants and run to Patsy with what you saw."

"Who's she?"

"This war with the coloreds isn't escalating fast enough for somebody. Whoever it is wants it to blow up big enough to wipe out all the small operators. Then when the smoke lifts he'll stroll in and scoop up the change."

"What'd he do, smear burnt cork on his face?"

"Muscle's cheap, and in this town it's mostly black. If I wanted you to think the coloreds were after you I'd put the hired help in big pimp hats and boost a nigger diesel and do it up brown; get it?"

"Who's *you?*" DiJesus was interested.

The inspector slid a four-by-six manila envelope from his inside breast pocket and tipped a stiff-backed photograph out onto the desk. It was a front-and-profile mug shot of a Latin face with thick gray hair in waves and sleepy-looking eyelids, an aging Valentino with numbers underneath stenciled white on black. "The picture's fifteen years out of date," he said. "I hear he's porked up lately on linguini and clam sauce. It was taken at the federal correctional facility up in Milan, just before the State Department shipped him off to Sicily."

He barely looked at it. "Everybody knows Frankie Orr. I thought he'd be dead by now."

"Frankie made a deal with Old Nick: eternal life in return for the soul of the City of Detroit. He means to make good on the contract. Ever meet him?"

"I never been abroad."

"How about Puerto Rico?"

No reaction. "Back home, I want to see spicks, I go down to Mexico."

Canada didn't pursue that line. If DiJesus was playing it ignorant it wasn't worth the trouble to confirm and if he really *was* ignorant, Canada didn't have a teaching certificate. "Frankie wasn't born behind a desk," he said. "By the time he was your age he'd committed two murders in front of witnesses, one in New York with a garrote and one here with a knife. Just now it's in his interest to let you go on breathing. As soon as it isn't you'll stop, simple as that. He's no bigot. He'd ice one of his own as quick as anyone if there's profit in it."

"Frankie Orr." The man in the chair chewed on the name. "It don't figure."

"Why not?"

DiJesus stopped there and Canada realized he was leaning forward off the desk. He relaxed. *Because I'm working for his son Patsy,* only DiJesus didn't say it. Suddenly the inspector had had enough of him. "Get out of here," he said.

"What about the niggers?" The other man stood.

"They aren't waiting for you. I just got through saying if they wanted you dead we wouldn't be talking now. The ones that peppered your car, anyway. I can't answer for Twelfth Street."

"What about my car?"

"It's in the impound. You can pick it up in a couple of days."

"Why not today?"

"What's your hurry? You're getting your interior cleaned for free, courtesy of the mayor. Remember that when you vote in November."

"Come November I'll be doing laps in the pool at the Flamingo." DiJesus left.

Lieutenant Coopersmith was reading the *Free Press* at a desk in the squad room when the inspector came out. "I sure hope the *News* doesn't go on strike," he said. "This liberal rag burns my butt. What'd you get out of our boy?"

"Oh, I'm his official biographer. Let me know if you turn anything." He started past the desk.

"I just got off the phone with the lab. They found a partial thumb on the Caddy's rearview mirror that doesn't match the owner's. I told them to run it over to the FBI. Probably belongs to the last mechanic who serviced the car."

"Okay, keep me up to speed."

"You want this squeal? I was going to drop it in Special Investigation's lap."

"Yeah, I'll take it."

Coopersmith shook his fair head. "Must be awful quiet up there on seven. You need any more open files, just buzz. I'll send them on up with a forklift."

Upstairs in the men's room, Canada took off his coat and shoulder rig, rolled up his sleeves and washed his hands and face, rinsing them first with warm water, then with cold, a ritual he'd observed ten or twelve times a day since his release from the Rabaul stockade. For sixteen months he'd shared a latrine with three other officers, eighteen inches from the filthy pad he slept on. At any given time two of the men had suffered from dysentery, and their aim was unreliable. He'd spent the last twenty-one years trying to scrub off the prison camp.

While he was combing his hair a toilet flushed in one of the stalls and Sergeant Esther came out to wash his hands.

"How's your daughter?" Canada asked.

"She brought her boyfriend home day before yesterday." The sergeant shook his hands dry and buttoned his cuffs. "He had on a belt buckle shaped like a cock."

"He probably just wanted to make a good impression."

"I'm pretty sure he busted her. If she gets knocked up I'll give her the boot. Find anything out downstairs?"

"Only that DiJesus is dumber than the average lifetaker."

"That's pretty dumb. Think we should haul Springfield in and sweat him a little?"

"Springfield doesn't know anything."

"That again." Esther put on his heavy-duty sportcoat. Everything he wore was either double-stitched or leather-reinforced; an iron ring protected the dial of his wristwatch from blows and scratches, as if his sedentary lifestyle exposed him to anything more hazardous than hemorrhoids. "Why would Frankie put the dump on his own kid's muscle?"

"Because it's Patsy's muscle. He's not a total washout; some of his younger lieutenants barely remember Frankie and they'd support the Crip in a war with the old man. A war between Patsy and Twelfth Street will clean out the coloreds and kick a hole in Patsy's set-up big enough for Frankie to step through and rebuild it from the ground up, Frankie's way."

"He can't show himself. The feds would just turn around and send him back home."

"He's had fifteen years to figure a way around that. My guess is he'll fight that old prostitution charge. That means a new trial, which costs money. His rake-off from a citywide policy racket ought to just about cover it."

"Pretty cold even for Frankie."

"He and Sal Borneo did the same thing thirty years ago when Joey Machine and Jack Dance were beating the hell out of each other. When it was all over, Dance was dead and Machine was out of capital. Sal's Unione Siciliana bought into his operation and when they didn't need him any more they blew him out from under his hat." Canada put away his comb. "The only thing about these Sicilians that ever changes is their tailors."

A uniformed officer came in to use a urinal. Canada and the sergeant went out into the squad room. "I hope to Christ you're wrong," Esther said. "Frankie's been gone a long time, he doesn't know what's been happening with the niggers. He could light a fire that you and me and the mayor and the whole fucking fire department couldn't put out."

"Let the boys in Civil Defense worry about that part. Worry about where Albert Brock fits into all this."

Later, in his office, the inspector watched a tide of rain blur the window on the other side of the steel mesh, like transparent silk dragged across the glass. His eyes were blurring too and he realized with a little start that he'd been at work since midnight and was halfway through a second shift. That wouldn't have happened before his marriage went bad, when home was more than just a change of walls. He yawned and reached in his pocket for his keys. His hand closed around a wad of paper. Instinctively he drew it out; he never wrote notes to himself and hated contraband in his suits. It was the napkin he'd gotten from Connie Minor, the retired tabloid reporter. The Cadieux shooting had driven it out of his mind.

He sat down and dialed the number written on the napkin. After two rings a woman's voice answered.

Chapter 24

They went to see *The Greatest Story Ever Told* at the Ramona. Krystal thought it was about Cassius Clay.

Afterward, walking down Gratiot, looking for a cab and not-listening to Krystal talking about her late mother's efforts to help her find Christ, Quincy stuck his hands in his pockets and breathed the brimstone air of a Detroit evening after a summer storm. The gutters were running and automobile headlights cast elliptical reflections in the puddles on the street. As his brain uncoiled from its long confinement, he considered that John Wayne in the armor and sandals of a Roman centurion still looked like John Wayne.

Gidgy Gidrey's Excalibur glided up alongside them like the *Queen Mary* on wire wheels. The drug dealer reached across the front seat and cranked down the window on their side. "Man, you tired of living?"

"What's happenin'?" Quincy leaned on the sill. Gidgy's dark glasses and darker face looked smoky in the shade of his Panama.

"You ain't heard?"

"Man, I been in the Holy Land the last three hours. If it ain't in stereo I ain't heard nothing."

"Somebody gone hit DiJesus this morning. I figured it was you."

"Dead?"

"All's I know is they shotgunned his car. You just walking around in the open, asking to get took down. Your clothes clean?"

Quincy sometimes had trouble following the train of Gidgy's conversation. The refrigerated air inside the car was thick with blue smoke, not tobacco. He said his clothes were clean. Krystal spoke up for her tank top and miniskirt. Her lack of underwear spoke up for itself.

" 'Kay, hop in. Wipe your feet first."

They got into the car, Quincy in front next to Gidgy. The seats were suede leather, soft as butter and the same shade of yellow. Gidgy fired a joint off the dashboard lighter, sucked in a lungful, and passed the joint to Quincy. It was better than the stuff he sold; when Quincy handed it to Krystal over the back of the seat, his lips stuck together from the resin. He pried them apart with his tongue. "Who hit DiJesus?" It came out in a wheeze.

"Don't look at me, blood. I ain't the gambler in this crowd." Gidgy accepted the joint from Krystal and wheeled out into traffic. "When Lafayette said it wasn't you, I figured Sebastian Bright, but he was with Joe Petite's old lady all day. Offering his condolences, I expect."

"Where is everybody?"

"My dump. That's where we're headed. We didn't think it was smart to meet at your place."

"Who's *we*?"

"Besides you and me there's Sebastian and Lafayette and Beatrice Blackwood and her pet Zulu and them wrasslers. Lafayette called them when he couldn't get hold of you. You should've told him which movie you was going to see. I been to just about every theater in town."

"What about Mahomet?" Quincy declined another hit. He was getting a contact high from the smoke in the car. It slowed his heartbeat and ordered his thoughts.

Gidgy steered with his wrists while he pinched out the joint and laid it in state in the ashtray. "Out speaking someplace, Lafayette said. Who you think done it if it wasn't us?"

"What kind of speaking?"

"Ask Lafayette. I ain't nobody's answering service. Maybe cops done it."

"Not with shotguns in broad daylight. See is anything on the radio."

Gidgy turned it on and ran the dial up and down AM and FM. He got a collage of rock, hillbilly, and classical and a stock market report. He turned it off. "There's a TV at my dump. We'll catch the eleven o'clock."

"Where'd you hear about it?"

"The six o'clock. They didn't know no more than what I told you."

Krystal said, in a voice blurred with muggles, "Krystal's got to pee."

"Wait till we get to Gidgy's."

Gidgy swung into a Shell station and set the brake in front of the rest rooms. "It ain't your upholstery."

Krystal came back after a few minutes and they drove the rest of the way to the Morocco Motor Hotel on Euclid, in which Gidgy owned a half interest. The other half belonged to nobody knew who and Gidgy wasn't saying, although rumor said it was a Detroit policeman whose name was expected to appear sooner or later in one of the little black books still under scrutiny from the Grecian Gardens raid. A white frame two-story building with green shingles and shutters to match, it looked better than its reputation: During one week the previous April, five arrests had been made on the eleven-room premises on charges ranging from prostitution to narcotics violations and the sale of unregistered firearms. The fact that Gidgy had been in Florida that week had seemed to confirm the suspicions about his silent partner's occupation.

In the garage, the drug dealer paused to cover the ostentatious vehicle with a custom-made tarp with Quincy's help and the three entered the motel through a covered walkway. Gidgy rapped twice on the door marked MANAGER, paused, and rapped once more. When it opened, Kindu Kinshasha wedged his bulk draped in the inevitable dashiki into the two-foot space. His big broken-knuckled fist was wrapped around a revolver with a large bore.

"Open says me," Gidgy said.

The ex-fighter identified Quincy and Krystal and opened the door the rest of the way. The office was actually a small living room furnished out of a rummage sale, with a closet-size kitchenette opening off to the right and gauchos poster-painted on black velour on the walls. The room was full of smoke, some of it tobacco, and people.

Lydell seized one of Quincy's arms in both hands and coughed. He coughed all the time lately, and in those new surroundings Quincy noticed that he'd lost weight. His gray vest hung in pleats and his wrists rattled in his shirtcuffs. A cigarette smoldered in the jade holder between the first two fingers of his right hand. "Man, I thought you was feeding the alley cats by now. Where you *been*?" His eyes lacked focus.

"Anything new?" Quincy glanced at the screen of a color console television set, the most expensive thing in the room. Dr. Richard Kimble was running down a long corridor pursued by cops, without a sound.

"News'll be on in a little. Man, I thought—"

"What's this about Mahomet speaking?"

"Wilson McCoy axed him to give a talk at his place on Kercheval. Man—"

"That hotheaded son of a bitch? Why'd you let him go?" McCoy, a former Black Panther, was self-appointed head of the Black Afro-American Congress—BLAC, in the papers—headquartered in a private home on Kercheval that had been raided in the past as a blind pig. McCoy's temper had threatened to escalate the routine arrests into something else.

"I look like his mama? Anyways, that was before we got word. Who done it, you think?"

"Since when's Mahomet make speeches?"

"Oh, that shit he fed Joe Petite at Congo's wake got around. Gidgy says he can get us all the guns we need."

"Handguns with a history, all name brands, hunnert apiece. Three hunnert you don't want them traced. Automatic weapons a thousand a pop." Gidgy took off his Panama and hung it up, exposing a head of carroty hair that compromised the solemn dark wood-sculpture of his face; hence the hat. "I got a dude in Chicago's been after me for months to trade him coke for guns. I tell him, 'What I want with guns? I get along with everybody.' 'You never know,' he says."

"*White* dude?" Sebastian Bright had joined them. Quincy might not have recognized him except for his shiny bald head. The gold-toothed grin that had won him his name was nowhere in evidence. He and Joe Petite had been tight.

Gidgy spread his hands. "Color don't figure. Man likes to throw snort parties, impress his friends with his big-deal connections. Who cares what color he is if his guns shoot?"

"Means he's white. Maybe his guns don't shoot. Maybe they blow up in our face."

"This ain't no race war."

"It ain't Ethiopians we're fighting."

"We ain't fighting nobody," Quincy said. "Not yet. We don't even know for sure what happened. Dude like DiJesus has got more enemies than brains. Maybe one of his own done him."

"Or maybe it was one of us."

They turned in a body toward Beatrice Blackwood, perched on the couch with her ankles crossed and a glass of amber liquid in her hand. She was wearing a white blouse with a lace yoke and a full black skirt. She cropped her hair close to the scalp, accentuating the Egyptian cast of her Jamaican features.

"Anybody can buy a shotgun," she went on. "He wouldn't even have to tell anyone about it."

"Not much percentage in a one-man war," Quincy said.

She sipped her drink. "Maybe he didn't think it would stay just one man."

"You saying somebody done it just to start the ball?" Quincy was looking at Sebastian.

After a long moment the gold tooth broke cover. Sebastian shook his head. "I got no stomach for that. Never did."

"Don't take no stomach to hire help." Gidgy had taken a seat next to Beatrice on the couch and poured a quarter-teaspoon of white powder out of an envelope onto the scratched glass top of the coffee table. From an inside breast pocket he produced a straight razor with a mother-of-pearl handle and proceeded to divide and subdivide the powder into a series of thin lines.

Sebastian said, "It weren't me."

" 'Course not." Lydell coughed. "Everybody knows Sebastian never spends his own money on nothing. I heard a lady bought him that tooth."

"One *sweet* lady. She went and married a repo man." The bald man was sanguine.

Beatrice said, "Sebastian wasn't the one that invited us to the wake."

"I was to go after DiJesus I'd of done it after he hit my place," Quincy said. "I only knew Joe to talk to. I sure wouldn't of killed for him."

"There's the news." Lydell turned up the volume on the set. At that moment James Brown started wailing "I Feel Good" in the room next door. Gidgy hammered on the wall with his fist until someone turned down the music. On the TV screen, a GI in combat fatigues winked as he walked past the camera carrying an M-16 with a flower stuck in the muzzle.

Gidgy used a silver straw to ingest a line of powder into his left nostril. He sat back and let an uncharacteristic grin blossom over the lower half of his face, displaying the yellowest teeth Quincy had ever seen. "Don't nobody else want a toot?" he asked.

Beatrice shushed him. The flower-carrying soldier had given way to a tight shot of a jagged hole in the rear window of a parked automobile. The camera prowled the length of the car, lingering on a spray of oval holes in the sheet metal on the driver's side. ". . . at the intersection of Cadieux and Mack Avenue," thundered the voiceover. "The driver, identified as Harold DiJesus, thirty-one, a resident of Nevada, reportedly emerged unscathed and was released from custody after questioning. Police declined to speculate on the motive for the attack, but did not rule out the possibility that drugs were involved. In a related story, Detroit Police Commissioner Ray Girardin today announced the adoption of a plan to protect citizens and private property in the event of a civil disturbance . . ."

Lydell turned off the set just as Girardin's basset-hound visage appeared. "If they get the guy they better not count on a confession," he said. "Ain't nobody going to admit he missed twice't at that range with a fucking splattergun."

Quincy found a bottle of Vernor's in the kitchenette and poured it into his sour stomach. "Least we know who's going to be coming at us." He belched.

"Won't be DiJesus," said Sebastian. "Cops'll be on him like flies on a pig's asshole. For a while anyways."

Krystal leaned over Beatrice. "I just love your blouse."

The telephone rang. Lydell picked it up. "That's probably Mahomet. I sent them wrestlers to fetch him back here."

"We still don't know who did it." Beatrice ignored Krystal.

"That don't matter no more." Gidgy was coming down. "We want them guns or not?"

Lydell hung up the receiver. "Shiiit. That was Mighty Joe Young." Quincy gave him a stupid look. "The wrestler, you know. The meeting was over when they got there. They missed Mahomet."

Quincy said, "He'll head for our place. DiJesus might have somebody there. You bring the Sting Ray?"

"It's parked out back." A fit of coughing bent him double.

"Throw me the keys. You can't even walk."

"I can shoot." Wheezing, Lydell handed Quincy the ring. "I got my Bulldog."

Krystal rose. She had Gidgy's straw in her hand. "I'll go too."

"It only seats two." Quincy watched as she dropped back down and raised the straw. "Go easy on that shit. I don't want to scrape you off the ceiling when we get back."

He drove the Corvette flat-out. The moisture in the air beaded up on the windshield and made crooked tracks toward the frame.

Lydell held his hat and looked back. "You just busted a red."

Quincy said nothing. He down-shifted for a curve, then banged the stick back up into fourth. The engine harrumphed and whined. Traffic was sparse.

"Man, I hope you drives like this for me when my time comes."

"Everybody I hang around with needs to be took care of," Quincy said. "I should start a mission."

"That's what you been running right along, brother. You just serves liquor instead of soup and sells numbers instead of Bingo. You the Saint fucking Francis of Twelfth Street."

Collingwood was quiet at that hour. A light burned behind the window of the Jiffee Coin Laundromat & Custom Laundry to discourage burglars, illuminating starkly the rows of washers and dryers inside, like white marble slabs in a mortuary. Only two cars were parked in the block. One, a stove-in Ford Fairlane with two flat tires and a square of clear plastic taped over a missing window, had been there for three weeks and sported a police tow sticker on the windshield. The other, snugged against the curb across from the laundromat, was a new black Plymouth Fury. Someone was seated behind the wheel.

"Don't look till we get past." Quincy kept his eyes on the street ahead.

At the corner, Lydell lit a cigarette. His hand shook. "All's I know is he's white."

"We'll go around the block, see can we spot Mahomet."

"Maybe he went up already."

"Maybe. I don't see no lights."

They turned down Twelfth, doubled back on Calvert, and parked on Fourteenth near the corner. From there they could see the Fury. A couple with their arms around each other walked past them swinging white cardboard cartons bound with string, trailing the sweet-sharp aroma of ribs in barbecue sauce.

"Think Mahomet's up there?"

"One way to find out." Quincy opened his door. "Give me your piece."

"What you fixing to do with it?"

"That ain't up to me." He held out his hand. Lydell laid the Bulldog in it. It felt cool and heavy. Quincy got out and put it in the side pocket of his linen jacket, leaving his hand on it. He leaned his hip against the door until the latch caught. "If anything moves, blow the horn."

"Okay if I wets my pants first?" Lydell's grin flickered and went away.

Quincy tried to walk normally, but the weight of the revolver threw off his rhythm. He turned the corner onto Collingwood opposite the parked car and tried not to look in that direction, tried not to look like he was trying not to look; so of course he looked. From that angle the interior was full of shadows. He kept walking toward the door that led upstairs to the blind pig. His footsteps clapped back at him as if he were walking down an empty corridor. He thought of Dr. Kimble. He turned to grasp the door handle.

The Sting Ray's horn honked.

He heard the creak of the car door opening, a new set of footsteps shuffling on asphalt. He drew the Bulldog out of his pocket and turned toward the street. A man was standing in the middle with his feet spread and a gun extended in both hands.

"Police!" shouted the man. "Drop it!"

Chapter 25

The address Canada had written in his notebook belonged to a new brick ranchstyle in Allen Park, one of those architectural one-sided coins with fretwork and built-in flower pots in front and a back as plain as a Dixie cup. The flagstone path that ran past the picture window had been claimed by an overgrown juniper hedge. With an oath, Canada surrendered his shoeshine to the grass, still wet from the day's rain. Evening shadows made black shag of the lawn.

The doorbell brought a small woman in her middle thirties to the screen. He took off his hat. "Miss Niles?"

"Yes. Are you Inspector—?"

"Canada. Thanks for agreeing to see me."

Her short laugh was husky and entirely mysterious. She reached up and unhooked the screen door and he pulled it open and stepped inside.

Susan Niles had on a simple knitted dress—taupe, if he remembered the name of the color correctly from his married days—cinched at the waist with a pleated belt. In low-heeled slippers she was almost a foot shorter than her visitor. Her hair was ash blond, nape-length and swept to the side in an almost careless fashion that he liked, and her chin came to a point; the only fault he noted on short acquaintance. She turned away without offering to take his hat.

"We'll talk in the living room. Can I get you anything?"

"Thanks, I just had supper."

She stepped down carefully into a sunken room containing a lot of heavy furniture that appeared to be suspended a few inches above the pile carpet until he got close enough to see the thin steel legs. The walls were bare, but painted in soft colors that lessened the effect of no pictures, and where a television set would have stood in most households was a stereo in a walnut cabinet and a rack filled with LPs. Although the lights were on, she reached out and felt the wall switch. Canada knew then that the blue eyes were sightless.

"How is Connie?" She touched the arm of a plaid sofa and sat down.

He trusted his weight to a tulip chair and laid his hat in his lap. It occurred to him that he could just as well have put it back on. "He ought to get out of the lawn mower business. He hates it."

"He needs the money. And he won't go back to newspapers."

"Did he tell you I'd call?"

She nodded. After a little silence she said, "I'm not Connie's mistress, if that's what you're thinking. He knew my Aunt Harriett."

"He said something about almost marrying your aunt." He wondered where this was going.

"Long was her last name."

He nodded, then remembered the uselessness of gestures and said, politely, "Oh?"

She smiled in his direction. "There's a scrapbook on the table by your chair. I hope it isn't too dusty. I got it out after you called. I memorized everything in it long before the glaucoma."

He'd noticed it when he sat down, an old-fashioned ledger-size volume with thick boards bound in raveled green fabric. He transferred it to his lap and lifted the cover carefully to avoid smearing his hands. A brittle brown clipping from the old Detroit *Times* was pasted to the first page. The picture, taken with a flash and rubbed and faded with years, was of a woman in a cloche hat with circular penciled eyebrows, beestung lips, and Susan Niles's pointed chin. Madam testifies in m'donald case, read the block headline. It was dated October 2, 1939.

He looked up. "You're Hattie Long's niece?"

"I thought you might recognize the name, being a policeman. Just about no one else would. She died when I was thirteen."

"Some of the older officers were still talking about her when I joined the department. She ran a blind pig back when blind pigs were blind pigs. The Rooster."

"The Cock," she corrected. "The newspapers cleaned it up in print. It was named after the stuffed rooster in the window of whatever building she happened to be using between raids. You forgot to add that the blind pig was also a whorehouse."

"I seem to recall that it was more than that."

"It was where every politician and policeman above the rank of sergeant went to get paid off in town. When that came out during the grand jury a lot of vacancies opened at City Hall."

"Thirteen Hundred too," he said. "That's how I got into the training program."

"Until the day she died, Aunt Harriett thought I thought she was a stenographer. Young ladies didn't read newspapers then. It's funny how naive the truly jaded can be. All that time I was keeping that scrapbook. She was my father's sister; if my mother ever found out I visited Aunt Harriett in her apartment—well, she didn't. When Hattie died, I inherited a cigar box full of photographs. They're all in the book."

He turned pages. More clippings from the grand jury investigation into events surrounding the suicide of Janet McDonald, the jilted mistress of a corrupt police official, sprinkled among black-and-white snapshots with serrated edges of mixed groups seated around bar tables and smiling in front of automobiles with running boards and bullet-shaped headlights and picnicking on a younger, cleaner Belle Isle. The articles told him, if he didn't know already, that the Grecian Gardens affair was nothing new in the history of the Detroit Police Department. Most of the people in the pictures were unknown to him. In one, Hattie Long, in a low-cut gown with silver clips at the shoulders, sat at the back of a horseshoe-shaped booth with her hands resting on the arms of a skinny young man in a tweed jacket and crooked bow tie and an even younger roughneck wearing a two-hundred-dollar suit and the broadest grin Canada had ever seen. His curly hair needed trimming. Canada commented on the picture.

"The one on the left is Connie," Susan Niles said. "The big one is Jack Dance."

He looked closer at the roughneck, at the expression and posture of a youth well aware of his good looks. Nothing in his appearance suggested that he was the man the press had dubbed Jack the Ripper after bullets from his gun cut down a teenage girl by accident during a gangland assassination attempt on Sylvester Street. "He looks like the captain of a college football squad."

"Aunt Harriett said he received more fan mail during his murder trial than Valentino."

He turned over a few more leaves, questioning and commenting as he went. He didn't know what he was looking for and the blind woman was no help. She seemed to be waiting.

By the time he found what she was waiting for he had seen so many lost faces he almost went past it. Two men were seated at a Formica-topped table with schooners in front of them and a forest of tall-necked beer bottles standing between. They appeared to have just noticed the presence of the camera and were turning in that direction when the picture was taken. The man on the left, dressed in a forty-dollar suit and the characteristic white socks of the last working-class generation, was Albert Brock; twenty-five years younger perhaps, dark-haired and powerfully built rather than stocky, but Canada had been staring at his likeness too much lately not to recognize him. The other man, older and dressed more expensively but constructed along similar lines, looked vaguely familiar. He had

dark thinning hair cut short and a five o'clock shadow. Recognition
nudged gently at the inspector's memory.

Susan Niles interpreted the long silence. "You found it."

"Harry Bennett. That's Harry Bennett. When was this taken?"

"Connie asked the same question the first time I showed it to him.
It's dated on the back."

He dismounted the photograph from its corners and turned
it over. The notation, written in blurred pencil, read "Roseville
5/28/37." He read it aloud.

"Aunt Harriet was operating a beergarden in Roseville then.
How's your UAW history?"

He ran a silent check of his knowledge of the United Auto
Workers and caught himself shaking his head. "Not as good as yours,
I bet."

"On May twenty-seventh, nineteen thirty-seven, Walter Reuther,
Richard Frankensteen, and other union officials gathered in front of
the Ford plant in Dearborn to hand out leaflets. A gang of thugs
hired by Harry Bennett beat them up and threw Reuther down the
steps of the Miller Road overpass. The Battle of the Overpass, it was
called."

"That much I know. I didn't know the date."

"Not many do. You also might not know that a number of other
unions went out on strike in sympathy as a result of the action. One
of them was the Steelhaulers."

It was as if a door in his brain had been opened to a room full of
light. The blind woman sensed it; nodded.

"Brock was a shop steward for the Steelhaulers in nineteen thirty-
seven," she went on. "The question is, what was he doing having a
beer—several beers—with the man responsible for the overpass
fight when every other union man in town was burning Bennett in
effigy?"

"We could ask Bennett." But the answer was no less rhetorical
than the question. Henry Ford's strongarm chief, long since forced
into retirement by the old man's grandson, was an aging recluse,

decomposing bitterly inside a ring of his own security men in a castle he had built for himself in Ann Arbor, turrets and all. Canada fingered the snapshot. "Who took it?"

"Aunt Harriett. She was a shutterbug after Repeal. I think she knew about the cancer early and wanted to leave some kind of record behind. She used to say the marks a prostitute makes generally burn away with the first cigarette. I was her favorite family member, so she left it to me."

"If it can be proved Brock made some kind of secret deal with Bennett, the union will dump him in the next election. It wouldn't matter how long ago it happened; the majority of the rank-and-file are old enough to remember Bennett and hate his guts. I wish there were some way to verify the date."

"There's a newspaper in the frame. Is the date visible?"

It was folded lengthwise on the table by Bennett's elbow. The partial masthead identified the paper as the *News*. Part of a headline said something about Spain. Bennett's left hand rested on the corner where the date would appear. "No," he said. "But if this headline is about the Spanish Civil War, that would narrow it down to thirty-seven. We could blow it up, match the issue to the one on microfilm in the library or at the *News*. Bennett would probably be carrying around that day's newspaper, but it wouldn't matter if it were a week old. He certainly wouldn't have it *before* the twenty-seventh, when keeping company with him wouldn't be so incriminating. Can I borrow this?"

"You can keep it. I have no more use for anything in the book." The blue eyes, entirely ornamental, were shadowless.

He placed the picture carefully in his billfold, closed and returned the scrapbook to the table, brushed the dust from his trousers, and used his handkerchief to wipe his hands. With nothing more to do, he stood. Her face followed him up. "Personal question," he said.

"Why."

"Yes. I don't think you care about Albert Brock one way or the other. You're not arbitrarily malicious."

"You don't know that."

"I was a cop before I became an inspector. When you lose that you're through." He waited.

"That scrapbook is Hattie Long's life," she said. "As long as it just sits there she's dead, really dead. This way—well, whatever the result, it's like she's still out there somewhere. Of course you'll let me know what happens."

He promised he would, and took her hand when she started to rise. She squeezed her thanks and let go. Her fingers were strong and calloused lightly at the tips. "What do you do, Miss Niles?"

"I teach Braille at Cranbrook." She smiled, suddenly and dazzlingly. "Aunt Harriett might approve. I think."

"I'll bring back the picture."

"You don't have to."

"I'd like to."

"All right."

She walked him to the door. He put on his hat and opened it. "You see plenty for someone without sight."

"I'm blind," she said. "Not stupid. Good night, Inspector."

Chapter 26

Gerald W. Lilley—Mahomet to his new Twelfth Street friends—walked the five miles from Kercheval to Collingwood. Wilson McCoy had offered him a lift, but he'd said no. It was a nice night after the rain and he wanted the extra time to come down from his high.

Not from drugs. He had given those up in all forms when he read *The Autobiography of Malcolm X*; impressed with the ethic of the Black Muslims but with no clear idea of how to join formally, he had jettisoned his Christian and family names and adopted a variant spelling of Mohammed. The change was easy because both his parents were dead and his siblings scattered, and he had no friends. The degree from Wayne State University, for which he had washed dishes and bused tables for six years, had cut him off from others of his race. He'd thought of enrolling in divinity school after graduation, but when a distant cousin was lynched in Georgia because he resembled another Negro overheard shouting drunken obscenities at a white woman on the street, he decided that God had abandoned his people. Rising tuition costs and a discouraging academic record in his senior year ended subsequent plans for a career in teaching.

A stint at singing, involving a six-record contract based on an audition at Motown, went the same way when Barry Gordy laid an arm across Mahomet's shoulders and said, "Man, you can diagram a sentence, but you ain't got *soul*." The records weren't released.

He let his life slide after that. When jobs he applied for, and for which his education qualified him, went to white men who had barely finished high school, he came to wish that he had never opened the books; they merely promised worlds that were closed to him. About the time he read Malcolm X's book he learned of Mrs. Rosa Parks, a Negro seamstress who had stood trial in Alabama ten years before for refusing to sit in the back of a bus. Rosa Parks had given up her back seat for one beside Malcolm in Mahomet's esteem. Although he had lost his faith, he had continued to sing in Baptist choirs as an outlet for his voice and training. But his bitterness at sermons preaching brotherhood and mercy—things plainly denied everyone in the congregation—had begun to boil over in the form of impromptu speeches needled with invective and blasphemy. He was asked to leave. Deprived of that forum, he had carried his anger to restaurants, private clubs, and nightspots where Negroes were tolerated only in the livery of service. Inevitably, he was ejected. Just as inevitably, he had returned, to be beaten and arrested for creating a disturbance. It was a slow, passive form of suicide that would eventually have fulfilled its purpose had not blind luck—he resisted God yet—flung him into a cell opposite Quincy Springfield's.

When, the day after their brief first acquaintance, a turnkey opened his cell door and told him that Springfield had bailed him out, he'd experienced a lightning revelation of the sort that he had only read of in eighteenth-century British novels: *Only your own will look out for you.* Nothing he had learned since joining Springfield's loyal little group had changed that impression. Certainly not Krystal, who had formed the habit early of sharing with Mahomet the cash that Springfield gave her in hopes she might spend some of it in shops that wouldn't dress her like a Twelfth Street whore.

He had invested some of that money in the suit he was wearing, white linen with a pinched waist and flared trousers, woven so tight it felt like cool silk against his hot skin. Walking along with the jacket flung over his shoulder, he admired his reflection in store windows. The contrast between white vest and pink shirtsleeves and tie made a bold statement that matched the defiance of his verbal message. The fag tailor had tried to sell him a Panama, but he'd refused; hats left ugly ledges in his painstakingly relaxed and brilliantined hair, like laminated porcupine quills. The suit, along with the high-heeled black patent-leather boots he always insisted on regardless of the condition of his finances, added inches to his stature.

The talk had gone well. Wilson McCoy, a firebrand barely out of his teens whom Mahomet distrusted instinctively, had been enthusiastic about the reception and asked him to come back Saturday night when he could promise more than fifteen listeners. Mahomet had said he'd get back to him. Even then he knew he'd accept. He had found his calling.

He barely remembered the words he'd used. They were but fuel to get him around from behind the long table that served as a bar after hours while the fifteen in their folding chairs listened at first with skepticism, then swelling anticipation and finally, as he bore down on them, with the rhythmic, junglelike grunts of acquiescence he'd heard so often from congregations in the thrall of the Reverend Otis R. R. Idaho those Sundays when the fever was truly upon him. The words didn't matter in the end, only the fire and the spirit. He had struck Soul, and the vein was deep, deep. Sex was never as draining nor as satisfying; although he had to admit that most of the sex he had experienced was part of a monetary transaction, and its passion therefore suspect. Women had wanted him, for his looks and his hair and his voice, but *that* kind of transaction called for a sacrifice after the fact. Once sated, Mahomet's appetites turned in new directions.

Yes, it was a changing fate that had ushered Quincy Springfield into the life of Gordon W. Lilley, Jr.

A pair of headlights on high beam swung around the corner, blinding him momentarily and shrinking his vitals; the thing with the Sicilians was always a dash of cold water in the face of his good fortune. Despite his fistfights with the Man in all his many incarnations, Mahomet was not physically brave. He felt a warm release when the vehicle, a sport model of some kind on a short wheelbase, sped past. Then its tires shrieked and it reversed directions in a shower of flaming rubber. The door on the driver's side sprang open. Someone bounded out and seized him by the shoulders.

"Jesus, we been looking for you all over the West Side! You just shufflin' along, gots all the time in the world."

The wasted features staring down at him were Lydell Lafayette's.

"What happened?"

"Quincy got busted is what. Looking for you. The war's on. We gots to get down to the police department and post bond. How much cash you carrying?"

He pried himself free and picked his jacket up off the sidewalk. He found six dollars in a side pocket. Lydell coughed disgustedly.

"I got about a hunnert. We'll go up to the place and get what's in the box. *Shake* it, brother! That nightside's hell on niggers." He was climbing under the wheel.

Mahomet got into the passenger's side carefully. He'd wet himself when Lydell grabbed him.

The name on the watch desk at 1300 was O'Pronteagh, but the sergeant's accent was flat Midwestern and he had the patrician features of a Roman senator, all high cheekbones and eagle's beak and a shock of salt-and-pepper hair on a tall tan forehead. Despite the airlessness of the big room with a single fan humming in a distant corner, his collar was buttoned and his necktie snugged up under an Adam's apple as big as an eightball.

"Your boy's being booked downstairs," he said. "Carrying a concealed weapon. You can visit him in the morning at County."

Lydell said, "We're here to post bond."

"Sorry."

Lydell took the roll from his pocket and thumped it down on the counter. "They's a thousand here. That ought to cover it three times and change."

"Son, are you trying to bribe a police officer?"

"I ain't your son."

Mahomet laid a hand on Lydell's arm. They had begun to attract the attention of the other officers in the room. "Excuse me, Sergeant, but regulations say we can post bond on a misdemeanor."

O'Pronteagh took in the white suit. "If you're selling Ajax, where's your horse and lance?"

One of the uniforms snorted. Mahomet said, "How much is bond?"

"I'm a peace officer, son. It's not my job to let you people run around with firearms."

"What you mean, 'you people'?" Lydell gripped the counter.

The sergeant made an infinitesimal movement of his head. One of the uniforms standing nearby stepped in, grabbed Lydell's wrist, and jerked it behind his back. His other arm went across Lydell's throat. The prisoner stopped struggling.

O'Pronteagh handed the roll of bills to another officer behind the counter. "Count it and tag it as evidence. Attempted bribery and resisting arrest."

"Call Gidgy," Lydell croaked. "The Morocco Motor Hotel." His eyes were starting from his head.

Mahomet went to a booth near the door. He was reaching for the receiver when someone pulled him out of the booth. A fist plowed into his stomach. His knees lost tension. Someone caught him before he hit the floor.

"Another resisting." The sergeant's voice, far away. "Book them both and make it stick."

"Jesus fucking Christ. Jesus fucking goddamn Christ."

The other plainclothesmen in the seventh floor squad room stood around in silence. They had never heard the neat quiet inspector raise his voice before. Now he was standing over a goggle-eyed

Sergeant Esther, both hands clenching the sides of the sergeant's desk to avoid seizing the sergeant's fat throat.

"It wasn't me, Inspector. I just found out about it myself."

"O'Pronteagh and the others just got bored, decided to kill some time with a little nigger-baiting?"

"Not exactly, no."

"What, exactly?"

Esther took a deep breath and exhaled. Canada smelled stale coffee. "Wasylyk busted Springfield at the stakeout in front of the place on Collingwood; Springfield had a piece. When he came in I told O'Pronteagh to hold him no matter what. I knew you'd want to talk to him. But I never said to rough anybody around."

"Where are they now?"

"Holding."

"Kick 'em."

"Inspector—"

Canada shoved a finger in the sergeant's face. "Kick them. Give back the money and the gun; it isn't as if they couldn't score another one thirty feet from the door. Tell O'Pronteagh if I even see erasures where their names were on the blotter I'll have him up on charges so fast his shorts will ride up. The whole fucking thing never happened."

"That might not be so easy, Inspector. There was a reporter downstairs when it happened."

"*News* or *Free Press?*"

"*News.* It was Conger."

"That's a break. They don't go to press till afternoon. Cut a deal."

"What kind of deal?"

"Use your imagination. Offer him first look at the final I.A.D. report on Grecian Gardens. That ought to hold him for a couple of months."

"These aren't exactly leaders of the Negro community, Inspector. Springfield's and Lafayette's priors would fill a drawer and this Mahomet character's a born troublemaker. I bet he's the one started it."

"I don't give a fuck if he started the New York blackout. Any rookie knows you don't muss up coloreds on the ground floor of Thirteen Hundred in a hot month like July. Especially not when the Orrs and the Springfields are stalking each other all over town. You want Joe Weaver and a Channel Two camera up here on seven?"

Esther lifted his receiver. "Give me the desk." He made eye contact with the knot of the inspector's necktie. "Coopersmith heard back from the FBI."

"What?" Canada was disoriented.

"Just a second," Esther said into the mouthpiece. "On that partial thumb the print boys found in that stolen Caddy. DiJesus, you know? I started to tell you when you came in, but—"

"What'd they say?"

"Belongs to somebody named Curtis Dupree, Negro, did a nickel in Jackson for opening up some poor schnook's skull over a fender-bender on the Lodge. Works at McClouth. He's a Steelhauler. A.P.B.?"

"Let me." He went into his office.

After he got off the telephone to Dispatch, Canada took the photograph he had gotten from Susan Niles out of his wallet and stuck it to the center of the bulletin board covered with mug shots. He resisted the temptation to drive the thumbtack grinning between Albert Brock's eyes.

Chapter 27

The Tigers lost, but Rick and Pammie got to overhear Jim Northrup negotiating to buy a used Chevy from Norm Cash next to the dugout. During the game, Pammie ate a prodigious number of hot dogs, drank three Cokes, and visited the ladies' room at least six times. She wore a Tigers cap as promised and a Snoopy T-shirt over a pair of tight green shorts that pushed the fat on her thighs into white ridges. Her knowledge of history at the corner of Michigan and Trumbull made Rick want to run home and bone up on his ten-year collection of programs. When the players went to the showers the two remained in their seats while most of the crowd hurried to join the crush of traffic leaving the parking lot. An old Negro worked his way down the bleachers, spearing paper cups and hot dog wrappers with a nail on a stick.

"I wonder if he bought it," said Pammie.

Rick rested his head on the back of his seat and watched clouds boil past the quarter moon. The night was warm. "I doubt it. Sounded to me like the block's cracked."

"Maybe it didn't sound like that to Northrup."

"He's been in the game too long not to know anything about cars. Everybody misses the bus from time to time."

"I don't think it's the block at all. The plugs need cleaning." She grinned when he turned his head in her direction. "I got three brothers. I spent more time in garages than Parnelli Jones."

"That how you wound up at PG?"

"No, I'm just staying out from under foot during summer vacation. I start Eastern Michigan in September."

"Everybody in the office seems to be on his way somewhere else," he said. "Lee's joining the Peace Corps, I'm going into politics, you're waiting on a baseball scholarship—"

She giggled. "I watch. I don't play. I'm majoring in Business. Either that or Elizabethan Poetry. I haven't made up my mind yet. Did you go to college?"

"U of D, two years. I'd have thought you'd been around longer. You run the office when Wendell and Enid are out."

"Oh, I've been there two years, nights, weekends, and vacations. My pop thinks I'm being taken advantage of, not getting paid and all. I keep telling him, money doesn't motivate our generation."

"Now you sound like Lee."

"You sound a lot older than thirty sometimes."

She was pouting now. He changed the subject. "Enid isn't on her way somewhere else."

"Enid was born rich."

"You say that like you're sorry for her."

"I am, sort of. It sure hasn't made her happy."

"She and Wendell got something going?"

She looked at him quickly, then at the infield. The grounds crew was unrolling the tarp. More rain was predicted. "I wouldn't know about anything like that."

"Come on. You know everything."

"You ask too many questions. Lee says it's because you were a reporter, but I think you're just plain nosy. Everybody should do his own thing and leave everybody else's alone."

"That's Lee talking. He reads all that stuff they hand out on street corners." He shrugged. "I just don't like being the only one who doesn't know what everyone else knows. Personally I think she likes women."

"Why, because she wouldn't give you a tumble?"

"Hey, I never asked."

"What was that needlepoint thing all about then?"

"It was a joke. Are you sore at me for something?" He sat up.

She didn't answer. She took off her glasses and wiped them with the tail of her T-shirt. She rubbed both eyes and put them back on. "They're going to kick us out of here." She stood.

"Sit down. We're not the only ones waiting for the parking lot to clear."

She sat down. She was still looking at the grounds crew.

"I'm sorry," he said.

"Sorry for what?"

"For being a jerk. A guy isn't supposed to talk about other women when he's on a date."

She smiled then, without looking at him. "I thought this was a buddy thing."

"If it were a buddy thing I'd have asked Lee. Him I could win an argument with on who leads the Tigers in bases on balls."

"You still owe me a Coke." She'd forgotten about the infield. "I thought you were interested in Enid. Just about everybody who comes to the office is. I might as well be a file cabinet when she's around."

"She scares the hell out of me."

She beamed. "You?"

"These fashion mannequins with their eyes locked on their goals always do. Enid never doesn't talk shop. When you're a guy that's intimidating."

"That's nothing. Well, you met Caroline." She had shifted gears into gossip.

"I don't see her every day."

"Enid had a tragedy. I shouldn't talk about it." The eyes behind the glasses said she couldn't wait to.

"She told me about her parents. I don't think that explains it."

"Well, you were warm before." She got up. "I think you can get your car out now."

He didn't bring up the subject again. The hook was set; from here on she would reel herself in.

In the car, Pammie said the hot dogs had made her hungry. They drove to Nicholson's Steak House on Woodward, waited a few minutes to be seated, and ordered two open-face steak sandwiches with fries. The other diners were in suits and crepe dresses and ballpark casual, like them. He watched her pour Heinz ketchup over her sirloin.

"Why Elizabethan Poetry?" he asked.

" 'Cause I don't know much about it and I sure won't read it unless somebody makes me. I know me." She offered him the bottle; he shook his head. She shrugged and set it down. "I'm sort of a poet. One of my poems got Honorable Mention in the *Detroit News* Scholastic Writing Competition last year."

"Congratulations."

"All I got was a Certificate of Merit and my name in the paper on a big list. Anyway, if I'm going to make anything of myself, I think I ought to try and understand it, don't you?"

"Absolutely."

She dipped a french fry in the ketchup and held it up like a scepter. "You're a writer, right? I mean, you wrote for the papers."

"Actually I just talked to people and took notes. Someone else did the actual writing."

She looked disappointed. Then she shrugged again and took a bite out of the fry. "Still, you're as close to a real writer as I ever got. Would you read my poems? You could tell me if they're any good."

"The Certificate of Merit ought to have told you that."

"That was high school stuff. I want to know how they stack up to the professionals."

"All I know about poetry is it doesn't rhyme any more."

"Oh." She concentrated on stirring the stub of potato in her ketchup.

"I'd be glad to read them."

"That's okay."

"No, really. It's just that my opinion isn't worth more than any-body else's."

"I haven't shown them to anybody else."

He stopped sawing at his steak. "They're not, like, personal, are they?"

"Just stuff that comes to me."

"You even sound like a writer." He took a bite.

"Really?" She brightened. "I'll bring them to the office tomorrow. Don't spare my feelings. A poet has to have a clear idea of her limitations."

"Who said that?"

"I just thought of it. Is it good?"

"It's a good simple declarative sentence. They liked those at the *Times*." The closest he had ever been to a newspaper office was an occasional cup of coffee with the police reporter from the *Free Press*. He had chosen the *Times* for his background cover because the paper had been defunct for six years, making his story difficult to check.

They ate their meals. Pammie sipped her Coke through a straw and wrinkled her nose. "Too much syrup. How'd you guess Wendell and Enid had—something going?"

"Do they?"

"I didn't say that. I was just wondering what made you think so."

He backed off again. "Just something I overheard her say to him on the phone once. Also I get the impression neither of them thinks too much of Caroline, except as a lawyer. Probably I've just got a dirty mind."

"I read a letter he wrote Enid." She took another sip.

"A letter?" He hadn't counted on letters. His inner antennae were tingling.

"It was an accident. She had to go out and asked me to file a bunch of letters on her desk. I guess it got mixed up in the stack. By the time I knew it didn't belong it was too late; I'd read it." She flushed.

"No, that's not true. I went on reading after I figured out what it was. I guess that's pretty terrible."

"What did it say?"

But she'd sealed off. "I put it back on her desk, under some other papers. I never said anything. I don't think she knows I saw it."

"Must've been pretty hot."

"It wasn't your usual office memo." She ate her last fry. "Do you think they have a dessert tray?"

He drove her home. He didn't bring up the letter again. "We'll get 'em Saturday," he said, referring to the game. "McLain's pitching."

"I like Lolich. I just wish he'd lay off the beers. He's starting to look like Jackie Gleason." She watched the scenery roll past, lighted shop windows and pools of light under the street lamps like the ones Jimmy Durante used to walk through at the end of his TV show. She turned her head suddenly. "What's this big idea you had that you wouldn't tell Enid about?"

"I'd better not say anything yet. It might not come off."

"Is it legal?"

"Not entirely."

"Wendell says we should be careful and not break the law. That's just what GM wants us to do so the government will shut us down."

"Right, like we could be any less effective if it did."

"Are you going to discuss it with him?"

"Sure. It wouldn't work without Wendell."

"Come on, give me a hint."

He chewed on it. "You like parades?"

"Not much. I'm too short. All I ever see of the J. L. Hudson parade on Thanksgiving is the back of people's heads." She paused. "That's your idea? A parade?"

"I just asked if you liked them."

"Thanks a bunch."

The house was in Melvindale, one of a row of narrow high-peaked residences, all painted white. Rick recognized the style. They had been built by the Ford Motor Company under the original Henry for the employees at the Dearborn plant. Blue light from a television screen flickered in one of the downstairs windows, the only illumination in the house. He walked her to the porch.

"Pop's watching Dean Martin. We better say good-bye here," she said. "I had a good time."

"Me too. I learned more about baseball than Al Kaline knows."

She smiled; then she frowned. "Don't tell anybody about the letter, okay? I shouldn't have said anything."

"Who'd I tell, Lee? He'd just shake his hair and say"—he imitated Lee Schenck's sleepy tones—" 'Everybody's got his own bag.' "

"You do good impressions." She giggled. "You should cut an album, like Vaughn Meader."

"Yeah, but who's heard of him lately?"

"Good night." She stood on tiptoe and kissed his cheek. The bill of her cap grazed his forehead. Then she went inside.

Back in the car he sat for a long time before turning the key. A light went on in one of the windows upstairs. He started the car then and backed out of the driveway. On Greenfield he reached up and flipped the mirror to the night side. That way he didn't have to look at his reflection.

Chapter 28

"**I** like it," Wendell Porter said. "But I hate it. The Porter Group has always stayed within the law."

They were in his office on the second floor of the house on Whittier—Porter, Enid, and Rick. The consumer advocate was half reclining with an open folder in his lap on a backless Victorian couch that reminded Rick of the one in a psychiatrist's office in a Jerry Lewis film someone had dragged him to see. It was a small room with one window, untidy bookshelves, and a cheap pine desk with a cracked top and warped drawers where Wendell claimed he'd written *Hell On Wheels* in longhand in a Nifty pad. Both the desk and the chair behind it were heaped with books and bound copies of the *Congressional Record*. The office had the contrived disarray of its occupant's trick haircut and shabby Ivy League dress. In reality Rick knew Porter did most of his work in a neat anonymous room in the same building where Caroline kept her legal offices. The garret was for receiving visitors.

"Within the law, always," Rick agreed. "Where's it got you? Waiting for the telephone to ring from Washington like an ugly girl on prom night."

"I think most ugly girls give up before the actual night." Porter's avuncular smile made it clear that homey comparisons were his territory. "I'd rather we held off on this kind of action until all legal resources have been exhausted."

"It's a misdemeanor at worst. There'll be a fine and a citation for not having a permit. You couldn't buy the same publicity for the amount of the fine."

"Why not apply for a permit?" This was Enid's contribution. Rick had declined to broach his idea until Porter was due in the office this Friday morning.

"We wouldn't get it," Rick said. "Cavanagh's running for the Senate. He's not about to allow an eyesore on Grand Boulevard. If he even gets wind of it he'll slap us with an injunction, and if we defy that we'll be in real trouble. If we don't ask, the city can't say no."

Porter said, "I'd like to hear Caroline's opinion."

"She'll say no."

He looked at Rick. "What makes you think so?"

"She's your lawyer. If she were my lawyer and she advised me to go ahead with a scheme like this, I'd fire her."

"It certainly wouldn't be the first time I went against her counsel. All the same I don't like going behind her back."

"That's your decision, sir. But if she knows, her assistant will too, and that's five people in on the secret. If it leaks to the press early the event will lose all its impact."

". . . Only if four of them are dead. I see you know your Franklin." Porter studied the folder in his lap, in which he had plainly lost interest. "It's medieval. No, it's older than that, it's Roman. The victorious emperor parading his prisoners and spoils down the Appian Way. Only we're hardly victorious, are we? What do you think, Enid?"

"I think it's harebrained. If it goes wrong it'll follow us around for years. Porter's Folly."

"Okay, that's one vote against and one for. Mine seems to be the deciding ballot." He returned his attention to Rick. "Is it feasible? Can you get your people to go along?"

"Thanks to Enid I've spent the last couple of weeks establishing contact with services in the area. When you come down to it, it's a simple tow job. It will run us a couple of thousand."

"Enid keeps the books."

"I'll draw it out of discretionary." She'd resigned herself to defeat.

Rick said, "It'd help if we could count on one favorable media source to cover the story, preferably television. Do we have anyone?"

"We've always gotten a fair shake from Ven Marshall at Channel Four. An impartial press is favorable when your cause is just." He managed to say it without pomposity.

"We'll call him an hour before we roll."

Porter closed the folder and rose. "Set it up for next Saturday."

"A weekday's better," Rick said. "We want to catch Jim Roche in his office." James M. Roche was chairman of the board of General Motors.

"How much time do you need?"

"Wednesday morning's good. That way we can make the news at noon, six, and eleven."

"Wednesday morning, then." He smiled. "Amazing what a little jolt in an automobile will do for your sensibilities, isn't it?"

"I considered suing you for whiplash, but that was before I met Mrs. Porter."

Mention of Caroline swung the mood back to business. "I always wanted to be in a parade. Should I participate?"

"No." Enid was firm. "I'll make an appointment for you in Washington that day. If I can't get anyone else I'll line up a Senate page. That way when it blows up in our face you can blame it on your overeager subordinates."

Porter became grave. "Kennedy's death changed everything. Doing good never meant being devious."

Rick would have corrected him, but couldn't think of a way to do it without blowing his cover.

After Porter left, Enid locked the office door. "Lee thinks knocking is Establishment," she said. "I assume you want to keep this secret from the others as long as possible."

"Okay, so you hate the idea. If anything goes wrong you can throw me to the wolves."

"Maybe it's not the idea I hate. Maybe I resent the new kid storming in and taking over like the rest of us have been standing around all this time with our thumbs up our noses."

"You're not that petty."

"You don't know how petty I am. You don't know anything about me."

"I know enough to look forward to seeing you every day."

It was like shooting craps in the dark. He couldn't tell how he was doing. The sunlight coming through the window behind her haloed her dark hair in red. She was wearing a light cotton dress with a dusting of tiny blue polka-dots and a half-slip underneath, silhouetted against the light.

"Mister," she said, "I'm not the least attracted to you. I like them dark and mature."

"You just described Wendell."

"I just described LBJ and Gregory Peck and half the male population. You're in the other half. If I wanted cute and boyish I'd date Ricky Nelson."

"Do you really think I'm cute?"

She pointed at him. "That's what I'm talking about. Just because you look like you belong in an Archie comic book doesn't mean you have to act like it. Got a sampler to cover that?"

"We'll have dinner, talk about Wednesday."

"I thought you were dating Pammie."

"Pammie's a buddy. What do you say? I'll even wear long pants."

"Wednesday's your baby. I've got an office to run. I'll start with a press release apologizing for Wednesday and saying it was arranged and carried out without Wendell's knowledge or consent. No sense waiting until the last minute." She unlocked the door. "Don't you have calls to make?"

"I'd better make them in here. Pammie's got ears she should leave to science." He lifted the telephone, standard and all, off the desk and carried it to the couch, but he didn't sit. "Is it the idea you don't like, or just me?"

"I don't like Soupy Sales either, but I don't let it get in the way of my responsibilities. You're just stopping in on your way to the White House. Some of us have to live here. Your cute prank could undo years of hard work."

"There's that word again. I'm wearing you down. I'll make a bet with you: Dinner with me Wednesday night if the thing comes off."

"Define 'comes off.' "

"At least one favorable comment from someone in authority, in the form of a telegram or a telephone call, after we make the news. In politics that's as good as an invitation to come in and talk turkey."

"What do I get if that doesn't happen?"

"It's what Wendell gets. My resignation, along with a signed confession that I undertook the whole mess on my own, without consulting anyone."

"Deal." She spat in her palm and held it out.

He looked at the hand. "Where'd you pick that up?"

"Sister Mary Pacifica. She coached the girls' softball team at Blessed Sacrament."

They shook.

After she left, Rick spent an hour on the couch with the telephone standard in his lap. He wasn't listening to himself during the last half-dozen calls; by then he had his spiel down like the Lord's Prayer. Only one of the people he spoke with refused the transaction, and that was at the beginning when he was still feeling his way.

Pammie was waiting for him in the downstairs office. For an instant he thought he had a visitor. She had on a yellow dress with bows on the shoulder straps and a pair of red pumps whose three-inch heels had her swaying like a tug in a heavy sea. She'd brushed her hair down from its customary Alice the Goon topknot and tied it with red ribbons a shade off from the shoes. She was holding a sheaf of papers to her bosom.

"I typed them up," she said. "My penmanship's pretty hard to follow."

"Typed what up?" He took his place at the card table.

"My poems, silly. I was up most of the night." She laid the sheaf in front of him.

He riffled the edges. There were thirty pages easy. "I'll have to take them home."

"Of course. You'll need to, like, evaluate them. Reading poetry takes almost as much concentration as writing it."

He smiled and set the papers aside. She was still standing in front of the table.

"Well?" she said.

"Well."

She stuck her arms out to the sides and twirled around. She caught herself before she fell off the heels. "How do you like it? I only wore it once, to my high school graduation party. Pop bought it for me."

"It sure is yellow."

"Saffron, the man called it. At HughesHatcherSufferin." It came out as one word. "I don't wear dresses much. They bunch up on me when I sit down."

"It's nice." She looked like a school bus.

"Free for lunch?" she asked. "I mean, this is no place to waste a dress."

"I've got a lot of calls to make; this survey thing. I'm going to have to work through lunch."

"After work, then. You'll be starving."

"I've got an appointment."

"Oh. Politics?"

"Sort of." He was planning to wash and wax the Camaro.

"Dinner? Corky's Sandwich Shop is open late Fridays."

He was silent for a moment. Then he got up. "Let's go to lunch."

"What about your calls?"

"They can wait. We have to talk."

"Oh."

"Corky's Sandwich Shop sounded like a good idea," he said.

She looked down at her poems. "You don't have to feed me, Rick. I've been dumped on an empty stomach and I've been dumped over a meal and dumped is dumped."

"Nobody's dumping anybody." It sounded like an admission even to him.

"Stupid cow."

"What?"

She said it again. "That's what somebody called me once. He was right. One ballgame and a steak sandwich and Pammie's ready to go steady. Stupid, stupid, stupid." She snatched up the pages and ran out. The front door banged.

Enid was looking at him over her Smith-Corona when he came out into the entryway.

"Say it," he said.

" 'Pammie's a buddy.' " She returned to her typing.

Chapter 29

Mike Gallante said he'd rented the house in Highland Park for its kitchen.

It was the largest room in the house, a big, sunny, old-fashioned place of the kind where families used to gather before television turned the living room into a shrine: black-and-white checkered linoleum and sturdy wallpaper with blue cups and saucers printed on it and a big oak table in a bay window with chairs all around. Patsy Orr sat on one of them, feeling exposed despite the reassuring view from the rear of Sweets's massive conical body and pointed head hovering outside the window. Patsy's canes leaned against the table where he could get to them in a hurry, the way he preferred them when not in the security of his home or his office in the Penobscot Building.

Gallante, in his shirtsleeves and sheathed in a white apron from neck to knees, waited until the sweep hand on his wristwatch reached the six, then flipped off the burner on the gas stove, lifted the pot bubbling there, and dumped its tangled contents into a colander standing in the sink to drain. "The secret to *al dente* is in the timing," he said, turning to stir a smaller pot simmering on a low flame. "You can pay more for linguini marked *al dente* in a supermarket, but if you cook it ten seconds too long you might as well have bought Prince's spaghetti to begin with."

"I don't cook," said Patsy.

"It's a valuable skill, particularly when there are no women around. I picked it up in fifty-seven when Genovese and Costello were at war. It was self-defense; you can only eat so many sardine-and-mustard sandwiches. Your boy's invited too." He began setting the table.

"Sweets stays at his post. You know how many *capos* have been shot over dinner?"

"That only happens in restaurants. Governor Romney should have the security system I put in here."

"I don't know why we couldn't meet at the office."

"My father worked two jobs, seven days a week. My sister and I never got to see him. When I bring my wife and kids here from New York, that's one mistake I'm not going to make. I'm establishing the habit of staying away from offices on Saturdays." He filled two stemmed glasses from a bottle of burgundy and lifted one. *"Salute."*

Patsy didn't touch his. "Wine screws up my digestion."

Gallante shrugged, drank, set down the glass, and used serving tongs to heap both plates from the colander. He turned off the burner under the smaller pot and ladled clam sauce from it over the linguini. Removing the apron, he took his place at the table and scooped pasta into his mouth. "Perfect," he said. "Directions say eight to ten minutes, but that's at least two minutes too long. What are you doing about DiJesus?"

Patsy poked at his linguini. Spiced sauces were almost as bad as wine for his system. "What's to do about him? He's doing a good job."

"Just as long as he doesn't take it into his head to hit the coloreds ahead of schedule. Some of these hitters are pretty independent."

"They tried to hit him. I guess he's got a right to hit back."

"He shouldn't have gone after Joe Petite. Was that your idea?"

"The niggers needed another lesson. They were spitting in our face with that funeral." He wasn't about to inform Gallante that the Petite killing had come as a surprise.

"If you hold off long enough, I'll hand you Twelfth Street without firing a shot. All DiJesus is doing is stirring them up, giving them a reason to fight."

"We'll rip them up if they do."

"Why rip anyone up if we don't have to?"

Patsy pointed his fork at Gallante. There's no *we* about it. You're just the East Coast help. You're only here because the Commission outvoted me."

"I don't like it any more than you, but they gave me a job to do. I studied at Princeton. I'm front man for the organization's legitimate interests on the Atlantic Seaboard; you think I asked to come here and count pennies in niggertown? If they wanted a war they'd have sent some Apache from Hell's Kitchen."

"Don't throw the Commission in my face. My father helped build the Commission."

"Your father's methods went out with Joey Machine. That's why the government sent him back to Sicily."

Patsy said nothing. So far only he knew that Frankie Orr was on American soil.

Gallante had a few more forkfuls and topped off his glass from the bottle. A thick gold wedding band winked on his ring finger. Patsy despised men who wore them. "It would be different if this were between Italians, or Italians against Jews," Gallante said. "The blacks are headline news. Just yesterday a jury in Georgia convicted a Klansman for civil rights violations in the murder of a Washington educator. A couple of years ago that would've been a simple homicide beef and no one would have heard about it outside Georgia. The feds are cracking down. That's good news for us, because it means Uncle Sam's only interested in the boys in sheets and dunce caps. If we mix in this race thing, though, he'll turn his gun on us."

"I'm not going to sit by and hand everything over to the coloreds, government or no."

"They're not trying to take anything over. They're just trying to hold on to what they've got. And right now the country's on their side."

"Whores and pushers, the bunch of them."

"That's the kind of fine distinction that gets overlooked in the current climate," Gallante said. "My advice is to call off DiJesus. Send him back to Vegas. Let me deal with Springfield and I'll give you Twelfth Street for Christmas."

"The motherfuckers opened up on him with shotguns. My man. They'll be coming after me next."

"I doubt it. They made their pass and it came up craps. They'll draw their horns in now. I know Springfield. He won't fight a war he can't win. If we dictate terms now—peacefully and with tact—he'll accept them. But you have to give me time."

"What time is it?"

He blinked and checked his watch. "A little after one."

"I've got an appointment with my physical therapist at two." Patsy reached for his canes and rapped on the window. Outside, Sweets turned around, looked, and started toward the front door. By the time he joined the others in the kitchen, Patsy had secured his leg braces and was standing with the aid of the canes. "Tonight's the money night," he told Gallante. "Tell Springfield and his people we're taking ninety-five percent from now on. Tell them to pass the word to the rest."

"I can't do that!"

"My father taught me never to tell a man to do something twice. He said that's why God made undertakers."

"Why ninety-five? Why not a hundred percent?"

"Lincoln freed the slaves." He clanked toward the door. Sweets stepped past him to hold it.

"What if they decide to send you ninety-five percent of me instead?" Gallante asked.

"Take DiJesus with you."

When they were through the door, Patsy remembered his manners and sent Sweets back to thank Gallante for lunch.

Canada showed the uniform at the barricade his badge and ID and joined the group gathered by the parked Studebaker with its trunk lid standing. A passenger jet shrilled overhead, dragging its shadow across the long-term parking lot; one of the new 747s. Flies swam in the stench from the car trunk.

"Shut it, for chrissake," Canada said.

One of the uniforms slammed the lid. Everyone was smoking, including Sergeant Esther, who didn't have the habit. He coughed a lot and his face was red. Canada, who had given up cigarettes five years ago, bummed one off the uniform holding the pack and lit it off Esther's. The smoke helped kill the stink. He watched two morgue attendants in gas masks preparing to lift a stretcher on the ground containing an oblong in a black zipper bag. "Is it him?"

Without warning, the sergeant bent down and unzipped the bag twelve inches, uncovering a face bloated like bread dough, the blurred features of which vaguely resembled the mug shot of Curtis Dupree; also half the Negro population of Detroit and a manitee Canada had seen once in a picture in the *National Geographic*. Stench rolled out like smoke from a broiler. One of the uniforms turned away and threw up on the asphalt.

Canada, his lungs filled with smoke, motioned for Esther to close the bag. He nodded to the attendants and they lifted the corpse and carried it to the coroner's wagon parked in the middle of the aisle.

"It's him okay." The sergeant walked with Canada toward fresher air. "We'll need a positive ID from his wife, but Dupree's name is on the registration in the glove compartment. Airport cops figure it's been parked here three days. In this heat they don't take long to turn."

"That would make it the day after the try on DiJesus. What about his partner?"

"Holding down the bottom of Lake St. Clair, maybe, if he didn't get smart and blow town." He threw away his cigarette. "Springfield's had a couple of days to get over Wednesday night. I think we ought to pull him in and sweat him."

"He wouldn't know anything."

"Just because Dupree paid his union dues doesn't mean he was Brock's man. If you took all the blacks out of the Steelhaulers you wouldn't have enough men left to get up a bowling league. He wasn't any stranger in the numbers parlors around town."

"That's a real coincidence, that is. A Negro who plays numbers." Disgusted to find that he was still smoking, Canada dropped the butt and crushed it out. The heat rising from the pavement billowed the cuffs of his trousers. Esther was sweating heavily. "Find out who Dupree hung out with," the inspector said. "I want the partner."

"We'll need a medium."

"Maybe not. Maybe he skipped town like you said. If so he left a trail."

"If we're going to take over all of Coopersmith's cases I hope he remembers us come Christmas."

"Christmas, that's the other side of the elections. Another country."

They had reached Canada's car. "Anything else?"

"Put the whole squad on the partner." Canada opened the driver's door; the handle was white-hot. "Meanwhile I think I'll go pay a visit on the Steel Behind the Steelhaulers."

Gallante unfolded himself from the passenger's seat of the Cobra, a tall, square-jawed, thick-necked man in blue gabardine who looked like a retired athlete gone into a successful business. Harry DiJesus, wearing tight Wranglers and a white see-through shirt that showed off his pecs, joined him on the sidewalk. The short-barreled .32 he carried when he wasn't doing heavy work made a clear outline in his right hip pocket. He narrowed his eyes speculatively at the holes in the Cobra's sheet metal. A garage connected with the Orr organization had managed to replace the rear window the day after the shooting but was waiting on a new trunk lid and door from Shelby before completing the repairs.

"Should've brought Max and Georgie along," he said.

"No, I know these people. They won't give us as much trouble if it's just two. If they think we're afraid to come here alone there's no telling how they'll react."

"Devlin's safe at home, I bet."

"Devlin pushes pencils."

They climbed the narrow rubber-runnered staircase next to the laundromat. No light showed under the door to the blind pig. Gallante's knock went unanswered. He inspected the luminous dial of his watch. 1:36. "They should be in there setting up." He tried the knob. It turned and the door opened.

DiJesus put a hand in front of Gallante and tugged out the .32. He went in ahead.

The room, like any other in a city at night, wasn't entirely dark. Light from windows in other buildings made swollen shadows in the quiet bar and gleamed fuzzily off the rows of bottles on the back shelves. DiJesus closed the door behind him noiselessly, leaving Gallante out on the landing, and moved away from it along the wall before hitting the light switch. An uninhabited room glared at him under the ceiling bulbs.

Staying close to the walls, he took five minutes working his way behind the bar and into the pool room, where the fixture suspended over the table bounced and swayed after he jerked its chain, splashing light up this wall and that. He was alone with the cues and secondhand music drifting from Twelfth Street. The hot stagnant air told him the windows had been shut for hours. A mirror inside the open door of the single bathroom reflected a sink and toilet as old as the building; otherwise it, too, was unoccupied.

He went back and admitted Gallante, who went straight to the bar and leaned over it to lift the White Owl cigar box from the shelf underneath. It was empty. He let it fall.

"Cleared out." DiJesus returned the revolver to his hip pocket. "I guess they spooked when they missed me."

"I wish I could believe that."

The killer blew into a glass, sniffed at a bottle of Jack Daniel's, and poured himself two inches. "The coloreds got no guts for gun stuff. Blades are more their speed."

"I didn't figure Springfield for your average colored."

"So you want to go into the saloon business?" DiJesus drained the glass.

"That's up to Patsy."

"Sebastian Bright and the rest'll fall into line now. Springfield was their leader."

"I guess."

"It's too bad. I wanted a shot at him bad."

"Go back to Vegas."

He helped himself to another inch. "Too hot there this time of year. I think I'll hang around for a little."

"Don't start anything." Gallante was looking at him. A window was at his back with the lights of Detroit scattered across it like dirty sequins.

"I get paid for finishing things, not starting 'em." He finished his second drink.

The two men came out of the door next to the laundromat and got into the Cobra. The engine growled to life and the car took off with a gasp of rubber. It was barely out of sight when Lydell fired up his Zippo, punching a hole in the shadow of the doorway he shared with Quincy. Quincy stepped out onto the sidewalk. The lights were still on in the second-story windows across the street.

Lydell blew smoke with a sigh. "Think they bought it?"

"Who knows how them people think?"

"I do. They all carry on like Rome never fell. They bought it all right. Ain't no way they could ever think it would go any different." He coughed and spat. The spittle hit the warm concrete with a crack. "Question is, what do we do now?"

"Nothing."

"Nothing?"

"For now."

"That's the trouble with doing nothing," Lydell said. "You never know when you're through."

Chapter 30

The reporter sent by Channel 4, a former J. L. Hudson's mens-wear salesman in his twenties who wore his hair and dressed like JFK, complained that he had landed the parade beat; Rick overheard him telling one of the technicians that he had covered a Negro funeral procession on the Fourth. The cameraman, a white-haired Wallace Beery type in a Hawaiian shirt and baggy-kneed slacks, groused that the sun was too bright and the shadows too sharp. The sound engineer, nineteen and covered with acne, snarled that he'd been rushed out of the station with only two reels of tape. They were the bitchiest crew Rick had ever encountered. He paced the sidewalk in the shade of the Fisher Building, ignored by the TV people, checking his watch every few seconds and ducking into the building periodically to call the office from a pay telephone. The security guards had begun to take notice of the young man in jeans and a gray work shirt with the tail out and the sleeves rolled above the elbows.

So far it was a disaster. One truck had vapor-locked on the Lodge Freeway, creating a backup from Howard Street to the Edsel Ford interchange, two others had been stopped by the police for minor traffic infractions and detained because their work orders were

incomplete—discount towing services, Rick was learning, didn't
save enough to offset the hassles—and most of the rest were late.
He'd hoped to line them up on Third and bring them *en masse*
around the corner and down Grand Boulevard between the erect
finger of the Fisher and the accordion construction of the General
Motors Building, but the scant four tow trucks he had waiting there,
with their crushed and wrinkled burdens suspended by their rear
axles from chains, suggested nothing more out of the ordinary than
a bad accident. He'd arranged for fifteen, down from the original
fifty because of the logistical problems involved. He'd already broken up two fistfights among the drivers, who had been waiting more
than an hour in the ninety-degree heat. Now a couple of them were
arguing spiritedly about whether Chester Goode or Festus Haggen
was the better sidekick for Marshal Dillon on *Gunsmoke*. Rick had
thought the jig was up twenty minutes into the vigil when a police
cruiser pulled up behind the last truck and two officers got out, but
the older of the partners remembered Rick from his Plainclothes
Division days and agreed, no questions asked, to hold off any more
inquiries pending the outcome. So far he had proven as good as his
word, Rick's first break that day. But it couldn't last, and anyway if
they didn't get rolling soon they would miss the Twelve O'Clock
News and the event would lose a third of its impact.

He wondered what had been so wrong with working part-time at
the Kwik-Pro Garage.

The young Kennedy look-alike approached. "What's the holdup?
I'm covering a Democratic fundraiser live at noon."

"Can you give me a half hour?"

"I can give you twenty minutes. As it is we're going to have to make
a flying run past the station to drop the stuff off for editing."

"I'll check on my people."

Inside the cool marble walls of the Fisher Building, Rick turned
his back on the guards and dialed the office. Enid answered.

"Anything?" he asked.

"I just got off the phone with five of the services," she said. "Four of them haven't had radio contact since the last call, but that truck on the Lodge is back on its way. Are we paying traffic tickets?"

"Tell them only if most of our players are here in fifteen minutes." He hung up.

He went out the Third Street exit, past the arcade of glassed-in shops and the parking lot, where the asphalt pulled at the soles of his shoes and the rows of stationary vehicles appeared to be losing their vertical hold in the heat ribboning up from the pavement. Horns were honking in the street. When he got there the tow trucks were lined up along the curb to the corner of Lothrop and beyond, sealing off traffic behind the Fisher; new red GMCs and old green Dodges and blue Fords with the names and telephone numbers of the services lettered neatly on the doors and rusting Internationals with wired-on license plates and fenders missing. Thirteen in all, the idling of their engines sounding like lions snoring in a pit. Each one had in tow a late-model General Motors car in need of body work: *Corpus delicti,* physical evidence of accidents foreordained the moment they left the plant.

As he walked around to the Grand Boulevard side to tell JFK Junior to get his people ready, Rick caught himself singing under his breath. "Seventy-six trombones led the big parade, with a dee-dee-dee-dum-dum-dum-dee-dee-dum. . . ."

Enid had a portable Sylvania on her desk with built-in rabbit ears extended almost to the ceiling and she and Pammie and Lee Schenck were gathered in front of it when Rick got back to the office. When he saw the young reporter onscreen he was afraid he'd missed it. Then he recognized the dining room of the Pontchartrain Hotel in the background and realized he was looking at the political fund-raiser. A well-known local lobbyist wearing a straw boater with WILLIAMS lettered on the red, white, and blue band had a hand on the reporter's shoulder and what looked like the start of a three-day drunk.

"Did they show anything yet?"

"Just a teaser." Enid straightened. She wore a violet silk suit and a floral-print blouse with an open neck that showed cleavage. "It came and went so fast you couldn't see anything. What *are* we going to see?"

"This for starters." He unfolded a citation for holding a parade without a permit and laid it on the desk.

"That's *all*? After all that advice I gave you about going limp when they carried you away?" Lee was disappointed.

"Maybe it'll come in handy some other time. I was too close to it to tell how it went. I about had a heart attack when the lead truck started coughing and sputtering in the middle of Grand. The gas gauge was laying on empty. But it made it through."

He looked at Pammie, who was absorbed in a commercial. She hadn't said ten words to Rick since Friday when she'd run out of the office clutching her poems. She had on shorts and a gray sweatshirt with the sleeves cut off at the shoulders. No more dresses.

"What did the police say?" Enid asked.

" 'Get these buckets of shit out of here.' Which I did, at about five miles an hour. It looked—"

Lee said, "Cool it." Speedy Alka-Seltzer's beaming face had been replaced by Ven Marshall's stern one. But the next story was a man-on-the-street interview spot gathering local reaction to Monday's march by Martin Luther King to the Chicago City Hall, where thousands of Negroes and whites had cheered as he taped a list of demands to the front door in emulation of his namesake, Martin Luther.

"There's a man," Lee said.

Rick said, "I wonder if he got a permit."

And then they were looking at the pasture-wide expanse of Grand Boulevard and the angled verticals of the General Motors Building, before which crawled a phalanx of trucks towing the carcasses of automobiles sacrificed on the altar of speed before safety. The angle of the shot made the procession appear to stretch on forever.

"Corvairs, Chevelles, Impalas, Toronados, Furies, Coupe de Villes," intoned the young reporter's voice from off-camera, deeper and more authoritative than it had sounded in person. "The top of the GM line, none of them more than a year old and all of them, according to a spokesman for the Porter Group who asked to remain anonymous, badly damaged in accidents that could have been prevented on the assembly line. Based on statistics gathered by the controversial organization of consumer advocates, each of the fifteen demolished cars in the parade represents sixteen hundred accidents annually. . . ."

"Where'd you get those figures?" Enid asked.

"Same place he got the other two cars," Rick said. "Thirteen's unlucky, so I included the no-shows. These TV people can't count."

". . . is not known whether General Motors Chairman James M. Roche, who was unavailable for comment, was in his office at the time of the demonstration," finished the reporter, now onscreen. "In front of GM World Headquarters, this is Robert Wicks, reporting for Channel Four News."

The anchorman came back on. "Who is Wendell Porter? Tonight at eleven, Channel Four examines the career of this modern-day David locked in a struggle with an industrial Goliath."

Even Enid cheered.

Lee disappeared into the kitchen and came back a minute later carrying a champagne bottle and four water glasses tucked in the crooks of his arms. "This has been in the fridge since *Hell On Wheels* went bestseller." He set the glasses down on the desk. "He had to go to Washington and we called off the party. It's Establishment, but what the hell."

They cheered again when he freed the cork. It dented the plaster in a corner of the ceiling and landed on the file cabinet. "Only a splash for you, Pammie," he said, wetting the bottom of the fourth glass. "You're a minor."

"Guess I always will be." Her eyes made brief contact with Rick's. Then she snatched up the glass.

Lee raised his. "Confusion to the enemy."

They drank. Rick looked at Enid. "To dinner."

"You forgot the terms," she said. "One favorable comment, in the form of a telephone call or a telegram, from someone in authority. That hasn't happened."

The telephone rang.

Chapter 31

The *Iocaste* was a converted navy minesweeper, stripped of armaments and painted white with jaunty red trim over the original battlewagon gray, but still martial-looking in its spartan lines and belligerent prow. A stiff breeze—the only one blowing within miles of Detroit on this blazing Wednesday in mid-July, wrinkled the aluminum-colored surface of Lake St. Clair and set smaller craft swaying, but the *Iocaste* sat like so much pig-iron in its slip while frustrated waves thudded its hull. In this, Canada thought, she was much like her master.

The inspector walked out on the pier carrying his jacket over one shoulder and stopped at the foot of the gangplank, wondering if he was supposed to ask permission to come aboard. He had not been on a ship or a boat of any kind since he'd returned from the Philippines. Finally he went up. A large young man in a blue suit blocked his path at the top. He had fair hair and the beginnings of a sunburn on his cheeks and forehead. Canada showed his badge. It had as much effect as the sunburn.

"It's a cop, Mr. Brock." The young man raised his voice without turning away.

"He's expected."

Canada followed the young man along a new teak deck to the stern, where the president of the American Steelhaulers Association was sitting in a deck chair with his ankles crossed and a glass in his hand. Brock wore a white cotton short-sleeved shirt, pleated khaki shorts, a long-billed fisherman's cap, and deck shoes on his bare feet. Small shoes, small feet. Canada wondered how a man could spend years double-clutching eighteen-wheel rigs and walking picket lines without pounding his feet as broad and flat as Swiss steak. The shoes were wearing through at the toes, the shorts and cap were dirty, the bill finger-marked and creased down the center, and the shirt was smeared with something that looked like old blood.

"Go find a movie," he told the young man.

"Sure, Mr. Brock?"

"I get along with cops. Now."

The young man started back toward the gangplank.

"Something with Dean Jones," Brock called after him. "He goes to see those old gangster shows in the art houses, thinks he's Mike Mazurki," he told Canada, sitting up to shake hands. His grip was a knuckle-buster, the result of union election campaigns rather than truck driving, which he hadn't done in decades. "Sit down, Inspector. In my work we do everything on our asses."

Canada moved an empty deck chair into the shade of the aft cabin and sat. The change of angle gave him a view of a man in his middle fifties starting to take on flesh over large biceps and thick hairy thighs and around his waist. He had a healthy-looking tan and his face was handsome in a broad, solid, American working-class kind of way. He looked as if he could still clear a bar with very little help.

"Thanks for the time, Mr. Brock. I know you're on vacation."

"Vacation, hell. I'm getting the old girl ready to take some board-room Hemingways up to Port Huron after salmon. They can't fish for shit but you'd be surprised what you can do with them once you get them out of their air-conditioned offices and into some real clothes. Neckties just cut off blood to the brain."

"I didn't know you fished." Canada was now sure it was fish blood on Brock's shirt.

"I grew up in Rouge, you kidding? If I ever tried to dip a worm in that water he'd've crawled back up the line and slapped my face. My doctor told me to find a hobby for my gut. Slug of milk? It's ice-cold." He indicated a pitcher full of white liquid on the folding table next to his chair. When Canada shook his head, Brock topped off his own glass. "Too young, I guess. My theory is everyone who grew up during Prohibition is fighting ulcers. We thought we had a special obligation to drink as much liquor as possible, and some of that stuff they were passing off as Canadian would eat a hole in a brass bucket. What's on your mind, Inspector?"

"I work for Jerry Cavanagh."

The union leader showed his bottom teeth. "Guess I shouldn't have sent Dan to the movies. You figuring to weight me down and drop me overboard or just leave me here for the gulls?"

"Of course I'm not here to shoot you."

"Don't act like it never happened. Well, it must be blackmail, then, because if it was a payoff he'd send a lawyer."

"What have you got against the mayor? Don't bring up that business about the city labor contracts; I don't buy it."

"I don't like him."

"You supported him the first time he ran."

"I hated Mariani worse. That was then. I can't stand the mick bastard. Let's leave it at that."

"I never thought I'd hear a politician say he wouldn't support someone just because he didn't like him."

"I'm not a politician."

"How long's it been since you ran steel?"

"Politicians lie for votes; I never did. I won't say I never lied. But not to the union. That kind of lie is like atomic fallout. You can duck it for a long time, but it's still waiting for you when you come out."

It was an opening, but Canada didn't step through it. The photograph Susan Niles had given him remained in his wallet. So far Brock had navigated the course of the conversation. Canada changed that by changing the subject. "Are you acquainted with a man named Curtis Dupree?"

"Sounds French."

He took the mug shot from the inside breast pocket of his coat hanging on the back of the chair and reached it over to Brock, who studied it.

"Well, he's not French." He handed it back.

"You don't know him?"

"Never saw him. What's he wanted for?"

"He belonged to the Steelhaulers."

"There are two million Steelhaulers. Do you know every cop in Detroit?"

"We pried this one out of the trunk of his car at Metro Airport last Friday. He had a thirty-eight slug in the back of his head."

"Then I guess I never will know him. What's Cavanagh's interest?"

"We're pretty sure Dupree was the wheel man in an attempt on the life of one of Patsy Orr's men last week."

"I don't know Patsy. I knew his old man, just to talk to. In the old days you had to know all kinds of people."

"I think you know him better than that."

Brock whisked away his milk moustache with a finger and set his glass on the table. "Why don't we step on the gas? We'll get there quicker."

"Frankie Orr wants to start a war between the local mob and the Negro numbers operations citywide. The Negroes would lose and while his son Patsy's recovering, Frankie plans to nail down the policy racket for himself. He couldn't very well arrange the contract through his son, and any connected operation he went to would run to the Commission, who would have Frankie hit rather than take the heat from a race war in Detroit. I think he went to his only other local contact who could set up something this big. That'd be you."

"I don't owe Frankie Orr anything."

"You owe him this boat and your office downtown and everything you've got on down to your skivvies. Everybody in town knows that except your biographer."

"Can everybody in town prove it? Can you?"

"I'm not here to prove anything," Canada said. "Dupree's partner the triggerman could, if he's still alive, but I don't need him. I brought everything I need to stop this war."

Brock watched him rummaging in his coat. "Thought you weren't going to shoot me."

Canada found his wallet, took out the snapshot, and handed it to the union leader.

"The whore," Brock said after a moment. "She was always taking pictures. You stopped noticing after a while."

"You have a good memory."

"It was the only time I ever met Bennett. The miserable son of a bitch is hard to forget." He turned it over and read the date.

"We tracked down the newspaper in the picture," Canada said. "Friday, May twenty-eight, nineteen thirty-seven. The day after the Battle of the Overpass. I guess a dead cockroach would have beat out Bennett in a union popularity contest that day."

"That was a UAW beef. That horse's ass Walter Reuther wouldn't have anything to do with me when I was working at Chrysler; thought I might snatch his goddamn presidency right out from under him. Would have, too. Anyway there wasn't any love lost between him and the Steelhaulers. I thought I could negotiate a separate deal with Ford's, but Bennett wasn't having any. The stupid bastard thought he'd won that war. My guess is you made copies." He gave back the picture.

"You should've grabbed the camera the minute it was taken."

"Where would she go with it? The press was on Bennett's side. Not that the picture means anything."

"The rank and file might not agree. When one union goes out they all follow. Solidarity."

"Bullshit. We fought each other as much as we fought the shops.

Every third man was a management spy, and half the scabs who drove trucks when the Steelhaulers went out were UAW men who'd been banned from the auto plants."

"That was then."

Brock filled his glass with milk and drank it off in a draft. But for that he seemed as unagitated as when Canada had arrived. "I've been around too long. I'm working with business-school graduates who don't know a gear box from a cigar lighter who keep telling me the history of the union I built. I always learn something new. Just yesterday one of them told me I ought to buy stock in one of the steel companies and run for a position on the board. It would give us a say in how the company's run, he said."

"Makes sense."

"My folks kept ducks and chickens during the Depression. Fox killed the hen and all but one of her chicks. That chick started hanging around with the ducklings, ate with them and followed the mama duck all over the yard with the others. One day it followed her down to the river and drowned. Forgot it was a chicken, see. No," he said, "you got to keep your ducks and chickens separate."

"Ever considered retiring?"

"And leave it to those whelps? In six months you couldn't tell it from General Motors."

"Except for the Mafia."

"They'll get their hooks into GM too. I've been fighting those guineas straight uphill since nineteen thirty-one."

"The strike at the Chrysler plant," Canada said.

Brock tilted his head back, taking his face out of the shadow of his cap. The sun found pleats there that the cameras missed. "You did your homework. I've still got a scar on my scalp where one of those headbusters sapped me. It didn't used to show."

"That was before they switched sides."

"They came around when everyone else did, including the papers. There's no money in losing."

"A race war's too high a price to pay for Frankie Orr's past support, Mr. Brock. It wouldn't stop with the numbers parlors."

"Don't go Pat Boone on me, Inspector. I was getting to like you. You wouldn't be here if your boss didn't want to be President."

"You don't have a picture. I do."

"It isn't evidence."

"Evidence is for lawyers. You know how it goes in politics. All you have to do is open a crack."

"I guess you didn't catch the news this morning. The union voted to kick into my re-election fund."

"The shop stewards voted. They vote the way the rank and file tells them to, and the rank and file hasn't seen this picture. Those business-school graduates you mentioned aren't alone. Half the present membership wasn't born when you were elected to head the local. They don't know how bad things were before you became national president. But they all know about Harry Bennett and the Battle of the Overpass. That's how it is with legends."

"What's your pitch?"

"The next time Frankie calls, you don't know him."

"If it was that easy, I mean, assuming he ever calls," Brock said, "there wouldn't have been any reason to deport him in the first place."

"If it were that easy I wouldn't need this picture for leverage. Taking orders from Frankie Orr or anyone isn't your long suit."

The union leader took off his cap, ran his fingers through his graying brush-cut hair, and put the cap back on. "I guess all this is off the record. Extortion isn't covered in the police manual."

Canada shrugged. He felt a confidence coming like cold metal against his spine.

"I always could bargain with Frankie," Brock said. "We both knew if he pushed too hard some of it would slop over into the papers, and after the stink that went up when Joey Machine bought the farm he treated headlines like the clap. Now it's like he doesn't care. You can't dicker with a man who thinks he's got everything to gain and nothing to lose."

"Can you hold him off ?"

"That depends on how long."

"Just through the hot weather. It's hard to get up a good riot when you're standing in snow ass-deep."

Brock spread his hands, an eloquent move on the part of someone who understood the magic of gestures. It was good enough for the inspector, who held out the snapshot.

Brock took it. "What about the copies?"

"I didn't make any."

"Risky."

"I didn't think so."

He tore it in half, then quarters. He put the pieces in his shirt pocket and patted it. "Wouldn't want to be arrested for polluting the lake. What about the mayor?"

"You can only buy so much with a picture." Canada rose.

"It'll be business as usual when I get back from Port Huron. From here to election time I don't plan to let up on him."

"He'll survive."

Brock shook his hand. "You fish?"

"Never cared for it."

"Too bad. Look me up if your tastes change."

Chapter 32

"**S**enator Hart called just before quitting time," Enid said. "I made an appointment for him to see Wendell Friday. At PG. That's the first time a politician has offered to come to him."

"What's that make, three?" Rick asked.

"Four, with Romney. That was just a courtesy call, so he can tell the press he's been in touch when they ask. But he's a Republican governor, and he was president of American Motors. He must have been swallowing bile the whole time."

Rick had never seen her so animated. They had had dinner at the Grecian Gardens in Greektown, a tough place to get a reservation since the notoriety of the Christmas list, but the only restaurant in town where Rick could be certain they wouldn't encounter any of his old police acquaintances; then gone to the Lafayette Bar to hear the Greek band. They had ouzo brought to their corner table, where Rick liked to watch the clear anise-flavored liquer cloud up when water was added. He was surprised when Enid drank hers straight. Ouzo was slightly less treacherous than the Viet Cong.

Orange light from the candle in the cut glass on the table crawled over her interesting bone structure as she watched the band getting ready for the next set. She had changed at the office into a ruby-colored silk dress with a V-shaped neckline that didn't plunge as far as the blouse she'd worn earlier, but that for some reason Rick found sexier. He poured more water into his drink. "What did Wendell say?"

"He was still in his meeting last time I called. I left a message for him to call me at my place after eleven." She looked at the thin gold watch on her wrist. "I assume we want to watch that special report on the news."

"I was going to ask your TV set or mine."

She let that slide. "Just because I didn't welch on our bet doesn't mean I've forgiven you for throwing dice with PG's future. You've only been with us a couple of weeks. What do you know about the years of work that made your little parade worth more than three lines in the police column?"

"My high school algebra teacher defined 'work' as an act of accomplishment," he said after a moment. "If nothing is accomplished, what you've been doing isn't work. All I did was kick the chocks out. You built the wheels."

"Everything you do and say comes down to wheels. I know the real reason you joined Wendell's Wonders."

He made his face expressionless. "I'm listening."

"You wanted a job where you could talk about cars all day without being told you're boring. You couldn't care less about politics. You haven't discussed them once since I've known you, but I could write a book about cars just from what you've told me."

"*Son of Hell On Wheels?*" His grin was genuine, fueled by relief.

"I went out once with a young man who loved old movies," she said. "The older the better. They were his whole life: *Citizen Kane, The Birth of a Nation, Stagecoach*—you name the picture, if it was more than twenty years old he could replay it scene by scene and recite the credits down to who catered the wrap party. It turned out his parents fought all the time when he was growing up and the only theaters he could afford to hide out in were the revival houses. The night before the morning his parents decided to file for divorce he saw *Anthony*

Adverse and *War and Peace* back to back. What were you hiding from?"

"No hiding. My father worked at Dodge Main. When he had enough saved up to buy a new Dodge on his employee discount he gave me his old Model A to fool around with. I was thirteen, and what I didn't know about cars would fill Cobo Hall. By the time I got that piece of junk back on the road and sounding like anything but a bucket of nails falling downstairs I qualified for master mechanic."

"Sounds like hell."

"To you maybe. I was in heaven the whole time. First day I took it out was the best day of my life. If it wasn't for gas rationing I'd have driven clear to Chicago."

The band started up, the manic strings banishing conversation. Enid looked at her watch again and jerked her head toward the door. He paid up and they left.

Above the lights of Greektown, the night was a narrow black shaft with stars punched out of it. A young man with a tattered beard and hair to his shoulders passed them, humming "Summer in the City."

Enid said, "There wasn't any gas rationing in nineteen forty-nine."

"Sorry?"

"I worked it out. If you're thirty now like you wrote on your application, you were thirteen in nineteen forty-nine. The war ended in forty-five."

"Whoops."

"How old are you?"

"Thirty-seven."

"You sold yourself short. You could've gotten away with twenty. On your looks, anyway. I suspected for some time you were older than you said. Why'd you lie?"

He told the truth. "I thought Wendell would be more likely to take on a kid."

"Thirty's no kid."

"It is from this side."

They stopped at the Camaro. "We don't have time to drive to the office and pick up my Mercedes," she said. "Would you come by and give me a lift in the morning?"

"I still don't have seat belts." He unlocked and opened the door on the passenger's side.

She climbed in, and this time he got to see her legs. "You can't be a fanatic all the time."

The house was in Highland Park, a brick colonial on a half acre with a car port and cedars in the yard. He parked in the port and she let them in the side door. They walked past an automatic washer and dryer and up a step into a kitchen full of stainless-steel appliances. It reminded him of the kitchen in a new restaurant.

"Was this your parents' home?"

"Yes. We had a cook but I let her go; I don't entertain much. This room always makes me feel guilty. I never learned to cook. I make a great pot of coffee, but you know that. Shall I?"

He said yes and leaned on a counter while she charged an electric percolator. "What's it like to grow up rich?"

"I don't have anything to compare it to. My parents argued about money, and I'm told that's universal. By the time I knew we were wealthy it was too late to take on airs."

"Any sisters or brothers?"

"None. You?"

"One sister. She left home before I got to know her. She's a grand-mother now. I guess that makes me a great-uncle, but I haven't seen her since our father's funeral. Her husband drives a Rambler."

"Do you judge everyone by the car he drives?" She plugged in the percolator.

"Pretty much. I paired you with the Mercedes in the PG parking lot the moment I saw you. The Volkswagen had to be Pammie's." He felt a twinge when her name popped out.

"What are you going to do about her?"

"I'm taking suggestions. No one ever had a crush on me before."

"Talking helps."

"Believe it or not, I thought of that. She won't talk back."

"An unnatural state for Pammie. Keep trying. That's a small room for the two of you to spend all day in not talking."

"I'd do better if she had a carburetor and a drive shaft."

"It's almost eleven."

They crossed through a foyer with a curved staircase and antique chairs against the walls and entered a parlor with a fireplace, chairs of lesser vintage but more comfortable design, and a color television in a cabinet with doors that swung to, concealing the screen. Enid opened the doors and turned on Channel 4. Credits scrolled over a freeze-frame of Bill Cosby and Robert Culp.

The fireplace mantel bristled with family photographs in gold frames. In one, a grave little girl wearing a winter coat and knitted tam with her hands hidden in a white fur muff posed between a couple in their late twenties outfitted for winter. A church building reared behind them.

"Blessed Sacrament." Enid saw him looking. "Easter, nineteen forty-six. I've never known it to fall on a warm day in Michigan."

"You don't look happy."

"I wanted to be Jewish like my Uncle Hans. He took the picture. My father converted to Catholicism when he married my mother and Hans was the only one on his side of the family who'd have anything to do with us after that. He was my favorite person in the whole world. That's him on the end of the mantel."

It was a portrait in an oval frame of a Satanic-featured young man in a jacket and glistening tie. He had a cocky smile and Enid's dark coloring. "Was he killed in an accident too?"

"Somebody shot him to death in his home in nineteen fifty. They never convicted anybody, but the police thought it was one of his old partners who was paroled from Jackson earlier that year. Uncle Hans was a bootlegger," she said. "He and my father used the money to buy real estate during the Depression."

"I wondered where the capital came from."

She adjusted the color on the set during a Chesterfield commercial. "I never knew anything about it until my uncle was killed and reporters started hanging around. He and my father didn't talk like the Bowery Boys or carry violin cases. Anyway, maybe that's part of why I use my money and time in support of a good cause like Wendell's. If my parents weren't killed in an accident I suppose I'd be working for the March of Dimes."

They sat through a Vietnam report, an anti-war demonstration in Washington, D.C., and a gushy announcement that Frank Sinatra and Mia Farrow were engaged to be married, before the parade story came on, virtually unchanged from the noon presentation. When it was over, Ven Marshall scowled at the camera and said, "Who is Wendell Porter? A look at the career of the self-described consumer advocate after these messages." Then a pump jockey in immaculate coveralls and a bow tie offered to put a tiger in their tank.

Enid left the room and came back carrying the percolator, two cups, and containers of cream and sugar on a flat tray. Rick moved some magazines so she could set the tray on the coffee table. Pouring, she said, "We seem to have upstaged the political fundraiser."

"One drunken politician looks pretty much like all the rest." He sat back with his cup. Her coffee could float stove bolts.

The report was a three-minute montage of clips, with an objective voice-over, of Wendell Porter fielding hostile questions at a press conference, being interviewed outside a courtroom during one of his many appearances as the defendant in a lawsuit, lecturing on auto safety at Wayne State, and signing copies of *Hell On Wheels* for a long line of customers at the downtown Hudson's, as well as a glimpse of Caroline, eyes unreadable behind rose-tinted glasses, steering her husband through a gang of reporters in a corridor of the City-County Building, trailing a string of "no comments." It ended with a shot of the closed door of James M. Roche's office in the General Motors Building and the information that when the board chairman had finally been located and asked for a statement on Wendell Porter's parade, he had asked, "Who is Wendell Porter?"

"Yes!" Enid jumped up and flipped off the set. She leaned back against it with her hands on the top. "First thing tomorrow I want you to call the station and ask for a print of that film."

"Even the last part?"

"Especially the last part. We'll show it everywhere Wendell appears, including before Congress. A month from now, 'Who is Wendell Porter' will be as famous as 'Let them eat cake.' "

"Are we going to behead Jim Roche?"

"Better than that! We'll castrate the fucker." She stopped and raised a hand as if to clap it to her mouth. Rick didn't know if she'd been embarrassed by the profanity or her choice of *castrate*. Had she detected a reaction to Caroline's use of the word when they were in her office?

Before he could cover, a telephone rang. She left the room. He poured himself more coffee. Instead of perking him up it had the curious effect of deepening his ouzo buzz. He wondered if it was doing the same for Enid.

She returned. Her eyes were bright. "That was Wendell. He saw the story on Washington television. NBC picked it up. I told him about all the calls. I haven't heard him this excited since his book went into a fifth printing. He loves my idea of showing the film."

"Did you remind him whose idea the parade was?"

She hesitated only a second, long enough for him to stand up. They met halfway. Her lips were softer than he'd anticipated, her body harder; she was all supple muscle and nails puncturing his shoulders.

"Right now," she said when they stopped for oxygen. "You saw the stairs?"

"What's the hurry? We've got all night."

"If I change my mind we'll avoid doing something we'll both regret."

"Let's go."

His memory of her bedroom was cashmere shadows and platinum light and stretched satin where the shadows broke. She smelled of blossoms remembered on the dark side of a hill. On the bed they melded and separated and found the stroke and rode the shadows and the light. It was better than expected, better than shoving the Camaro flat-out down a long straight stretch of smooth road.

"Hello?"

"You motherfucker."

"Excuse me?"

"You back-stabbing bastard. You piss-poor excuse for an under-cover."

"Oh, hello, Dan. What time is it?"

"I didn't call you up to give you the time, you son of a bitch, you candy-assed—"

Rick laid the receiver bottomside-up on the nightstand, switched on the lamp, and looked at the alarm clock. Just past four. He'd left Enid's house at two and had been asleep forty-five minutes. He sat up and picked up the receiver. Dan Sugar had paused for breath.

"What's on your mind, Dan?"

"I been trying to get you all night. Where were you?"

"My mother lives in Miami Beach. You sure don't sound like her."

"Did you know what Porter was planning to pull today—yesterday? Because if you didn't, what the hell is Roche paying you for?"

"I'm the one who thought it up."

The silence on the other end ran long enough for Rick to wonder if they'd been cut off. "Dan?"

"You mother-fucker, you back-stabbing bastard, you—"

"You're stealing your own stuff, Dan. I'm supposed to be working for Porter, in case you forgot. Would you like it better if I sat around in a trenchcoat and dark glasses, taking notes and snapping pictures with a little Jap camera?"

"Nobody said you had to make GM look like shit. Porter was doing that okay before you came along."

"If I thought it would work as well as it did I might've kept it to myself," Rick admitted. "Anyway I'm in solid with Wendell. He'd trust me with the key to his wife's chastity belt." He felt his second twinge that night. It could have been the ouzo. He had a headache like an icicle pressing against an exposed nerve.

"So what do we get for all this trust?"

Rick told him about Porter's letter to Enid. He could almost hear Sugar rubbing his hands. But his response was guarded.

"Sure she ain't burned it by now?"

"If she hung on to it long enough for Pammie to get a peek at it, there's no reason to think she got rid of it since. It probably means a lot to her. And there might be others."

"Get it. Get them."

"I'm working on it."

"Fuck working on it. Steal it."

"I'm an undercover, not a second-story man."

"You're a thief that got caught with his hand in the glove compartment of a fucking T-bird. Get your hooks on the letters and shoot them to me. We got to get our licks in before this parade shit blows up too big to pop."

"I'll get them," Rick said.

"Good." Sugar breathed. "Sorry about that thief crack, but you need to remember you ain't working for the cops now. You don't get title free and clear to no Z-28s for smelling like lime water and lavender."

Rick said he'd be in touch and pegged the receiver. He sat up for a while afterward, hoping for his headache to get worse. He'd earned it that night.

At least that.

Chapter 33

Sergeant Esther was eating breakfast at his desk, three frosted bearclaws and a half-pint of milk in a cardboard carton. He was using a target silhouette for a placemat. *Dark Shadows* howled and creaked on the TV set atop the file cabinet, without an audience. As Canada approached he chewed rapidly and swallowed.

"Our only lead on Dupree's partner just blew up," he told the inspector. "Nobody in town's seen this buddy of his for a week, but turns out he's been visiting his sister in Alabama since before the try on DiJesus. Alibi checks out. I'm starting to think Brock went outside the Steelhaulers for his trigger."

"Forget him. Dary still heading up the Detroit bureau of the FBI?"

"No, he retired in January. Burlingame's in charge now."

"Get him on the horn."

"Something? How'd it go with Brock yesterday?"

"Just get him, okay? I'm pulling the plug on Frankie."

"I thought you wanted him right where he is."

"I changed my mind. You ever change your mind?"

Esther lifted his receiver.

In his office, Canada went through the mail on his desk, then went through it again to see what was written on the envelopes. He didn't open any of them. He sat there for a while looking at nothing. Then he made eye contact with the photograph of the young men in jumpsuits hanging on the wall. He got up and went over and lifted it off its nail and leaned it in a corner on one end, back to front. It left a lighter rectangle on the painted wall.

The intercom buzzed. He flipped the switch. "Get him?"

"Not yet." The sergeant's voice crackled out of the speaker. "The commissioner just called. He wants to see you in his office."

"Now?"

"Yesterday."

Ray Girardin's office had windows looking out on Greektown and Beaubien, a quiet room insulated by carpeting and soundproofed panels and blinds that Canada always felt gave its occupant as clear and unobstructed a view of the crime situation in Detroit as the bunker had given Hitler of World War II. He respected the commissioner for his thirty years' experience as a crime reporter for the Detroit *Times* and had applauded his appointment, but the glare of public office had exposed him as an indifferent administrator and a poor leader; despite an inspired effort to introduce modern methods of law enforcement to a department whose basic structure had remained unchanged since Prohibition, the twelve precincts had deteriorated for want of decisive guidance from 1300 into a feudal state, with each commander operating his fiefdom independent of all the rest.

Girardin was standing in the middle of the office when the inspector entered, and came forward to shake Canada's hand. He was a slightly built man of sixty-three with thinning gray hair, swollen eyelids, and a face whose bone structure appeared to have disintegrated below the cheekbones, the flesh withering from there down to his oversize collar like a dried stalk. He resembled a cancer-stricken Edward Everett Horton. But his grip was firm.

"How are you, Lew? You don't look like you've been getting enough sleep."

"I'm fine, Commissioner." Canada's response was automatic to a question barely heard. He was looking at the mayor seated behind Girardin's desk.

"Officially, Jerry's not here," the commissioner said. "He's supposed to be addressing the city council, but it isn't the first time they've been kept waiting. He asked for this meeting because he's concerned about the racial situation."

"Racial situation?" Canada didn't approach the desk. Cavanagh had made no move to rise and offer his hand.

"Twelfth Street." The mayor looked grim; but then he always did. His round Black Irish face inclining toward jowls, receding dark hair, five o'clock shadow, and gimlet, up-from-under stare lent gravity to his relative youth. This together with his programs to end polarization among Detroit's black and white population had won him a whopping sixty-nine percent of the vote in his re-election. In Canada's opinion he had overestimated his political popularity when he decided to challenge former Governor G. Mennen "Soapy" Williams for the Democratic senatorial nomination; but Canada had served on the department through many administrations and had witnessed the ego-distorting qualities of the office at close range.

"We haven't had any serious problems on Twelfth Street," Canada said.

"Don't be deliberately obtuse, Inspector. You know what I mean when I say Twelfth Street. Shall I call it the Black Bottom, or don't you go back that far?"

He said nothing. Opposition charges of inexperience during Cavanagh's first campaign had left the mayor resentful toward anyone with a proven track record. It was one reason why he had gone outside the usual political circles and placed a newspaperman in the office of commissioner.

"I don't need to tell you how much of my reputation rests on my record in race relations," Cavanagh went on. "After Vietnam, the American people are most concerned about the Negro situation in urban areas. Nobody wants another Watts."

Girardin walked across the room and sat on the edge of the leather couch, one elbow resting on his knee, the reporter waiting to jump on the sparkling quote. "You wouldn't have known that the first day I walked in here," he said, looking at Canada. "Do you know what Gene Reuter said when I asked to see a copy of the department's riot plan?"

" 'What riot plan?' " Canada had heard about the exchange between Girardin and the superintendent whenever the subject had turned to race.

"Exactly. Manual of procedure for crowd control was written in nineteen forty-two. It included special provisions for the arrest and detention of persons of Japanese descent. The weaponry was even worse: A few shotguns and twenty-year-old canisters of tear gas stored with the motor oil in the municipal garage. I stayed up all night getting that stuff fixed."

"You've done a fine job, Ray." Cavanagh hadn't taken his eyes off the inspector. "In the event of a civil disturbance on the order of what took place last year in Los Angeles, this department is reasonably prepared to restore order. However, I prefer that order be maintained and that we prevent any such disturbance from taking place. What's the name of this person we discussed?" He looked at Girardin.

"Quincy Springfield. Numbers boss, runs a blind pig on Collingwood."

"Drugs?"

"Not that I know of. Lew?"

"He's clean there," Canada said. "The associate too, Lafayette. Gamblers don't cross that line very often. If you're worried about Springfield's beef with the Orr mob, that's just street stuff. It isn't racial."

"Any Panther involvement?" Cavanagh asked.

"Definitely not. He's not political."

Girardin said, "That's not current. What do you know about somebody calls himself Mahomet?"

"Springfield's errand boy. We've had him here a couple of times. Assault, disturbing the peace. Nickel-and-dime pops."

"This incident last Tuesday at the front desk, was that nickel and dime?" The commissioner's tone was unreadable.

"Somebody overreacted. As soon as I heard about it I had everyone released."

"Did you order Sergeant O'Pronteagh to return an unlicensed firearm to Springfield?"

That son of a bitch O'Pronteagh had made an end run. Now he knew where this was going. "I thought it advisable that we treat the thing as a non-incident."

"You're not on trial." Girardin sounded exactly like a judge. "We're just collecting facts. You should have reported to me, but we'll talk about that later. You should know that this Mahomet character has been spending quite a lot of time lately at the headquarters of the Black Afro-American Congress on Kercheval. It's a blind pig operated by Wilson McCoy. We've quite a file on McCoy," he told Cavanagh. "He was formerly connected with the Black Panthers and we think this BLAC group is a politically sanitized Panther front."

"It's news to me. About Mahomet, I mean." Canada wondered where the commissioner got his information. Was there another secret squad buried somewhere on the force that answered only to Girardin? Mentally he upgraded the department's epoch from feudal to Borgian.

"In the light of this revelation," the mayor said, "would you care to re-think your position on whether Springfield's fight with Patsy Orr is racially motivated?"

"It's a dangerous assumption, based on the fact that a man works at one blind pig and socializes at another. Your honor."

"Jerry. We're in the team locker room now." The mood lifted slightly. Cavanagh stood and came around the desk and leaned back against it with his arms crossed. Canada admired the way the mayor's gray flannel jacket didn't gap or buckle. "Ray tells me you blame outside agitation for the shooting on Cadieux last week. What's your evidence?"

The inspector was prepared for that question. If he mentioned Albert Brock's involvement, Cavanagh would jump all over it, maybe even go public to discredit Brock. Fresh politicians didn't understand the importance of deals. "The car was a neon sign," Canada said. "Why steal an old Cadillac unless you want to leave the impression Negroes were involved? Also it's plain they weren't out to kill this trigger DiJesus or they wouldn't have missed with two loads of double-O buck. It's what we call a Boston tea party."

"Why?"

"Blame it on Indians," said Girardin, who knew the language. "Who do you suspect?"

"Frankie Orr."

Cavanagh made a noise of disgust and circled the desk. "He's been in Sicily since Truman."

"He's back."

Girardin rose. "Here?"

"Puerto Rico. A place called the Hotel Pinzón. He's been there at least a month."

"How long have you known?"

"A little over a week."

"You're an independent son of a bitch, aren't you, Inspector?" The mayor was back to titles. "You're supposed to report directly to me."

"Your honor, at the time we found out I didn't know if it came under the squad's jurisdiction."

"You knew about Orr's connection with the Steelhaulers and Albert Brock."

"Sir, with respect, I know the men in my squad and I don't know the people in your office. If it leaked out that Orr was on U.S. soil he might spook and run home and we'd be back to square one. I was planning to report as soon as we knew what he was up to."

"So now you know. Or think you do."

"Any way you shake it up it comes down the same: Frankie's the only one who stands to gain from a policy war."

Cavanagh stuck his hands in his pockets and gazed down on Greektown. The Grecian Gardens was visible from the window, the first cloud on his administration's horizon; some of the columnists had begun to hint at a connection to his office. When he turned back, first names were restored. "None of this is evidence, Lew."

"Evidence is for convictions, your honor. Jerry. I'm saying it doesn't feel like what it looks like." It sounded lame. It always did when he discussed gut reactions with people who weren't cops.

"Unfortunately, the people of Detroit don't share that feeling," Cavanagh said. "I can't afford to. If you're right, and Orr is stirring up a hornet's nest for his own ends, the situation remains the same. Ray?"

The commissioner went behind the desk and sat down. He lifted a typewritten sheet off the blotter and held it out. "I think you'll recognize some of these addresses, Inspector."

The first one on the list belonged to the Morocco Motor Hotel on Euclid. He knew most of the rest, and as he took them in he knew a mounting horror unlike anything he'd felt since the jump that had placed him in enemy hands in 1944; the sensation, like a cold fist clenching his entrails, of a tragic mistake in the making. "Blind pigs and dope houses," he said.

Girardin said, "I'm placing Motor Traffic and the Tactical Mobile Unit at your disposal, but don't call in the commandos unless you need uniformed backup, and for God's sake don't order Mounted without notifying me first. The last thing we want to do is look like Cossacks. I want a staggered pattern of raids, Saturday nights mostly between four P.M. and midnight when manpower is at the maximum, but not *every* Saturday night, so they'll be kept guessing. Now, that's not after hours, so there will be no liquor law violations except in cases where there's no permit to sell. Concentrate on known felons. I don't care if the arrests don't hold up, but don't take anyone in unless he's in possession of dope or a concealed weapon. These aren't rousts. And I don't want the switchboard jammed with complaints about unnecessary force or racial epithets on the part of the arresting officers. Two of those against the same officer is an automatic suspension. Oh, and if you do require backup, ask for black officers. That goes without saying."

"They'll riot."

The commissioner shook his head. "I've studied procedure in the Watts disturbance inside out, and most of the tactical errors had to do with misguided attempts to mollify the rioters, such as withdrawing from the scene once the trouble started in hopes the anger would burn itself out. Go in fast, avoid physical contact as much as possible, and get out with your prisoners before the reaction sets in. Make it look routine."

"We'll continue the sweep through August," Cavanagh said. "The strategy is to keep the agitators from settling down and gaining a following through the hot weeks, which is when these things boil over. The Michigan winter is our strongest ally."

"You don't understand these people, Mayor. They've been dealt off the bottom for a long time and they're just waking up to the fact that they're no longer a minority, not on Kercheval and along Twelfth. They don't need a tent meeting to get up a good mad. Riots aren't planned."

"Our sources say different." Girardin folded his hands on the blotter. "Wilson McCoy and this golden-throated fellow Mahomet have been exhorting anyone who will listen to secure weapons and go to war with whitey. They aren't singling out the Sicilians."

"What sources?"

"The usual. Paid informants, addicts busted for possession trying to deal their way out of custody before withdrawal. You know the animal."

"I know they're unreliable. They'll say anything you want to hear for the price of a lid. You have to know how to interrogate them if you're going to get anything worth using."

"I think there are others who are as qualified as you," the commissioner said stiffly. "I'm giving you this detail because of your experience and because you've been in on the situation from Day One. You can turn it down, but I can't think of anyone better equipped to handle the O'Pronteaghs in the ranks."

Suddenly Canada wanted out of that cotton-wrapped room. It was beginning to remind him of the nursing home where his Uncle Herman sat day after day with only his clear blue eyes moving in the withered skull; a place where dead men waited for the waiting to end.

He folded the sheet of paper and put it in his inside breast pocket. "When do you want me to start?"

"This coming Saturday, unless you need more time. You're the driver." Girardin grasped his hand. "Thanks, Lew. My first editor at the *Times* told me a great editor was one who could claim he had one reporter he could count on. That goes for police chiefs and cops. I'm a great police chief."

Cavanagh gave him the single-pump politician's handshake. "Good luck." Humming, he turned back to the window. Canada was out of the room before he recognized the tune as the mayor's favorite, "The Quest," from *The Man of LaMancha*: "To dream the impossible dream . . ." Rumor said he planned to use it in his presidential campaign.

On his way from the elevator to the seventh floor squad room, the inspector stopped at the vending machine in the hall and invested thirty-five cents in a pack of Camels. From April 1961 to last week, when he had watched them bag up Curtis Dupree's decomposing remains at Detroit Metropolitan Airport, he hadn't smoked so much as one cigarette. Since then he had gone through a carton.

Chapter 34

Of Wilson McCoy, Quincy Springfield had said, "Wilson ain't pissed because he's black. He's pissed because he's an asshole and everybody knows it." Lydell Lafayette had added that on five minutes' acquaintance he was ready to practice discrimination against McCoy "with a fry-pan upside his head." Now they were seated with him at the card table in the little utility room off the basement where McCoy sold drinks from 2:00 A.M. until dawn.

The block, bounded by Kercheval and Pennsylvania, was crowded with single- and two-family houses separated by strips of brown grass scarcely wide enough for a man to walk on without brushing against a wall on either side. The boards were parched and paintless and in the daytime old people sat on the sagging porches looking as bleached and gray as the horsehair sofas and overstuffed chairs that had grown too shabby for even the dark cramped living rooms and been exiled.

The house belonged to McCoy's mother, a nearly deaf woman of sixty-five who slept each night through believing her son worked nights waxing the floors at Felician Academy High School, a job he'd been fired from nine months earlier after an electric typewriter and a hundred dollars in staples and stationery disappeared from the office during his shift. At twenty he was the last of eleven children still living at home, a slat-thin, unlikely-looking Black Panther alumnus with a sunken chest, a straggly Fu Manchu moustache and chin whiskers, and an enormous Afro with a black beret clinging to one side at all times like moss on a boulder. Tonight he was wearing a dirty pinstripe vest over no shirt and bell-bottom jeans that looked as if they'd been urinated on by the Pistons bench. Quincy suspected the Panthers had turned him out for reasons of hygiene.

"You sure this is accurate?" McCoy dropped ash from his cigarette on the sheet of ruled notepaper in front of him and tried to brush it off. His hand was oily with sweat and he left a muddy smear on the diagram. The room had no ventilation.

"I drew it myself. Been there a hundred times." Quincy used his finger for a pointer. "This here's the express. It stops only two places, the ground floor and forty-three."

"Looks too easy."

"Well, there's security, and people going in and out all the time."

"Fuck the people. We need to know how many guards."

"Easy to get. What kind of guns you need? We got a connection."

"Full auto."

"Noisy."

"What we want," McCoy said. "Louder the noise, less pain-in-the-ass heroes we got to deal out. Plus we might not have time to play Annie Oakley. Spray and run."

"I don't want no bystanders hit."

"No big deal, blood. That time of day downtown, all's we hit is white meat."

"Hey, I ain't mounting no crusade for the fucking race. I'm just trying to stay alive."

"Okay, man. Everything's cool." Backpedaling. Quincy seemed to be the only man, black or white, whom McCoy feared to cross.

Lydell coughed; or maybe it was a laugh. The cough had become such a constant that Quincy never noticed it unless a third party expressed annoyance. The loss of weight was now unmistakable, and lately Lydell had complained of a sore back. He had taken to carrying a handsome walnut stick with a gold knob to help him get up and down. But he refused to see a doctor. The man who had escalated a few bar-splinters in his hand and wrist to the level of a Purple Heart now dismissed obvious serious illness as simple exhaustion. And he was smoking more than ever.

McCoy showed no irritation at the persistent coughing. He was the most perfectly self-absorbed individual Quincy had ever met. Quincy had heard somewhere that McCoy had been allowed to sleep in the same bed with his parents until age fifteen, at which time his sixty-two-year-old father had left home to move in with a waitress and part-time prostitute who lived down the street. After that, according to the rumor, Wilson had gone on sleeping with his mother. A few months later the father and his mistress were found shot to death in the bedroom of their apartment. The motive was officially recorded as robbery, but the police couldn't explain why the thief would have reloaded his revolver twice and emptied it three times into the couple on the bed. Wilson and his mother were questioned, but the murder weapon never turned up and the case remained open, as did so many others in neighborhoods like Kercheval.

"How many men you going to use?" Quincy asked.

"How many you want? We can go in with a dozen and cover all the exits."

"Too flashy. Cops might not spend too much taxes looking for whoever offed a bunch of thugs, but if we rub their noses in it they dog us into the ground."

"We can do it with three. Somebody got to cover your innocent lily-butt bystanders."

Their conversation was wrapped in the whooshing and thudding of the old gas water heater in the corner and a clatter of voices and music from the basement-turned-saloon outside, where a radio played straight Motown for the drinkers and dancers. When the noise swelled suddenly, McCoy leaned back in his chair and opened the door.

"Mahomet," he said. "That boy draws excitement like a knuckle-bone draws flies."

Through the opening the three watched Mahomet working his way through the brightly clad customers swaying on the linoleum and sitting on the sofa and chairs, pausing here and there to shake hands and flash his white grin, as brilliant as Sebastian Bright's in the reflected light of his suit. He wore white all the time now, even when he wasn't speaking; people who had never seen or listened to him recognized him on the street by his wardrobe and reputation. Behind him, dressed in dark suits and spread black collars like a rack of eight balls, trundled the exaggerated musculature of Mighty Joe Young, the two Bongo Brothers, and Anthony Battle, poor dead Congo's friends from the World Wrestling Guild. As bodyguards they managed somehow to look even larger than they were without dwarfing the compact Mahomet. It was a group calculated to turn heads away from the scene of a multiple accident.

"Looks like somebody done left Pat Boone in the oven too long." Lydell, who had developed a reluctant respect for Mahomet during the scuffle at 1300, still didn't like him.

The newcomer stopped outside the open door to the utility room. Hanging back a pace, the quartet of wrestlers stuck out four feet on either side of him.

"Quincy. Krystal told me at the apartment you were here." Mahomet seemed to be waiting for him to rise and approach.

Quincy, who unlike Lydell was more amused than irritated by his former inmate's ascent from jailbird to rib-joint messiah, stayed seated. "You spellbinding tonight?"

"Not tonight. I came to find out if you heard about Gidgy."

"Gidgy stays out of the news."

"That's changed. Cops hit the Morocco a little while ago. They arrested six for possession. One of them was the proprietor, the radio said. Isn't that Gidgy?"

Lydell put out his cigarette in a puddle of melted ice on the table. "They wouldn't take Gidgy. Gidgy's got a connection."

"I'm just telling what I heard."

"Where'd they take him?" Quincy asked.

"Police headquarters."

"Shiiit." Lydell clamped a fresh Kent into the holder and lit up.

"Gidgy was getting us our guns," Quincy told McCoy.

"Bail him."

"That ain't what I'm worried about."

"Think the cops know?"

"We only know one man likes to hear himself talk," Lydell said. Mahomet said, "It wasn't me."

"Fucking white police state, that's what we got here." McCoy studied the crude upraised fist tattooed on his left bicep. "We ought to go out and take over some stores, bring the TV people down here and tell 'em what's what."

Lydell grinned, ghastly in his emaciation. "Shiiit. You been talking about going out and taking over stores ever since I know you. Why don't you start one of your own?"

"They say who done the raid?" Mahomet shook his head. Quincy got up and peeled the back of his shirt away from his skin. "I don't like Gidgy getting took down. Wasn't no lieutenant from Vice called that."

"Mayor wants to go to Washington," Lydell said. "Elections fuck everything up."

McCoy folded the diagram sheet lengthwise twice and stuck out the flat tube. "Want to scrub?"

"Just get your people and go over that floor plan."

"It cost you. Where you going to get it now you're out of bidness?"

"How much to start?" Quincy produced a roll of hundreds.

McCoy combed his beard with his fingers. "Thousand. No, fifteen hunnert. That splits better three ways."

Quincy counted the bills onto the table. When McCoy reached for them, Quincy banged the heel of his hand down on top of the stack. "I hear them talking about this in the alley, I'm coming back."

"You won't hear."

"Let's split, Lydell."

"I don't think so."

"Quit fucking around."

Lydell's hand was clenched on the knob of his stick. He was still grinning. "Nobody's fucking nobody, bro. I can't get up."

Chapter 35

For two weeks after the parade, everyone at the Porter Group was kept busy.

Enid sorted the telephone messages, letters, and telegrams into her three *I* files: Important, Investigate, and Imbecile, and arranged for camera crews from Channels 2, 4, and 7 to be present when a smiling Wendell Porter handed a check to a nervous clerk in the City-County Building made out in the amount of his fine for conducting a public demonstration without a permit and creating a traffic hazard. Rick considered the second charge ironic.

Porter met for an hour in his office with Senator Philip Hart, agreed to see him next month in Washington to discuss an appearance before a special Senate subcommittee on automobile safety, and took Hugh Downs of the *Today* show on a tour of the Farm.

Lee Schenck filled one file with articles about Porter clipped from automotive journals published since the parade and started another. He had been working on the first file for more than a year.

In Grosse Pointe, Caroline Porter negotiated a thirteen-week contract with Kaiser Broadcasting in Southfield for a weekly ten-minute consumer advocacy program to be hosted by Porter on Channel 50.

Pammie ran errands.

Rick performed a telephone survey in the greater metropolitan area to find out how many people were aware of the Porter Group's efforts and whether they supported or opposed them. So far it was running forty percent favorable, with thirty percent—auto workers, mostly—against and another thirty percent declining to comment or professing ignorance of Wendell Porter's existence. Enid said, "If you asked half of them who's President, they'd answer Eisenhower."

On Saturday, July 23, when Channel 4's three-minute biography of Wendell Porter was shown to the Lions Club just before Porter spoke, the assembled members laughed loudly when James M. Roche was quoted as asking, "Who is Wendell Porter?"

Enid ordered five thousand bumper stickers with the question emblazoned in red capitals inside quotation marks, to be given out wherever Porter appeared.

Wednesday afternoon, Rick took a break from the telephone and wandered out into the entryway, where Enid sat at her desk slitting envelopes with a copper letter-opener with a handle shaped like a Corvette; a souvenir of the 1965 Detroit Auto Show. She snapped open a letter typed on heavy bond, read it swiftly, and handed it to Rick without comment. It was from a writer named Baedecker, requesting permission to interview Porter for a proposed biography.

"I've seen that name." Rick placed the letter on the desk.

"He wrote the authorized biography of Albert Brock. Fawning tripe. But maybe it's time someone fawned over Wendell."

"I'm glad it's working out. I like Wendell."

"Everyone does," she said. "Well, forty percent of everyone. A month ago they'd never heard of him."

He watched her open another envelope. "We haven't had a chance to talk in a couple of weeks."

"Talking isn't doing." She made a face at the letter, opened her deep drawer, and stuck it in the crackpot file.

"Doing is what I want to talk about," he said. "Specifically, what you and I did two weeks ago. Are you free for dinner?"

She resumed slitting. "Tonight I'm attending a meeting of the Detroit chapter of the D.A.R."

"I didn't know you were a member."

"My mother was. Last time I hit them up for a donation they were polite. They sent me an application to join. This time they called me. I figure they're good for a couple of thousand. More, if they're courting me to get Wendell to speak at their next convention."

"Can we go out for a cup of coffee this afternoon?"

She glanced at her watch. "I'm due at Porter Associates in half an hour. Caroline thinks General Motors is going to drop their suit and she wants me there when their attorneys call." She looked at him the same way she had looked at the watch. "Let's go up to Wendell's office." She put down the letter opener.

The room upstairs had been tidied since his last visit, the furniture dusted and the books returned to their places on the shelves. It was as if Porter in his new fame had decided he no longer had to pose as a man who didn't want celebrity; or maybe it was Enid making subtle changes in his image. Rick's small exposure to the eminent had caused him to wonder how much of what he admired or hated about certain public men had been manufactured by their women.

Enid assumed her favorite pose, leaning back against the desk with her ankles crossed. She had on a pale pink jersey top with a red pleated skirt and penny loafers, an outfit that made her look very young. She lacked only cotton socks and a plastic hairband to be taken for a cheerleader. "Wendell likes you," she said. "Not just because of the parade idea. He likes to work with people who aren't afraid to argue with him. He says that's what keeps a zealot from becoming a fanatic."

"I like him too. I said that."

"I love him."

He made himself comfortable on the Victorian couch. He hoped it made him look less like an interrogator.

"Not in that way," she said. "Oh, maybe once. Definitely once. I love him because he's a decent man, no kind of movie hero, who believes in what he's doing without setting himself up as the Way and the Light. Do you know how rare that is?"

"I'm more interested in hearing about the once."

She turned up a palm. "It's not exactly unheard of for a man and woman who spend a lot of time together in a common cause to fall in love. Especially when one of them is trapped in a cold marriage, not that he ever complained; it's been profitable for both of them and they went into it with their eyes wide open. But it's never enough.

"What happened ended months ago," she went on. "We agreed to end it because of what was at stake if the press found out about it. Thank God we were discreet. I didn't even know Caroline suspected until that little cat fight we had in her office. Was that when you caught on, Sergeant?"

He had started to form a response when he realized what she'd called him.

"If we're bestowing rank now, I think Lee should be sergeant," he said carefully. "He's got seniority."

"Sergeant Amery, wasn't that your title when you were with the Detroit Police Department?" She placed her hands behind her on the edge of the desk, her knuckles clenched. "You must have been a good cop. I didn't suspect anything until you made that age slip, and even then it didn't bother me until after we—until later. That's when I started working on Pammie. It didn't take long to find out she told you about that letter."

He hadn't budged from the couch. "How'd you find out I was a cop?"

"I had you investigated. It was easy. You should have used a phoney name, but I suppose that leaves you open to more slips. Once the detective found out you'd quit your last job and moved to a better apartment I knew you'd found a job that pays more. There's only one other kind of work you're qualified for, and half the personnel in security at GM are former police officers. Would you care to save PG the expense of further investigation and admit you're a corporate spy?"

"I prefer 'undercover,' " he said.

"I'm sure you do, you son of a bitch."

He got off the couch. "It's just a job, but I guess I can't make you understand that. I was at low ebb when it came along and Wendell Porter didn't mean any more to me than King Farouk."

"I'd be interested in reading the job description. I'm surprised they're not lined up all the way down Grand Boulevard hoping for openings."

"What happened at your place wasn't planned. The dinner was, but that wasn't. And it had nothing to do with getting my hands on the letter."

"I got as much out of it as you did. I'm not a heroine in a Faith Baldwin novel, I don't give a damn about my virtue. But when you screw Wendell you're screwing a million people you don't even know and never will, because that's how many people will die this year because the cars they're riding in are rolling death traps."

"Don't think I haven't thought about that. I've been thinking about it a lot ever since Wendell ran into those sandbags at the Farm. I didn't come up with that parade idea just to get in solid with him."

"Bullshit."

"Why lie now?"

"It's what they pay you to do," she said. "But it backfired, mister. People are listening to what Wendell has to say, and they know it's more important than who's saying it and what he does when he isn't out testing cars or scratching for attention."

"If that's true, you've got nothing to lose."

"You're right." She produced a ring of keys from the pocket of her skirt, went behind the old desk, and inserted one in the top drawer. She rummaged a moment, then withdrew a packet of envelopes tied with a piece of cord and held it out across the desk. "Take them."

"What are they?"

But he knew what they were. He recognized Porter's scrawl on the top envelope and the address.

"Eight letters. I got them all in the space of twelve days; I don't know where he found the time. There's enough here to nail us both in divorce court, if Caroline wanted a divorce. I doubt she will now that the Porter Group is picking up speed. I gave them back to Wendell when we broke it off. I watched him put them in this drawer and lock it. He should've burned them, but I knew he wouldn't. Go ahead, take them. Publish them. This is nineteen sixty-six. Everybody's into fucking."

"Why are you giving them to me?"

"To prove to you and General Motors and this whole goddamn one-wheel town that auto safety is coming and nobody can stop it. Not with nine-and-a-half-inch drums and certainly not with a bunch of starry-eyed scribbles. Wendell Porter's just a man, he can be destroyed. But you can't stop this thing that's started."

"This is what you had in mind when you invited me up here, isn't it? You didn't just decide to do it."

"I'm sorry I can't give you dinner too," she said.

He took them.

Something went out of her eyes then, like a light going out in a window just as he was coming up the walk. He had a sudden wild urge to return the letters. But he knew even if he did the light wouldn't come back on.

In the parking lot he sat for a full minute before starting the Camaro. The packet of letters rested on the passenger's seat. Finally he turned over the engine and pulled out.

He drove down the straight, smooth shotgun barrel of his thoughts, not paying attention to anything outside, trusting his hands on the wheel and his feet on the pedals to guide him scratchless through the physical world. The yelp of his tires as he stopped at a sign jerked him out of the barrel and he looked around at an unfamiliar neighborhood of horizontal houses and new trees planted in twin straight rows. The four lanes and long stretch of pavement ahead and behind, unbroken by curves or angles as if it had been laid out with a T-square, told him he was on Woodward, somewhere north of Highland Park. He didn't remember leaving Jefferson and the route didn't lead to his apartment. Freed of thought, his hands and his feet had headed toward Mrs. Hertler's house and his old room.

A horn blatted behind him and a car pulled out into the inside lane to pass. When he stopped at the sign the driver glared across at Rick, then smiled. After a beat Rick recognized him, the long black hair pushed back behind his ears, the mirrored glasses. The black Mustang confirmed it. He was the young man Rick had drag-raced on Woodward the day he had learned that he would have to give up his room and use of the candy-apple red GTO to Mrs. Hertler's son. A thousand years ago.

The young man slid his glasses down his nose and looked over them at the silver Camaro, frowning appreciatively. Then he slid them back up, showed his teeth, and gunned the Mustang's engine.

Rick flipped on his indicator and turned right, leaving the black car grumbling at the sign. On the way back to his apartment he stayed under the speed limit and obeyed all signs and traffic signals.

Chapter 36

Quincy found Lydell's new room at Detroit Receiving by tracking the music all the way from the nurses' station. Lydell was propped up in bed with his eyes shut and his hands folded on his stomach. He looked like a corpse. On the TV mounted near the ceiling Bugs Bunny was giving the Tasmanian Devil a nervous breakdown, but in mime; there was no room for any sound but the Supremes shouting "Itching in My Heart" from the transistor radio on the bedside table. Quincy picked it up and dialed it off.

Lydell opened his eyes, saw Quincy, and grinned. His friend was getting used to his resemblance to a skull when he did that. "Hey, bro. That there's my life support."

"When I brought it here I didn't think you was going to use it to drive out cockroaches," Quincy said. "The nurses was doing odds and evens to see which one was going to get to throw it out the window and you after it when I come along."

"You should of let them. Maybe that Shannon'd win. She likes me."

"She the one with the tits?"

"They all got tits; that's why they call them nurses. Last time she give me a sponge bath I tried to impress her, but I think they put saltpeter in my IV."

Quincy pointed his chin at the curtain dividing the dim room. "Who's next door?"

"Search me. I think he died."

"How's the food?"

Lydell lifted a hand with a flexible tube taped to the underside of the wrist. "I'll ring for a straw and you can try it yourself."

"Guess I wasn't paying attention to what I was saying."

"No good, man. *One* of us got to listen."

"Krystal says hello."

"That's nice. She never said it when I was around."

"Well, you know Krystal."

"Too short. How's the old lady?"

The woman Lydell boarded with had been too stiff with arthritis to come visit. "The joints, you know." Quincy shrugged.

"I bet she been sleeping with that hot water bottle. I told her that wet heat just makes it worse."

"She says she'll be off her butt to cook you kidneys when you get out. She says they're your favorite. I didn't know that."

"I ain't getting out."

"Want me to open them blinds? View from up here's better than what you had on three."

"You bring the cigs?"

"Now, what you want with them? They're what put you in here."

Lydell grunted in disgust, rummaged in the drawer of the table, and fell back. "C'mon. They only put me to sleep so's they can sneak in and take 'em away."

"Ain't you dying fast enough?"

"Dogs. The boy went and said the word."

Quincy took the pack of Kents out of his shirt pocket, opened it, and gave him one. "I never knew you to just up and roll over." He held the match.

The smoke came out in a sigh. Lydell put his head back against the window. "I seen about a thousand numbers come up. I figure mine's past due."

"Doc says it's operable."

"He tell you what they got to take out?"

"Well, there's always craps."

Lydell grinned, puffed, and plucked a shred of tobacco from his lower lip. He frowned. "Some son of a bitch stole the jade holder my daddy give me."

"You won it off Joe Petite on three straight throws."

"My daddy'd of give me one like it if he didn't run off. Hear from Wilson?"

"Too early."

"I see on TV the cops hit Beatrice Blackwood's place."

"She made bail. No big thing."

"Three raids in two weeks. I figure the cops know. That Wilson's all mouth and no balls."

"If that was the case he'd be in jail all the time."

"Maybe that's how he stays out."

"They ain't arrested me," Quincy said. "No reason. For just about the first time since I can remember I ain't doing nothing against the law."

"How's it feel?"

"Not as bad as I thought."

"I hear once you get used to it you don't never want to go back."

"That's cornholing."

"I never done that either."

Quincy stuck his hands in his pockets. "I'm thinking maybe I been wasting my time with numbers. I'm thinking maybe Mahomet's on to something with this civil rights thing."

"Forget that racket. The money's for shit and the cops bust sticks on your head."

"I ain't thinking of making money at it," Quincy said. "Didn't you feel nothing at all when the police was slapping you and Mahomet around?"

"I felt a cop's arm across't my throat and my arm getting busted."

"I don't know, Lydell. You and me we always laughed at Wilson

McCoy and that bunch, marching and throwing bricks and getting the shit beat out of them for no money. Maybe they been right all along. Not about what they been doing, but why they done it. Maybe change is coming."

"Take a hot bath and forget about it."

"No, really. I been studying on it a lot lately."

"Don't turn Christer on me, Quincy. You're all I got." Lydell held out the cigarette. "You better put that out now and find me a nurse. I ain't feeling too good."

Quincy got one from the station, a small dark woman of about thirty with a nice shape, and waited in the corridor while she went in. A white man in his fifties shuffled past in paper slippers and a checked robe, using his IV stand as a walking stick. He had a little hole in the white gauze wrapped around his throat, and from time to time he inserted the filter end of a burning cigarette in the hole. Smoke blew out.

Quincy felt heat between his fingers, looked down, and saw he was still holding Lydell's Kent. He dropped it quickly and mashed it underfoot.

He felt conspicuous. He was wearing his chalkstripe double-breasted over peach silk. Suddenly he was convinced he looked like a pimp. He wanted to go home and change clothes, but he hadn't a gray suit or a white shirt to his name.

The nurse came out. She had large chocolate-brown eyes. "Someone's been smoking in there."

"Sorry."

"You'd better finish your visit. That sedative will take effect in a few minutes."

"Thanks. You Shannon?"

She put a hand on her hip. "Now, what's that boy been saying about me?"

"He'd rather be kicked by you than kissed by Diana Ross."

"One of you lights up in that room again he'll get his wish. You, too. I've carried around bigger men than you."

"I'll tell him."

"I already did." She touched his arm, then walked away down the hall.

Lydell was lying flat with the TV off. From the doorway, Quincy noticed for the first time that his friend was going bald in front. He hadn't seen him often without his hat. Quincy approached the bed. "I see what you mean about that Shannon. A man could get took care of by worse."

"You ought to see what I get at night."

"Cuter than Shannon?"

"Like Moms Mabley."

"Want me to bring you anything next time?"

"Pack of Kents."

Quincy rested his hands on the bedrail where other hands had worn the white enamel down to bare metal. "You got any ideas at all about why you and me are friends?"

"You used to wail the shit out of the big kids when I couldn't talk my way clear."

"That's why I'm *your* friend. How come you're mine?"

" 'Cause you're too big, and you're uglier than you are big. I bet Krystal puts a bag over her head too just in case yours comes off."

"You don't know, do you?"

"No."

"Me either."

Lydell closed his eyes. Quincy was about to leave when they opened again and turned his way. "What's that you said once't about a Viking funeral?"

"I don't recall it."

"Sure you do."

"It was in *Beau Geste*," Quincy said. "When Gary Cooper and his brothers was kids in the movie they thought that was the best way to go out, burning in a boat cast adrift on the water. That's what his brothers done to him in the end when he got killed. It didn't mean nothing. I was just talking to hear myself."

"Think you can fix up something like it for me?"

"In twenty or thirty years, when it's time."

A hand too bony to support Lydell's World Series ring closed on one of Quincy's. "No shit, Quincy. This here's Lydell. We went in together on our first whore."

"Man, she was ugly."

"First whores is supposed to be. I ain't much for water. A fire'll do. Make it kind of big, huh?"

Quincy laid his other hand on top of Lydell's. "I'll burn down the town."

"Shiiit." Lydell grinned and went to sleep.

Chapter 37

The little man behind the counter was getting to be a rarity in Greektown, an immigrant who didn't go home to the suburbs after dark. His scalp glittered in the fluorescent light through curly hair gone the pink of his skin and the weight of his moustache seemed to be pulling his flesh away from the bone. His eyes, one of them cataracted, looked a question that through the years he had pared down to no words at all.

"Ouzo," Rick said.

The Greek glanced at the clock at the end of the counter—two minutes to 2:00 A.M., closing time—seemed to shrug, and bagged a plain bottle off the shelf behind the cash register. He made his only comment as he was handing Rick his change. "Drink a hole in a clear morning."

Rick drove home, poured two inches of the clear spirits into a tumbler, and added water, watching the liquid cloud up. That part always fascinated him. The first sip tasted like licorice. By the fifth the taste was no longer noticeable.

In high school, when the Model A died finally, he had worked nights pumping gas until he'd saved $150, enough to buy a 1939 white Oldsmobile coupe off a widow in the next block who hadn't had it out of the garage since her husband died. For weeks he'd haunted every junkyard within reasonable driving distance of his parents' home, picking up a carburetor here, a set of plugs there, and when he was finished with the Olds he had what he still liked to think of as the first genuine hot rod in Detroit. He'd have framed his first speeding ticket—ninety-two in a twenty-five—if he hadn't had to send it in with his payment. It had cost him the price of a new set of tires and the use of the car for one whole summer when his father found out.

Sitting there drinking he could smell the Olds's mohair interior.

He hadn't had a drink alone since leaving the police department. Not that he had any such problems, but he had seen good officers under hack for some chickenshit complaint drink themselves right out of society, and he hadn't been about to give those maggots at I.A.D. the satisfaction. He topped off his glass from the bottle.

With his first paycheck from the city he had made a down payment on a 1957 Chevy, red and white with tail fins till hell wouldn't have them and a speedometer that topped out at 120, although he had found out on the John Lodge that it would do better. Within six months the car was repossessed for missed payments. It was the memory of that, being dropped off at home by his partner at the end of a double shift to find the Chevy gone and a note from the finance company, that had changed his view of department regulations prohibiting the acceptance of gratuities.

He could read the shelf clock that had come with the apartment without turning on a light. Outside the window the night sky was beginning to peel away from a pale horizon.

In between there had been a Buick sedan, black, with a profile like the tortoise leaning forward at the starting line and three silver holes on each side of the hood and an exhaust that sounded like a twin inboard. He had wrapped that one around a telephone pole in rural Oakland County, total wreck and ten days at Receiving with his jaw wired shut and one leg in a cast. A salvage yard had given him forty dollars for what was left of the car, just about what Rick had paid for anesthesia.

Cars were his life, the little bratty fast ones and the big chesty loud ones, the high-strung foreign jobs that spent most of their time on hydraulic lifts and the Norman Rockwell workhorses that idled their way up vertical hills and kept on going miles after their crankcases squeaked dry and all the water had boiled out of their radiators. He would rather spend Sunday under a greasy chassis with particles of rust falling into his eyes than a week in a whorehouse, and what did he have to show for it, this lifelong love affair with the internal combustion engine? A leg that still throbbed every time it rained and a furnished apartment with a bum shower. And a stack of letters just now catching the light on the writing desk by the window.

He poured another two inches, without water. The letters interested him more than the chemical reaction now.

Man Killed in Puerto Rican Coup Attempt

SAN JUAN (UPI)—A 64-year-old man was slain in the crossfire between bodyguards of Governor Roberto Sanchez Vilella and rebels during an attempt to assassinate the governor on the veranda of the Hotel Pinzón late yesterday afternoon.

A group calling itself the People's Army for the Liberation of Puerto Rico (PALP) is believed responsible for the assault by four men with revolvers on the governor while he was having tea with friends and associates in the open-air café. Vilella, uninjured, was rushed from the hotel by members of his bodyguard while the others exchanged gunfire with the rebels, all of whom escaped. The victim, whose name is being withheld pending notification of his family, died instantly when bullets struck him in the head and chest . . .

"I'll take a wild guess." Lew Canada leaned forward in his chair and laid the long sheet of newsprint on the desk. "The victim's name was Francis Xavier Oro. Frankie Orr for short."

The man behind the desk put aside the sheet. "He was traveling under a Brazilian passport in the name of José Antonio Pérez. That's the name we're releasing. The story's just going out over the wires now. It'll be in the afternoon papers and on the Six O'Clock News."

"Who fucked up?"

Randall S. Burlingame stuffed an ugly black pipe from a leather pouch with a history. He was tall even when sitting, broad-shouldered, and built, like most of the FBI bureau chiefs Canada had known, along the lines of J. Edgar Hoover; thick through the middle and short in the neck. He had an impressive head of thick red hair graying at the roots and a granite cast to his features from years of Washington infighting.

"Officially, of course, there were no fuck-ups," he said. "Some nut group tried to take out the head of government and nailed a citizen in the confusion. Just between you and me and Dean Rusk, the State Department bobbled the ball. Standard procedure in a deportation violation is to make a simple arrest using Justice Department personnel; us. But that thing in Santo Domingo last year made State nervous, so they handed it to the San Juan city police with instructions to transfer Orr to federal custody later. The bonehead play was in failing to find out who the collar was having tea with."

He lit the pipe and got it drawing. "We don't know who made the first wrong move, Orr's personal bodyguard or one of Governor Vilella's men or some green cop. We're still investigating, not that it will change anything or that anyone will read the report outside of Hoover and a few staple-counters at State. You can bury a lot of corpses in a file drawer."

"How long do you think this one will stay buried?"

"As long as it counts. Vilella's happy; he stands to gain a couple of million in federal highway funds if he and his people can keep their mouths shut. That isn't easy for a Latin, but politicians are the same all over. He'll clam."

"What about this People's Army for the Liberation of Puerto Rico?"

He smiled around the pipestem. "I understand some grunt in media liaison suggested adding the Liberation part just before the release went out. Calling it PAP would have been asking for trouble."

"So Frankie goes out without even a whimper," Canada said.

"Oh, in a couple of years some journalist or other will throw his curiosity into gear and track him as far as San Juan, maybe even make the connection between Orr and the poor stiff who stopped lead for *el excelencio*. There'll be a stink, but nobody really cares how a gangster gets it, especially not in a place like that. Thirty percent of Americans surveyed think Puerto Rico is the capital of Peru."

Canada stood. "Thanks for calling me, Mr. Burlingame."

"Call me Red." He put down his pipe and got up to grip the inspector's hand. "I've got my orders not to share any of this with you, but Hoover doesn't have to work with the local authorities. I do."

"Of course, there's one possibility we haven't considered."

"Maybe nobody fucked up after all," Burlingame supplied. "The Commission has contacts there like everywhere else. Maybe one of those cops got the nod."

"You have considered it."

"I got hung up on why. Unless they just didn't want him in this country, I couldn't figure out where they stood to gain by dealing Orr out."

"It wasn't that," Canada said. "It's what they stood to lose if they didn't."

Patsy's idea was to subdivide the city into districts with one man in charge of each, answering only to Patsy, after the fashion of Roman legions and their emperor. From the time he was old enough to understand, Patsy's father had drilled him in Plutarch and Gibbon and Caesar's *Conquests,* and it was the one lesson that had penetrated the imagination of a sickly youth terrified by his parent's energies and reputation and taken hold. But Mike Gallante, with the tact of a born courtier, had gently steered Patsy away from that tentacled structure toward a more flexible system based on corporate industry. Once the merits of the plan were explained to him, the crimelord couldn't veto it without looking like some kind of dinosaur, but inside he was bitterly disappointed. For most of his adult life he had seen himself as Augustus to his father's Caesar, needing only an empire of his own to prove himself greater than his predecessor. Now that he had it he would have to settle for Henry Ford II.

They were using the conference room off Patsy's office. Patsy sat at the end of the long walnut table with a map of Detroit spread before him, marked all over with lines and circles in red ballpoint. Gallante stood over it in his shirtsleeves, making fresh marks and illustrating his theories of organization with sweeping gestures of the hand holding the pen. Patsy only half followed what he was saying. He felt as he had the summer he was nineteen and he sat in on a poker game with members of his father's troop, older men mostly with spaghetti bellies and salty stains on their underarm holsters. None of the games was familiar to him. Losing the money hadn't upset him half as much as not knowing why he was losing it.

"We'll want to hire coloreds for the menial jobs," Gallante said. "Runners and bag men and collectors. That leaves our people free to administrate and gives the neighborhood coloreds the impression they're still participating."

"No colored bag men." Devlin, seated bearlike in a wallow of his own fat across the corner of the table from Patsy, showed interest for the first time. Despite the air conditioning he had sweated through his polyester sport shirt. Even his necktie was sopping. "Springfield's courier ran off with fifteen hundred dollars."

"No colored strongarms either," Patsy said. "When they forget to pay I want everyone in the neighborhood to know who they owe and who collects."

"They might not be as eager to play if they suspect the operation's all white."

"They can't stay away. That's what made the policy business beautiful from the start."

"Things were different in those days. Coloreds stepped off the sidewalks when they saw a white man coming. Now they'd cut you as soon as look at you."

Patsy slapped the table hard enough to sting. "No nigger lays a hand on any of my people. They like cutting so much we'll cut the balls off the first buck that tries it."

"You're the boss, Patsy."

"I am. And Twelfth Street's going to know it." Patsy fumbled for the button under the edge of the table. Sweets came in, dry as cut paper in his sack suit and old-fashioned tie. "We're leaving." Patsy adjusted his knee braces.

Gallante folded the map. "We'll ride down with you."

Sweets helped with the canes and when Patsy was standing went out ahead of them to ring for the elevator. It was an express, a feature that added five hundred dollars to the monthly rent.

The bullet-shaped accountant heaved himself to his feet and he and Gallante followed Patsy out of the room, hanging back to avoid stepping on his heels. Slowing other people down was the only good thing about his affliction; it reinforced his leadership.

Gallante had overstayed his welcome, Patsy thought. He had hoped the Princeton prick would return to New York after Springfield cut and ran, but the Commission refused to recall him, explaining to Patsy in the infuriatingly pedantic droning way of that East Coast cabal that he needed a good administrator to smooth the transition in the Detroit policy business. He wondered where the Commission had been when his father tore the racket out of Joey Machine's dead bloody grasp. No smooth transitions there.

The elevator doors opened just as he got to them and he went in ahead of Gallante and Devlin and Sweets, who pressed the button for the ground floor. From the back, the bodyguard's pointed head looked just like an onion.

Nothing changed, Patsy thought. It was almost as if the war had ended in a draw instead of the victory he knew it was. And nothing ever would change if somebody with balls didn't take them in his hands and show Gallante's corporate structure what the Orrs were made of. It struck him then, leaning on the handrail to take the weight off his crippled legs, that he was glad Harry DiJesus hadn't gone back to Las Vegas after all. Gallonte was an easy kill. He thought pleasantly about the words he would use to break the news to his father the next time he called.

The car stopped with a hydraulic sigh and the doors knifed open. Patsy felt a flash of irritation when their exit into the crowded lobby was blocked by three black men waiting to board, one of them a tubercular-looking Dizzy Gillespie type with a black beret and a ratty goatee beard; it was the guard's responsibility to inform people the elevator was private. He just had time to wonder why the three were wearing heavy raincoats on a blistering August day when the coats flew open like wings and the car filled with noise and stinging heat.

Chapter 38

Quincy Springfield was seeing things he'd never seen before.

The tired front porch of the house on Kercheval, for instance, was decorated in the upper corners with that old-fashioned gingerbread that looked like spiderwebs. He hadn't noticed it on his previous visits, yet from its weathered condition and the festooning presence of the imperfect real thing it was obviously not a new feature. But then the last time he'd been there Lydell had accompanied him. He wondered when he would exhaust the store of places to go and think, *The last time I was here* . . . Lydell had been dead six hours. One moment it seemed like a year, then in the next he would catch himself making a mental note of something to tell Lydell next time he spoke to him, and the realization was like the ground opening under his feet.

"You cheap son of a bitch," he said. "You always did light out ahead of the bill."

"What, sugar?" Krystal clung to his arm in her white go-go boots and a silver lamé shift that just covered her pelvis and looked like Reynolds wrap.

"I was just saying I don't know why we got to be out tonight."

"You got to get out of your head for a little. I hear Mahomet puts on a show."

There was a knot of people standing on the porch, looking more garish than usual in their exaggerated Afros and bright nighttime clothes with the sunlight not quite gone. Quincy knew some of them and nodded to them on his way to the door. It was locked. He looked at his watch. A few minutes past eight. "Wilson's still at his day job," he told Krystal.

They went back down the steps and wandered up to the corner, where two men and a woman in short-shorts and a halter top were passing around a cigarette. The bright-metal heat of the day was mellowing. Quincy could feel the moisture in the air condensing on his skin. Dusk had been Lydell's favorite time of day. "You can see the brothers and sisters coming out of the cracks and taking over. The Man done grabbed the daytime for hisself, but he forgot about the night." Quincy wondered if he'd settle for ordinary crema-tion. Elrod Brown had given him a demonstration that afternoon and it was just like feeding rubbish to an incinerator.

"Krystal's thirsty, sugar. You gots a little taste?" She felt inside his breast pocket.

He handed her the hammered silver flask, a gift from Lydell with someone else's initials engraved on it. It gurgled once and she handed it back. He helped himself before putting it away. So far he'd managed to keep his buzz at the same pleasant level.

A police cruiser coasted past on a grumbling ripple from the crowd, the white officer behind the wheel hanging his big face out the open window and committing features to memory. At the corner he accelerated. One of the men on the corner spat after the car.

When he and Krystal turned around to walk back, the crowd on the porch had swelled to twice its original size and spilled out on the sidewalk and burned-out front yard. Quincy saw Sebastian Bright surrounded by his people. He hadn't been out alone since Joe Petite's murder.

A white stretch limousine came around the corner from Pennsylvania, seeming in its exaggerated length to flex in the middle like a snake. As it slid to a stop in front of the house Quincy recognized the plate. It was one of the Fleetwoods he'd rented for Congo's funeral. A white chauffeur in livery got out and opened the back door on the curb side. The Bongo Brothers alighted first in their dark suits and spread collars and stood glaring at the crowd with their hands open at their sides while Mahomet stepped up onto the curb. The light was fading quickly now and his white suit seemed to glow under the street lamps, which came on just then. Quincy wondered if he'd timed that or if God just naturally smiled on the small man with the straight slick hair and bottomless baritone. The crowd pressed in, but Mighty Joe Young and Anthony Battle had come around from the other side of the car and joined the others in forming a protective seal around Mahomet.

He spotted Quincy then and said something to Mighty Joe Young, who dipped his head with its elaborately beaded coif to listen, then nodded. The group approached Quincy. His hand was seized in both of Mahomet's.

"I heard about Lafayette."

"Doc says his heart just went," Quincy said. "Saved him some pain, I guess."

"He didn't care much for me, but I'm sorry just the same."

"Lydell was tough to get on with."

"Remember me, Mr. Big Stuff ? I bought you your first ice cream suit."

Mahomet let go of Quincy's hand and embraced Krystal. They were the same height. He left one arm around her waist. "Staying to hear me talk?"

"Well, the line was too long at the Poitier picture."

"I'll try to make up for it."

Wilson McCoy, in his dusty coveralls from his job at the brick factory, made his way through the crowd, jingling his keys. For once he wasn't wearing his beret. "Fucking bus was late," he told Mahomet. "Let's go in." He turned to mount the porch without acknowledging Quincy's presence. By agreement, they hadn't had direct contact since before the shooting at the Penobscot Building.

Police had counted 147 holes in the elevator car. Pasquale Oro and Michael Nicholas Gallante were pronounced dead at the scene and Herschel Schmerer, alias Sean Devlin, died in the ambulance on the way to Detroit Receiving. Ovid "Sweets" Sito, the bodyguard, lived for two hours with bullets in his brain, chest, and stomach, then expired without having regained consciousness. Being sought were three Negroes in their early twenties and a security guard named Paul Arnet, who had disappeared from his post earlier that afternoon and was still missing from home. Quincy had thought McCoy an idiot to go on operating his blind pig and conducting BLAC meetings, but since the artists' renditions that had appeared in the papers and on TV of the killer in the beret didn't remotely resemble him, maybe he was wise to go on as if nothing had happened. Quincy himself had been questioned and released when a waitress at the Butcher's Inn on Winder confirmed that he'd been eating there when the incident took place.

The crowd outside thinned as people entered the house. Just as Quincy and Krystal turned away from the street a blue car blatted past and he looked, his body tensing, just in time to see a taillight flick around the corner. He made himself relax. Everywhere he looked lately he was seeing blue Cobras.

McCoy, having unlocked the front door for his guests, was standing on the porch talking with Sebastian Bright. They both turned when Quincy and Krystal started up the steps, but they weren't looking at them.

"Wilson McCoy?"

The man who had called out, tall and white in a neat black suit and narrow-brimmed hat, climbed past Quincy accompanied by two Detroit police officers in uniform, both white, and another white plainclothesman, shorter and wider than Sebastian Bright, wearing a wrinkled jacket and double-knit pants and a hat with a five-inch brim like they didn't sell any more in stores. Quincy recognized

Inspector Canada and the fat sergeant with a woman's name, what was it, Ethel or Edith. Esther.

"This a private party." McCoy started to go inside. One of the uniformed officers grasped his arm.

"You're wanted for questioning in a quadruple homicide," Canada said. "Let's go downtown."

"Whitey's going to kill me!" shouted McCoy.

One of Sebastian Bright's men tried to seize Canada's arms from behind. The inspector elbowed him in the throat, cross-drew a short-barreled Chief's Special, and aimed it at the man's face. "Back down off the porch. Everybody off the porch," he barked. "This is police business."

"White motherfuckers!" Krystal lunged, her long-nailed fingers hooked like claws. Quincy caught her around the waist and dragged her, kicking and twisting, off the porch.

The crowd was surging back outdoors now, becoming vocal. The fat sergeant stood on the top step with his revolver out to cover the others' backs. The uniforms had handcuffs on McCoy, who kept saying, "Don't let them do this to me! You going to let them do this to me?"

A bottle sailed past the inspector's head and exploded against a porch post, showering glass and whiskey everywhere. "Radio for backup," Canada said. The sergeant retreated down the steps, backing and turning, and slipped around the corner of the house. Quincy had wondered where they'd parked the car.

There were people all over now. The porch boards groaned under their weight and they were standing in the yard and on the sidewalk and in the middle of the street, blocking the officers' way out. Many of them had come out of the other houses in the block.

"This is where it starts!" McCoy shouted. One of the uniforms slammed the prisoner's head against the wall of the house and he quieted down.

"Fucking pig!" Krystal's heels raked Quincy's shins. He cursed and held on. Sirens thrilled in the distance.

Mahomet's white suit appeared on the porch. He had his hands raised and his mouth was moving, but Quincy couldn't hear what he was saying.

The sirens were getting louder. They sounded like they were coming from all over the city, answering one another like wolves. Quincy transferred his grip to Krystal's wrist and pulled her a block and a half down Kercheval to where the Sting Ray was parked. He threw her across the seat and slammed the door. "Stay in there till I get back or you can pedal your ass from now on."

"Where you going?"

"Back to get Mahomet."

Blue-and-whites from Motor Traffic and the Tactical Mobile Unit were entering the block from both ends. More bottles had been smashed, their fragments twinkling in the red and blue of the strobes. One of the officers who had handcuffed Wilson McCoy pushed down his head and shoved him into the backseat of a cruiser. Other uniforms in riot helmets moved through the crowd with sticks and bayoneted rifles—bayonets, for chrissake—quartering it and isolating the hotspots. Quincy knew a flash of dread when he couldn't see Mahomet on the porch. Then he spotted him at ground level, a whitecap bobbing in a sea of bright shirts and halter tops, still talking with his arms raised.

Something struck Quincy hard between the shoulder blades. He stumbled and grabbed at the fender of a parked car for support. His legs were kicked out from under him and his hair was grabbed from behind and his face slammed into the hood. He felt his nose give. A hand frisked him from neck to ankles, his wrists were jerked behind his back and clamped together.

"Let him go."

Snuffling blood, Quincy turned his cheek to the warm hood. Inspector Canada was standing on the other side of the car. He'd lost his hat and his crisp black hair was in his eyes.

"Inspector—" The voice behind Quincy was muffled.

"He didn't do anything. Take off the cuffs."

His wrists were freed. He straightened up, leaned a hip against the fender. The officer who had cuffed him had on a white helmet with a tinted Plexiglas shield that hid his face. Only the hands sticking out of his blue shirtcuffs told Quincy the man was black. "Sorry, Inspector. I thought—"

"Get back with the others." Canada came around to Quincy's side of the car and gave him his handkerchief. "Is it broken?"

"Wouldn't be the first time." He blew into it and mopped the blood from his upper lip. The front of his face was growing numb, a sure sign.

"McCoy did it, didn't he?"

He tipped back his head and pinched his nostrils shut with the hand holding the handkerchief. "Did what?"

"You know damn well what. He shouldn't have worn the beret. Did you pay him, or is this one of those brotherhood things?"

"I just want to get Mahomet out of here. He gets beat up on a lot."

"That officer wasn't so far off. We'll just have to come back and do it all over again when McCoy talks."

Quincy lowered his head. "He won't talk."

"About what?"

"About nothing. This ain't no cops and robbers, Mr. Police Man. This here's war. You're the enemy."

"It didn't have to come to this. You had your chance to stop it when we talked back in June."

"It was already started." He held out the handkerchief. "Thanks."

"Keep it. It's bloody."

"Nigger bastard!"

Quincy turned toward the new voice just as the gun fired. He felt a hot wind on his cheek. Harry DiJesus, his face demonic in the light of the strobes, was standing in the middle of Kercheval with his feet spread and an automatic clamped between both outstretched palms. Canada's revolver was out and he returned fire. There was a moment of darkness while the beacons rotated away from each other, then when their beams crossed again the spot where DiJesus had been standing was vacant. "Get down!" Canada crouched behind the fender on his side. His head swiveled slowly from left to right. Bodies ran back and forth through the pulsating lights.

Four shots rattled, too close together for a revolver. The sound came from behind Quincy. He wheeled. Mahomet was standing in an opening created by the four wrestlers who never left his side, his arms still raised above his head. Four red spots the size of half-dollars had spoiled his white vest; Quincy thought crazily of straw-berries and cream. Mahomet, looking around, spotted Quincy and he started to smile. Then his knees bent and his head tipped forward and the rest of him followed.

DiJesus was crouched six feet away with his back to Quincy, still holding the pistol in target stance. He turned, his eyes darting, and the light when it struck them came back glowing green as from an animal's. Canada fired twice. The first bullet was high and struck DiJesus in the throat, neatly parting the gold chain around his neck. It glittered as it slithered down inside his T-shirt. The second entered his chest on the left side. He fell.

There was a lull in the shouting and running. Quincy walked past DiJesus' body without stopping to look at it and stood over Mahomet. Mighty Joe Young was kneeling with Mahomet's head in his lap. The eyes were already growing soft and glistening.

"What was he saying?"

One of the Bongos looked up, startled. Quincy repeated the question.

"Same thing, over and over," said Anthony Battle. " 'Be calm, brothers and sisters. This is the test.' "

Chapter 39

He slept, woke up, and went out and ate something at a counter, where the Marine type in the paper hat who took his order kept watching him out of the corner of his eye as he griddled the pancakes. Rick caught his reflection, unshaven and still wearing the shirt he'd put on the day before, in the chrome steel of a Bunn coffee maker behind the counter and sympathized. Back at the apartment he turned on the TV without turning up the sound and watched the Porter Parade all over again. Then Captain Kangaroo came on and he switched off the set. He had another drink just to maintain his buzz, then slept again. He woke up again in the afternoon and had another. In the evening when he woke up he felt like doing something.

"Hello?"

The voice in the earpiece sounded foggy.

"Dan, this is Rick."

"Rick. Jesus Christ, what time is it?"

Outside it was dark and he had left the lamps off, but the face of the shelf clock was visible in the flicker from the wastebasket. "A little after eleven. Did I wake you up?"

"That four A.M. shift's a pain in the butt." Sugar sounded wide awake now. "You get them? You get the letters?"

"Letters, who writes letters any more? It's a lost art, like undercover work in the age of listening devices."

"You drunk?"

He introduced water to the ouzo. The glass reflected the orangish, wobbling illumination that was growing now, making shadows writhe on the walls and ceiling.

"Have drunk," Rick corrected. "Pluperfect tense. The following is a list of words that require helpers: drunk, swung, hung, dung— help me out here. . . ."

"You are drunk."

"Spifflicated."

"What?"

"My mother's word. She used it when she chewed out my father so I wouldn't understand. They sold the stuff out of cars in front of Dodge Main and he never got past them walking a straight line. Spifflicated, I just remembered. Haven't thought of it in thirty years."

"You're celebrating, right? You got them."

"Got what?"

"The letters! Dear Love-buggy, your Wendy-poo misses oo. How many you got? They really hot?"

"Oh, yeah, they're hot." The next sip cleared his fog. "Listen, Dan—"

"Anything we can quote in the papers? We can use whatchacallum, asterisks for the really hot parts. That always makes 'em seem worse. Bring them over. No, better stay there. Where are you, your place? I'll be there in twenty."

"I don't have them, Dan. She burned them."

"She what? Who's she?"

"Enid. The Kohler woman. She burned them in her fireplace, every last one. Months ago."

"Bullshit. Broads don't destroy that kind of thing. My wife still has her wedding corsage and we ain't talked to each other in a year. You toss the place?"

"They're gone, Dan."

During the pause on Sugar's end, Rick leaned across the arm of his chair and slid the window up another few inches. The air in the room was getting hazy.

Sugar blew out. "Okay, we ain't dead, just crippled a little. Make her a deal. She want to be famous? 'Muckraker's Mistress Tells All,' we'll get her on magazine covers, TV. It could lead to a movie deal like that Keeler cunt. Tell her there's a couple of grand in it for her besides. No, shit, make it ten, we ain't cheap. They do anything, you know, kinky? Don't matter. We'll take her picture with a schnauzer. No kidding, I'm getting into this."

"I quit."

"Stop clowning around. We got work to do."

"I quit is what I said. Tell Jim Roche to stick it up his tailpipe. I'm hanging up my cloak and dagger. Don't bother with severance pay or references."

"Listen, we'll talk about this when you're not cockeyed. I had a nickel for every time I got a snootful and decided to tell the boss what I thought of him—"

"So long, Dan."

"Wait! What you going to do to eat?"

"I've still got my wrenches."

"You ain't got shit. The title on that Camaro? It's a fake. The car belongs to General Motors security. Answer the door, chump. That's the repo man knocking."

"He'll find the keys in the ignition. I've got enough put away for a used Buick I saw advertised in the *News*."

"That'd kill you."

"It won't, but the Camaro might have. A car's just something to get you around, hopefully in one piece."

"You motherfu—"

The flames in the metal wastebasket were dying down now. After

Rick hung up on Sugar he got a long-handled cooking fork from the little kitchen and stirred the ashes until the unburned portion of the letters caught fire, then doused the sparks with water from the pitcher. Black smoke boiled out and found its way to the window.

A few minutes later the landlady from downstairs tapped at his door and asked him apologetically to use the ventilator fan when he cooked.

Chapter 40

Smoke poured in a black column from the upholstery of an abandoned car someone had set fire to at the curb. The gasoline tank, like its tires and wheels and most of the engine, had been cannibalized weeks ago and none of the officers busy cordoning off that section of Kercheval was paying it any attention. Only Quincy was watching it when Krystal found him. On the other end of the block, glass broke with a long shivery tinkle. Most of the action had moved up the street.

"You okay, sugar? I heard shooting before but the police wouldn't let me through."

"You should of went home."

"You got the keys. Besides, you know Krystal don't like to sleep alone." She slid an arm inside one of his. "You sound funny. You coming down with a cold?"

He touched the back of a hand to his nostrils and looked at it in the firelight. The bleeding had stopped. "I'm okay."

"Radio says rain."

It was still playing. He could hear it in a Doppler effect from the Corvette parked several blocks down, Barry McGuire singing about the eve of destruction.

"Mahomet's dead."

"Somebody told me."

"I never did understand the crazy son of a bitch."

"Wasn't your fault, sugar. It was that white suit."

"Man ought to be able to wear what he wants without getting shot."

"Wasn't nothing you could do."

"I could of left him in jail."

Sirens swooped and fell. Somebody said something unintelligible into a bullhorn. Krystal squeezed Quincy's arm. "Riot's over, Quincy. Let's go home."

He let her steer him toward the car. Then he stopped, turned back, and fished something out of his pants pocket that caught the firelight in a red glint. Lydell had given it to him to hold when he went to the hospital because it didn't fit any more and he was afraid some intern might steal it. Quincy held up the ring, read the engraving: WORLD SERIES CHAMPIONS 1957. He threw it through the broken windshield into the burning car.

"The whole town next time, Lydell."

A few minutes later he helped Krystal into the Corvette and they drove back toward Twelfth Street.

Postscript

The so-called "Kercheval incident" of August 9–10, 1966—sometimes referred to as a "miniriot" but downgraded by the media from a full-scale civil disturbance at the request of Mayor Jerome P. Cavanagh and the Detroit Police Department—began Tuesday at 8:25 P.M. when a routine arrest in front of a private residence aroused the wrath of bystanders, and ended twenty-four hours later when a cloudburst drenched the spirits of even the most stubborn protesters. Mother Nature's intrusion was the last in a long line of fortunate coincidences—including the hour the trouble started, when the police force was at maximum strength, and the presence in the area of two squads of the Motor Traffic Bureau and both the first and second sections of the Tactical Mobile Unit—that enabled the police to restore order with a minimum of conflict.

The event has been called a dress rehearsal for the devastating riots that took place in the area of Twelfth Street during the week of July 23–29, 1967. A Sunday morning raid on a blind pig operated by the United Civil League for Community Action went wrong when customers attempted to prevent the police from leaving with their prisoners. Throughout the next seven days, the police engaged in running firefights with citizens on a street of flames. When local authorities proved incapable of containing the arsons, violence, and looting, Governor George Romney dispatched reinforcements from the Michigan National Guard and eventually requested emergency aid from President Lyndon Baines Johnson, who ordered tanks and paratroopers from the United States armed services into the area. When the insurrection had at last been put down, eighty million dollars in property had been destroyed and forty-three lives had been lost.

Mayor Cavanagh's hopes for national office died soon after the riots. Defeated by former Governor G. Mennen Williams for the Democratic senatorial nomination, he announced his decision in June 1969 not to run for a third term as mayor. His death some years later received minimal attention in the national press. Similarly, George Romney's dependency upon federal troops to quell a civil disturbance has been cited for his abysmal showing in the 1968 race for the Republican nomination for President. Detroit Police Commissioner Ray Girardin requested retirement in October 1967, explaining, "You've got to bleed some in a job like this, but, by God, I've been gushing."

In 1973, the year the Arab oil embargo and the resulting energy crisis ended the brief reign of the gas-guzzling "muscle cars," Detroit elected its first black mayor. Despite numerous federal and local investigations of alleged misconduct in his administration, Coleman A. Young remains in office as of this writing, the longest-serving mayor in Detroit's history. Under his leadership the municipal government and its police agency have come to reflect the city's predominately black population to a degree that would have been unthinkable in 1966.

Today, the biggest problem facing Detroit is not race but drugs, America's most enduring legacy of the 1960s. The fight for supremacy in the numbers racket has been supplanted by drive-by shootings and crack-house massacres over millions of dollars in controlled and illegal substances. There have been other changes as well. The music of choice is Rap. Video arcades outnumber neighborhood movie houses, and those automobiles not manufactured in Japan are built with foreign steel and assembled in countries other than the United States. By law, they are all equipped with seat belts and other features designed exclusively for the safety of the people who ride in them.

And Twelfth Street is now known as Rosa Parks Boulevard.